Dark Blood Curse

An urban fantasy

Michelle Corbier

Michelle Corbier

701 Green Valley Road, Suite 100, #325

Greensboro, NC 27408

www.MichelleCorbier.com

Cover and interior design by Cheri Lasota, Cutting Edge Studios

Dark Blood Curse

Copyright © by Michelle Corbier

979-8-9870408-6-7Dark Blood Curses, eBook

979-8-9870408-7-4Dark Blood Curses, paperback

979-8-9870408-8-1Dark Blood Curses, audio book

Books by Michelle Corbier

Write Club Mysteries

Murder Is Revealing

Murder In Gemini

Murder Between Neighbors

Mwindaji Urban Fantasy

Dark Blood Awakens

Standalone suspense novel

Hollow Voices

For Jean-Michel, all my love.

Acknowledgements

Special thanks to Dr. Jean-Ronel Corbier for his assistance with the Baoumali language and Haitian Creole translations. Dr. Corbier is a neurologist practicing integrative medicine. Visit his website at: https://brainrestorationclinic.com/

Chapter 1
May 2010

THE LATE SPRING MORNING brought sunlight streaking across Makeda's bed. She moaned and rolled over. Saturday mornings were meant for sleeping in—especially for nurses who worked third shift. Makeda didn't have that luxury—not this weekend.

Three weeks ago, her great-grandmother, Yewande, contacted her using *kasi kasi*. Appropriate, since she taught Makeda how to speak telepathically. But over two decades had elapsed since she'd spoken to her great-grandmother. Now, they planned to meet at nine a.m.

She recalled the tiny cottage home secluded in the western North Carolina woods. *What happened to it?*

No one had maintained the place since Yewande's death—at least not to Makeda's knowledge. Her parents kept information surrounding her great-grandmother's death secret. Makeda feared what had become of the house. She had no directions to its location.

Yewande's house wasn't on GPS. It had no mailbox or coordinates to reference. She would have to rely on memories and instinct.

Scented roasted meat tickled her noise and gave her the impetus to climb out of bed and into the shower. After slipping into jeans and a pullover sweater, Makeda sprinted out of her bedroom and across the living room. The home's great room included a kitchen, dining area, and living room. Her hand hovered over the doorknob as her mom called.

"Where are you going?" Mom stood at the kitchen island, filling a pot in the sink.

"Meria's," she lied. "She wants to go shopping. I'm going to hang out at her place."

Attuned to Mom's searching gaze, Makeda's countenance remained neutral. She cleared her mind of Yewande and the upcoming reunion. Mom didn't like Yewande—actually hated wouldn't be too strong a word. Makeda understood this fact from childhood. The two women barely tolerated each other. If Mom learned she planned to meet up with her great-grandmother...

And how would they meet?

Zaubers communicated via kasi kasi, but Yewande died decades ago. Would she be speaking with a spirit? *Figure it out later.*

"Gotta go," Makeda said. "Love you."

She sped outside and into her car, missing Mom's reply.

As she turned onto the main road from the dirt driveway, Makeda phoned Meria. On the second ring, her best friend answered.

"Hey, girl," Meria said, singingly. "What're we up to today?"

"I need you to cover for me. Mom thinks we're spending the day together."

"Okay. So what's going on and why can't your mom know?"

"It's not like that."

"Hooking up with Michael?"

"No. We haven't seen each other since I left Ramsey."

Memories of the handsome sheriff made Makeda's breath catch. She intended to spend time with him soon, only not this weekend. A vision of a hulking werewolf interrupted her romantic thoughts of Michael. *Figure out why a demon wants to kill you before planning a date.*

She peered along the narrow county road for landmarks.

"Why not? He's crazy about you."

A bend in the road required her attention and Makeda dropped the cellphone. With one hand, she groped along the seat cushion, hearing Meria's shouts.

"Sorry. I'm trying to find a house."

"Where?"

"I can't explain right now."

A few miles beyond the bend she noticed a familiar tattered wooden fence.

"Look, cover for me if Mom calls."

"Fine, but you owe me."

"Whatever," Makeda mumbled to herself.

"I'm serious. I want you to teach me magic spells—or make me a witch."

"I can't *make* you a witch."

"But you can teach me spells."

"Bye." She hung up as Meria continued listing demands.

While the area looked familiar, Makeda couldn't locate the house. *I'm lost.*

She shut down the phone and concentrated, sending a telepathic message for directions.

'Bajinu, mbabire.'

However, her great-grandmother didn't reply. If kasi kasi didn't work...

Makeda struck the car console with her fist. "Damn."

After pulling off the crumbling road onto a hilly shoulder, Makeda closed her eyes. *Concentrate.*

Lavender. The fruity herb reminded Makeda of when Yewande would pick her up from school. Mom often worked late or ran errands. Because he crafted furniture late into the night, Dad appreciated having a free babysitter.

Back then, Yewande drove a beat-up pickup. Plants, herbs, and other miscellaneous items filled the trunk bed. Inside, the cab smelled of lilac and lavender. A necklace draped with charms hung from the rearview mirror.

Once when Makeda struggled to attach her seatbelt, Yewande had glanced sidewise at her. "You don't need a seatbelt. We're *zaubers*. A car accident won't kill us."

Makeda still attached the seatbelt. Her parents had always insisted, and she hadn't believed her great-grandmother. Everyone died, including Yewande. So her grandmother had been wrong about at least one thing.

A maze of trees sped by. Nothing particular drew Makeda's attention. Smoke signaled someone was burning trash in the rural county. But nothing stuck out to identify Yewande's house. Makeda turned onto a smaller side road and drove east.

"I can't remember where the house is," Makeda huffed, straining to glimpse any distinguishing landmarks among the blur of trees.

This time, she strengthened her plea.

'Bajinu, mbabire!'

Again, no response.

Last night's hospital shift had been extra tiresome, and Makeda yawned. Her eyelids grew heavy. She seriously considered returning home.

I have to know why a demon wants me dead.

Makeda shook off her fatigue, stiffened her shoulders, and searched the narrow back roads for a house she hadn't visited in...too long. Her back tingled, and she adjusted her position.

"This is ridiculous." Looking for a spot to turn around, she piloted the car toward home.

'Hurry up.'

Makeda snapped to attention. 'Yewande, I can't—'

'Stop whining. This is your first lesson. If you can't identify the terrain, use *maji* to find the house.'

A saucy retort rested on Makeda's lips, but she held her tongue. Luckier people slept at home in their beds, but they didn't want to become sorceresses. And she desperately wanted to embrace her zauber heritage.

She refocused on the cottage house. Birds chirped and circled the clear blue sky. Perfume from lilac and lavender intensified. In her mind, a light materialized. It illuminated a tiny spot, which gradually widened like a stage scene.

"Got it!"

She executed a three-point turn and doubled back. A mile down the road on the right she spied a narrow gap in the foliage. Because she overshot the slim turnoff, she had to reverse. Leaving the paved road, Makeda's car swerved onto a rocky shoulder. The car tires squealed, jerking to a stop.

"What the hell?"

In the middle of the path sat a squirrel. Makeda's shoulders slumped as she waited for the critter to move. However, it stayed put. She tapped the horn. It wriggled in a small circle but refused to move.

Now what?

She exited the car and stared down at the rodent. "Move."

'I thought you needed help.' A creepy smile flashed across the squirrel's mouth.

'Big momma?'

'Don't call me—'

'Sorry, Yewande.'

'Well, don't stand there. Time for class.' The squirrel scampered around Makeda and darted inside the car.

Now, I'm communicating with a squirrel.

She shook her head and re-entered the car.

"If I speak normally, can you understand me?"

'Yes, but squirrels can't speak, so I'll have to communicate with kasi kasi.'

Makeda chuckled. "I have a feeling talking to a squirrel will be the least strange thing I will experience today."

Tree branches scraped the car windows as Makeda drove through a tunnel of trees and greenery. She frowned as the car bumped along the rutted road. *Please don't get a flat tire.*

Gradually, the foliage drifted aside, and the space enlarged. A miniature clearing in the dense forest. Between two spikey willow trees sat a perfectly square house. The cottage where she first studied maji.

'We're home.'

Because that was what it felt like, at least how she remembered it. A sanctuary.

Here, an atmosphere of invincibility enveloped her. A place of magical possibilities. She had learned gravitation, levitation, and manipulation of objects, skills which would serve her well as a *mwindaji*—if she relearned them. No, *when* she relearned them.

I can't accept failure, especially if a demon wants me dead.

The brick house had no windows on the first floor but on the second floor two elongated windows, resembling gawking eyeballs, watched eerily over the property.

Before Makeda exited the car with a swish of its tail the squirrel hopped down from the car's console and scurried outside. It waited beside the front door.

'You've become rusty. We've got work to do with little time.'

For the hundredth time since Yewande reached out to her in Ramsey, Makeda wondered why a demon wanted her dead.

Chapter 2

Despite the cool temperature, the Memphis sun beat down aggressively upon Allen's head. Sweat trickled down his spine. He zigzagged up the dirt path of Nesbit Park on his mountain bike. The trail weaved through the thin pines and over dry creek beds.

Tree canopy intermittently blocked the unrelenting sun's rays. An occasional sliver of water traversed under the narrow wooden bridges. Lush green forest gave the spring morning energy. Allen glanced over his right shoulder.

"Come on, guys."

"Slow down, man," one of his friends said. "This is a fun ride, not a competition."

But Allen relished the wind blowing in his face. With effort, his legs pumped harder. Exhilaration flowed through his veins. Cycling had always been his passion.

A quick glance at his watch reminded him of the ballgame that evening. After a long day cycling, he'd appreciate a cool beer and dinner with friends. His wife would probably expect him home early to help with preparations.

When Allen peeked over his shoulder a second time, his friends were no longer in sight. Gliding his bike next to a pine tree, he braked and rested it against the trunk. Near the exit of the trail, a large bridge covered a briskly flowing creek. His pulse pounded rapidly in his ears. With the back of his hand, he wiped his sweaty forehead.

Crunch.

Startled, Allen peered between the brush. "What's…"

Aww.

"Hello? Anyone there?"

Not receiving an answer, he tramped down the low-sloping bank, careful with his footing. Three feet down he stopped and listened, straining to perceive the slightest noise. Bramble and tree trunks complicated his descent. Ten yards ahead, Allen spied a body lying at the foot of a rotted tree trunk.

"Help," a low gasping voice croaked.

"Here I come," Allen said, sliding the final two feet and landing at the man's feet. "You okay, man?"

Bending down, Allen slowly reached forward touching the unconscious man's forehead. For a minute, nothing happened. The man didn't speak or move.

Allen shook him forcefully. "Come on!"

Though he knew CPR, Allen didn't relish giving mouth-to-mouth to a stranger.

"Hey, guys," he yelled up toward the trail. "I found someone—"

A guttural rumble leaked from the man's mouth.

As Allen leaned forward to check for chest movement, he spied a dark object inside a nearby bush.

He glanced at the man's motionless body before walking slowly over to the bush. A slimy gel covered its surface, and the body resembled a snake without scales. *Had the man been bitten?*

Hesitantly, Allen hiked up the path. "Guys! I'm down here."

Leaves and branches fluttered near the snake-like form. Curious, Allen climbed down and approached it again. As he peered ahead. His gaze widened.

Two brilliant yellow orbs glowed from one end of the creature.

"What the—"

Suddenly, the creature slithered and shot forward.

Using his arms, Allen shielded his face. "No!" Allen screamed as the creature smashed into his face.

Everything went dark.

Chapter 3

SOUND RICOCHETED OFF THE Raleigh nightclub walls like 1980's techno-pop, blaring Donna Summer's *Hot Stuff* around the room. People packed together, gyrating to the music. Among the throng, a slender woman with long, blond hair squeezed between dancers, searching for a seat at the bar. She zipped onto a vacant stool and periodically checked her cellphone.

A moment later, a gentleman in a sports coat and slacks nuzzled up beside her. "Lakesha?" he asked in a husky voice.

"Sean? Oh, hi." She popped off the stool, and they exchanged a brief hug. "So nice to finally meet you."

"Yes." At a half-foot taller than Lakesha, his dark eyes swept over her. "Yes, it is."

They sat and ordered drinks.

He scrutinized her while drinking beer. "Online pictures usually flatter appearances, but you're more beautiful in person."

She giggled. "You're pretty hot yourself." Lakesha glanced around the club as the bartender brought her a cocktail and Sean a beer. Before taking a sip, she asked, "Should we order something to eat?"

"I don't need food." Sean peered into her eyes. "Being here with you is enough. Now we've finally met in person."

"Online chats aren't the same thing."

His admiring gaze took in her entire body. Lakesha finished her cocktail and returned a comprehensive evaluation of her own. They drank each other in, oblivious to the frenetic surrounding atmosphere.

"Let's go," Sean said, gently assisting her off the stool.

Lakesha smiled. "Want to dance?"

Like a laser, his dark eyes focused on Lakesha. "I have something else in mind."

Sean leaned forward to make himself heard above the loud acoustics. His lips brushed her earlobe. "There's a bistro down the street. Better for an intimate conversation."

Heat made Lakesha's pulse thrill. She accompanied him out of the bar as if pulled by the weight of his words.

Breezy night air brought their bodies close. Lakesha blinked rapidly. As her vision adjusted to the darkness the intoxicated sensation diminished. She scanned the street.

"Where're you parked?"

Fingering her chin, Sean brought her face up to his. "The night's calm. Let's walk."

Lakesha walked beside him, occasionally observing traffic churning mere feet away.

"How far?"

"A little stroll." Wrapping a muscular arm around her waist, Sean led her toward an alleyway.

"What're you doing?"

"I know a shortcut. Those spiked heels aren't meant for hiking."

Though her smile faded, Lakesha followed. Halfway into the alley, she asked, "Are you sure?"

"Um hmm," Sean said, pulling her closer to his hip. "How about a kiss before dinner?"

Readjusting herself in his arms, she said, "Not a bad idea." Lakesha dangled her arms around his neck, gazing over his shoulders. "I didn't expect to meet such a gorgeous man online."

"Well, you can't always trust dating sites," he said, smirking.

"True. But this time, I got lucky."

He gazed down at the top of her head. "I feel the same way."

Sean traced a finger along her chin. Simultaneously, Lakesha stroked the side of his face.

"Ow," Sean cried, pushing her slightly away as a red linear streak pulsed along his cheek.

"Must've been my ring." She retreated a step.

"What's it made of?" He palpated his blistering skin.

"Silver."

His eyes widened.

Avoiding his gaze, Lakesha whipped a small pole from her purse, pointing it at Sean's chest.

Pointy incisors descended from his mouth. Light from the streetlamp magnified their cruelty. "Bitch. You're gonna pay for this."

She shook the pole, but nothing happened. "Dammit."

A crooked grin extended across Sean's mouth. "I'm going to teach you why online dating can be hazardous to your health."

He leaped forward but Lakesha sidestepped and smacked him on the head with the pole.

"Shit." Sean grabbed her wrist and hurled her down onto the pavement.

With her stilettos, Lakesha kicked toward his knee.

Sean swatted her foot aside, smacking the red stiletto into a trash can.

He leered down upon her. "Let's see if you taste as delicious as you text."

A thick, red tongue flicked between his lips like a whip. Sean bent over her and suddenly groaned. Blood and tissue spurted across the gravel, coating Lakesha's leg.

Frozen, Sean's eyes gaped. His spindly fingers palpated the silver lance protruding out of his chest. He grimaced before slumping to the ground.

"Yuck." She scooted away.

A thick-set man wearing glasses extended his hand. "Need help?"

Alarmed, she prepared to strike out with her lance but hesitated and glanced upward. "Zeke." She accepted his hand and rose.

"What took y'all so long?" She peeled off the blond wig and scratched her scalp.

Zeke watched the vampire disintegrate into a pile of sand. "I got tangled up in the crowd. Peter spotted you and alerted me," he said, displaying a walkie-talkie.

A voice blared over the line, asking, "Zina all right?"

"Yeah," Zeke said. "We're on our way."

Zina retrieved her stiletto, and they fled the alleyway. On the sidewalk, they blended in with the pedestrian traffic.

"What happened?" he asked, checking approaching vehicles.

"The stupid lance didn't work. It wouldn't extend."

"Did you check it before entering the bar?" Zeke asked, giving her a side-glance.

"No time."

A sand-colored van zipped in front of an idling taxi and braked, squealing to an abrupt stop. The side door slid open.

"Get in."

"About time," Zina said, squeezing inside with Zeke right behind.

"We're in, Thomas," Zeke said. "Tell your brother—"

Before they belted in, the van sped off. Thomas buckled into the passenger seat. Weaving in and out of downtown Raleigh traffic, the van rocketed onto Interstate 540.

Zina banged the lance against her palm. "What's wrong with this thing?"

"Give it here." Zeke examined it. "Always test weapons before a mission."

"I was texting Sean."

Zeke shook his head and worked on the lance.

Peter drove, methodically scanning the van's mirrors.

Seated behind him, Zina said, "Thanks for spotting me when we left the bar." She scratched her scalp, removing bobby pins that had held the wig in place. "Next time, Makeda can play the decoy."

"She's busy with nursing," Peter said.

"Humph," Zina huffed. "Why do I always have to play the victim?" She pulled out her cellphone and began texting.

"You make a perfect victim," Peter said, grinning. "The exact type of person to engage in online dating."

"Besides," Thomas said, regarding his brother, "since the incident in Ramsey—"

"You can't be an mwindaji and be scared of monsters," Zina interrupted.

"Easy to say when you weren't there." Peter sat up straighter in the seat. He and Thomas shared a glance.

"Over a hundred vampires and werewolves terrorizing a small Kentucky town," Peter said distantly.

"We barely made a dent in Ramsey's problem," Thomas said.

"Should've asked for help from the other mwindaji," Zina said, returning Peter's glare from the rearview mirror.

"Besides, you're proficient at anything internet," Peter said, gliding onto Interstate 40 West toward Asheville.

"It's useful. I've discovered several mwindaji groups."

"I doubt any legitimate mwindaji group would post to an online chat room," Zeke said, tinkering with her lance. "I can fix this, but next time, test out the equipment *before* the mission. What if I hadn't arrived in time?"

"Then you'd have to explain to my mom how you let me get gutted by a vampire."

"That's not funny," Peter said, observing traffic. "Sloppiness risks the entire group."

Zina stretched out her legs. "I'm joking. Lighten up."

Zeke glared at her. "Peter's right. This isn't a game." He retrieved several tools from the rear of the van.

"Why is everyone so extreme?"

Peter frowned. "You sound like the bimbo you played in the bar. This is real life."

"Whatever," Zina said, rolling her eyes.

"And stay away from online mwindaji sites." Peter gave her a stern glance.

"Daniel uses them to communicate with other groups."

"He knows what he's doing." Zeke shook the lance, fully extending it. "You don't."

"No wonder we lose members," Zina mumbled. "Too many stupid rules."

"The internet is dangerous," Peter said, changing lanes.

"With the internet we could easily locate monster cells, instead of relying on word of mouth or local contacts."

"Our system works," Zeke said, "and keeps us safe."

Peter glanced in the rearview mirror and noticed a glint in Zeke's eyes.

Chapter 4

I NSIDE A SQUARE, COZY study, Enu studied a ledger of financial accounts. Seated at a wooden oblong desk, he observed his brother scowling.

Korlemo stared vacantly at a cold fireplace. "Unacceptable. How did Herman expect me to live in this isolated hole under these circumstances?" His head shook. "Impossible."

"Herman had insufficient time to arrange suitable accommodations."

"Untrue." Korlemo stomped around the room. "Where are my pianist and valet?"

"Brother, this is not Ramsey. You cannot expect the same treatment as in Kentucky."

"I demand someone tend to my needs."

"Here, people will not work for the same wages we paid in Ramsey, nor will they submit to similar conditions."

Korlemo paused before a floor-to-ceiling bookcase behind the desk. "Our dear friend, Madame LaLaurie maintained her staff—even after she moved to France."

Enu grimaced. "Our friend? Are you referring to Marie Delphine MacCarthy?"

"When we dined in Paris, Madame LaLaurie recounted various methods she used to inspire her staff's obedience."

"*Your* friend lived in nineteenth-century slave state Louisiana. Besides, she fled America in disgrace and died over a century ago."

"How do you know? A *lupasteri* with her guile—"

"And if half the rumors can be relied upon, she mutilated and tortured her servants. They burned down the mansion, preferring death to life with her authority."

Shrugging, Korlemo said, "Whatever works."

"Does it not disturb you, Brother, that those enslaved people resembled you and me?"

"Fate rewards the strong. For centuries, Africans have enslaved and been slaves—as you well know."

"You seriously want to emulate a wretched, sadistic slaveowner?"

Korlemo circled the study. "I expect the same accommodations as before."

"It is not possible—"

"Do it!" Korlemo snarled, glowering at him.

Enu exhaled and closed the ledger. "Tantrums will not replicate the circumstances Herman created for you in Kentucky. We relocated at your insistence."

Korlemo lurched forward. "If servants cannot be hired to meet my demands, I expect my family to provide those services."

Enu gaped. "And function as servants?"

"If you do not want your wife and children cleaning the floors, I suggest you find a solution."

For a moment, Enu considered whether his filial obligations had finally exceeded their limitations. Resolved to complete the task at hand, he returned to reviewing the financial statements Korlemo provided.

"Well," the latter grunted, "are the funds sufficient?"

"Yes, but there appears to be a discrepancy in Herman's figures."

"Discrepancy? What do you mean?" Korlemo dashed over to the desk and peered over Enu's shoulders.

"I am not an accountant, however, it appears someone removed a significant amount of money from your accounts the day before the mwindaji slaughtered Herman and his family."

"Who?"

Enu stood and stretched his back. "I do not know."

"Figure it out."

"Hire an accountant if you want specifics." Enu sauntered over to a cushioned armchair beside the fireplace. "Otherwise, you possess sufficient finances for our present needs."

"Irrelevant." Korlemo's hands fisted. "I want the person who stole from me."

The door opened, and Zainabu entered. She glanced at Enu before pivoting toward Korlemo. "I heard shouting. Can I help?"

"No one shouted," Enu said, studying her. "Why are you here?"

In front of the desk, Korlemo held a chair out for her. "She will assist me since you refuse."

"Brother, I did not refuse. I merely stated an accountant can provide the details you require. I cannot."

"Perhaps I can." Zainabu smiled up at Korlemo. "If you wish, I will hire a forensic accountant. What else do you need?"

"I want to leave this retched place—immediately. But first, I must know who stole from me."

Tired, Enu headed for the study door. With his hand on the knob, he glanced back. "Our security should take precedence over your vengeance."

Korlemo sulked. "True." He turned toward Zainabu. "You will arrange for my personal security. The Baptistes have family along the eastern coast. What is the cousin's name, the one who heads their New York branch?" he asked Enu.

"Stefan."

"Correct." Korlemo addressed Zainabu. "He will assist you with the arrangements."

At the door, Enu spoke in Ibori, the language of their tribe. "Do you think it wise to trust this witch with these responsibilities?"

Korlemo snorted. "I do."

"We know nothing about her origins."

"Because of her vision, we left Ramsey before the mwindaji attacked."

"How do you know the mwindaji executed Herman Baptiste?"

"Who else?"

"You forget, Brother. Many *bindimèn* would love to see you dead, not to mention the demon."

Korlemo's jaw tensed. "This is not Zorulo."

"Are you sure?" Enu glanced at Zainabu. "Demons are clever and understand many ways to defeat an opponent."

He departed.

Chapter 5

T HE HONDA'S ENGINE IDLED as Makeda stared at the ramshackle house. Her chin quivered. Chilled, despite the warm spring morning, she recalled how lovely and delicate the home appeared to her as a child. She shut off the engine and exited the car.

Side by side, she and the squirrel surveyed the exterior. Minutes elapsed with the only sounds coming from rustling leaves and chirping birds. Makeda stepped onto the porch and prepared to open the door when a hawk swooped down and scooped up the squirrel.

"Yewande!" she shrieked.

The bird clutched onto the squirrel's body and soared into the sky. Confused, Makeda searched for something to hurl at it. Before she found an object, the tiny squirrel morphed into a ginger cat and snapped at the hawk.

Squawking, the bird released the feline, who fell toward the ground. Makeda rushed over toward the falling animal. She caught the cat and coddled it to her chest. Her heart raced as she stroked the cat's coat. The feline wriggled free and vaulted onto the ground.

'I'm fine. Let's get on with this.'

'Big Mom—Yewande, you could've been killed. Can't you assume a human body?'

'No, not unless I possess a bindimèn.'

Makeda frowned. 'A bindimèn?'

'That's what zaubers call humans.'

'Then why not a larger animal like a dog or cat?'

'Because stupid people kept trying to rescue me. I got tired of being dropped off at animal shelters.'

'What do you mean by possessing?'

'Forget it. Come on.'

Makeda unlocked the front door, and they stepped inside. Yewande, in the form of a cat, slunk through the door close upon her ankles.

Inside, drop cloths covered the few pieces of furniture. At least an inch of dust covered the surfaces. Beginning in the living room, Makeda removed the coverings and inspected the furniture. A half dozen photos lined a table near the front door.

One by one, Makeda admired the photos. In one, she viewed her great-grandmother as a young woman wearing a thin mid-calf dress with a blue beaded charm around her left ankle. Ten minutes passed before she realized Yewande had disappeared.

The small home had a rectangular living room. A narrow staircase led upstairs. Slightly off center of the front door, an arched doorway led into the kitchen. A door in the kitchen opened onto the back-yard. Makeda exited the house. Cautiously, she tested the splintered deck planks before proceeding outside.

On her left, a tangled mass of bramble and weeds choked the once-thriving herb garden. To the right, Makeda admired tall pine trees. At the far end of the yard stood a majestic oak tree. Kudzu draped down its tortuous limbs. She frowned.

'I loved this place. It seemed magical.'

'It will be again.' The cat slithered around her legs. 'Your first lesson.' Licking its paws, the cat stretched out along the creaking deck.

'An accomplished zauber understands magic *and* sorcery. Herbs play an important part in both. Now, clean up this mess.'

Makeda gazed at the cat. 'By myself?'

'Yes. You must prepare to face Zorulo.'

'Tell me about this demon. Who is he, and why would he come after me?'

'Why an enemy hates you makes no difference. Being prepared for battle does.'

With a deep breath, Makeda scrutinized the yard. She scratched her head. 'But I want to know why—' She looked down. The cat had disappeared.

'Yewande?'

In addition to wondering why a demon wanted her dead, Makeda failed to understand how cleaning up a garden would improve her sorcery. For a moment, she stared into the sky.

Would being a zauber help the mwindaji? What other sacrifices would she have to make?

As she re-entered the house looking for tools, Makeda mentally formed a list of questions to ask her great-grandmother.

First question, what did she mean about possessing bindimèn? Next, why did a demon want me dead?

Chapter 6

Inside the Ramsey Sheriff's Office, Michael Wilson propped his feet up on the desk and laughed. "So, when will you finish the yard work?" he asked, speaking on his cellphone.

"I'm not sure, but not before this weekend," Makeda answered.

Birds squeaked in the background.

"What about your brothers?"

"Peter's busy with wedding plans."

"Thomas?"

"It's complicated."

"Too busy with video games, right?"

"It's only one weekend."

"Don't forget your promise."

"I haven't," Makeda said before hanging up.

Reclined in a chair, Michael fantasized about his upcoming plans with Makeda. Since the mwindaji left Ramsey, most of their interactions had been telephonic. They shared one brief Saturday, discussing current events and making plans. He had no intention of letting Makeda forget about her promise. Knowing he would soon spend time alone with her made the monotony of Ramsey tolerable.

Michael grabbed his hat off the desk and exited his office. "Anything happening I should know about?" he asked a room full of deputies while zipping up his jacket.

"No, Sheriff. It's been quiet," a deputy said while filling out a form.

"Ramsey usually is," added Carlotta, their dispatcher.

"Anything from Bowling Green?" he asked.

"Naw. They've probably wrapped up the Baptiste murders by now," a deputy said.

"Any news about the dog?" he asked, glancing at the German shepherd sitting at attention beside the entrance.

"No, sir," a deputy replied.

"She's all yours," Carlotta said, grinning.

"I can't take care of a dog," he said.

"If you don't, we'll have to send her back to the breeder." Carlotta slipped on headphones and answered an incoming call.

Whistling for the dog to follow, Michael departed.

Outside, he inhaled crisp morning air, reflecting on events of the past month. The chief medical officer of the local hospital had been indicted for embezzlement after she fled with millions of dollars. Two of the most prominent families in the county had been slain in their own homes. *And* he learned his girlfriend belonged to a group called mwindaji, traveling the country killing monsters. April in Ramsey had *not* been boring.

Before starting his patrol car and phoning Bowling Green Homicide Division, he opened the back door for the German shepherd to hop inside.

"Hello, this is Sheriff Wilson in—"

"Oh, hey, Mike. What's up?"

"Hey, Ryan. Nothing much here. I wanted to check in. See how the Jason Tupelo investigation is going."

"That's been officially closed as of five o'clock yesterday. The DA issued a public statement."

Michael checked his watch. "I didn't see anything in the paper about it."

"Yep. The news will eventually trickle over to Ramsey. They concluded Jackie Baptiste murdered Jason Tupelo, and the gang she was associated with committed the homicides at the Baptiste and Senegal homes."

"The state attorney didn't contact us."

"I'm just a homicide detective," Ryan said. "They probably figured it wouldn't matter."

"Strange." Michael considered how the state attorney could close a homicide case in Ramsey's jurisdiction without contacting the sheriff's department. *Why would the state attorney rush such a significant investigation?*

Jackie's father, Herman Baptiste, had been the chief financial officer at Lebanon Memorial Hospital. From Makeda, Michael learned how Mr. Baptiste and his family of werewolves preyed on hospital patients. His stomach churned at the memory of the hospital refrigerator.

"Well, now Ramsey can go back to being sleepy, small-town America." Ryan chuckled.

"I guess. Hey, let me know if anything changes."

"Will do. Call when you're in town. We can throw a couple burgers on the grill and watch a game."

They chatted for another minute before Michael hung up. Staring out of the windshield, he considered what Ryan had said.

Fortunately for the mwindaji, authorities had no idea of their group's involvement—or existence. It irked Michael though that the state attorney's office closed the case without consulting his department. Another peculiar thing about Ramsey. He started the cruiser and began his patrol.

The car dashboard clock displayed 5:28 p.m. After a brief call to his dispatcher, Michael headed toward southwest Ramsey. Though not gated, the area clearly represented a higher economic area of town. Spacious lots held old colonial homes. A few still had separate functional servant quarters.

He'd stopped calling them slave quarters because it irritated the owners. Amid this display of opulence sat an older, sturdy brick house with a huge, gnarled oak tree anchoring the front yard.

Michael parked in the 1950's ranch home's driveway, ambled up to the entrance, and rang the bell. Less than a minute elapsed before the door opened.

An older man with light blue eyes squinted. "Hey, Mike. Come in. It's chilly."

"Thanks, Doc." Michael entered, careful to wipe his feet on the mat. "Oh, can Daisy come in?"

"Sure. Your sidekick's welcome." The doctor wiped his glasses as he entered the living room.

Michael and Daisy followed. The former admired the classical interior before taking a seat beside a wall of windows at the rear of the room.

Over several minutes, the doctor arranged a small card table and another chair across from Michael.

"Need any help, Neil?" he asked.

"I'm good. What can I get you? Wine?"

"Beer for me." He stretched his legs beside the table and gazed into the backyard.

Neil returned with a can of beer and a bowl of pretzels, took a seat, and placed a deck of cards on the table.

"To friendship," he said, holding up a glass of brandy.

"And honesty." Michael tapped his beer bottle against the doctor's glass.

With a side grimace, Neil asked, "What does that mean?"

Michael drank while studying his friend. "Simply what I said. Truth between friends."

Without replying, Neil dealt the cards. Both men picked up their hands and play began. Several hours of brisk gin rummy ensued. Neil won the last hand.

"You're off your game tonight, Mike."

"I've been distracted."

"How's it working with your canine program?" Neil said, tilting his head toward Daisy.

He exhaled. "Fine, except no one wants to take care of the dog. I don't know what Carlotta was thinking signing us up as a K-9 unit."

Neil frowned. "I thought you liked dogs."

"As pets. This dog will bite your face off. Besides, we don't have a kennel for her."

"Take her home."

Michael shook his beer can and discovered it was empty.

Neil stood. "Want another?"

"No, I have to drive home."

With a mischievous grin, Neil said, "The mountains are nice in the summer. You planning a trip soon?"

"How did you find out I was planning a trip?"

"It's no secret you and Makeda are involved."

"Careful," Michael cautioned.

The doctor's blue eyes lit up. "Makeda's a decent girl. Besides, her brothers will look after her."

"Does everyone in Ramsey have to know my business?"

"No." Neil shuffled the cards. "But they do." He dealt another hand of gin.

Michael crunched on pretzels, tossing several to Daisy.

"If you don't want people to know your business, don't live in a small town." Neil swallowed the rest of his drink, and they both considered their cards.

After another hand, play ended. Neil returned to the mini-bar and prepared himself another drink. "Sure you don't want another beer?"

"I'm good." Michael reclined in the chair. "Have any suspicious corpses showed up in the morgue?"

While sipping brandy, Neil retired to the kitchen. "No." Neither spoke until he returned to the table.

"Look—"

"Mike, trust me. I'm in control." Neil removed his glasses and wiped the lenses with his shirttail.

He studied Neil's profile for a second then stared into the woods. "I can't keep Ramsey safe if I don't know what's going on."

"I remember how this town suffered before the mwindaji arrived. We're in this together." He raised his glass.

In return, Michael raised the empty beer bottle. "Thanks. I had to be sure."

At the door, they shook hands.

Michael sauntered over to his cruiser, surveying the neighborhood along the way. Daisy hopped into the passenger seat. As he strapped in and reversed down the driveway, he glanced at the 1950's ranch.

"What are you lying about Neil?" He sighed. "Time will tell."

Woof.

He patted Daisy's head, reached over, and removed two guns from the glove box, one a department-issued weapon and the other a gift from Makeda. The second gun held silver bullets. Michael checked both weapons.

"Let's go home."

As he headed west, an unsettling thought arose. He knew his life would change again. *For better or worse?*

Chapter 7

Jules Senegal paced before terrace windows overlooking a rainy Manhattan skyline. He reviewed the information his sister had shared.

In April, Svie unexpectedly arrived on his doorstep from Kentucky alleging malfeasance by Herman Baptiste against the *ajabu* community of werewolves and vampires. She claimed Korlemo's actions jeopardized their existence.

Svie took drastic actions to protect their community, embezzling money from Lebanon Memorial Hospital to support the ajabu. Jules barely had time to process the information before she had fled. Her safety remained his primary concern.

The assaults in Ramsey killed their father and brothers. Initially, he had discounted Svie's concerns—her story sounded fantastic. Their family had never run afoul of law enforcement. They kept their affairs private and supported the proper charities *and* politicians. Jules marveled at how anyone could associate them with illegal activities.

Have we been targeted? But by whom?

In one day, they had lost their patriarch and respectable name. Now, Svie risked losing her life. The day after his sister flew out of JFK airport, the Kentucky State Police arrived at his door inquiring about her whereabouts.

Straightforwardly, Jules had explained to the authorities how Svie requested his assistance. At the time, he had no knowledge of any improprieties concerning Lebanon Memorial Hospital. Further, he asserted Herman Baptiste instigated his sister's involvement.

In Jules' version, Svie discovered discrepancies with the hospital's finances. Because she feared Baptiste framed her for embezzlement—or at least incompetence—she had fled. Svie had pleaded for time to sort out the situation.

He offered her a place to stay while he consulted an accounting firm and obtained legal advice. Svie had declined to wait and contacted a friend, who drove her to the airport. Jules hadn't spoken with his sister since.

The NYPD, along with a representative from the Kentucky Bureau of Investigations, searched his home. Once confident Jules hadn't hidden his sister on the property, the authorities departed.

Staring at the cellphone in his hand, Jules grudgingly made a call.

The phone rang once before a voice asked, "Hello?"

"Stefan? Jules."

"Are you calling—"

"It's a burner phone."

"Good. Still under surveillance?"

"Not since I called my lawyers. You?"

A slew of curse words erupted over the phone. "Police are parked outside our New Jersey estate."

"And in Ramsey?"

"The KBI blamed the murders on Jackie's friends, some gang out of Cincinnati."

Jules sat on the sofa. "It's possible. Jackie—"

"They're wrong!"

Seconds passed. Jules didn't want to upset Stefan. Jackie had associated with the scum of society, but he needed to tread carefully. Stefan wouldn't want his sister's reputation maligned.

Herman Baptiste, Stefan's father, had lied to the quorum and betrayed the *ka'trete*, an ancient agreement between Korlemo and the ajabu. Svie proved Baptiste's duplicity with hospital financial documents. However, right now Jules needed Stefan's help to protect Svie. He didn't want to sever their mutually beneficial relationship—not yet.

While he understood Stefan mourned the death of his father, Jules needed answers—especially concerning Korlemo. The more Jules understood about Korlemo's plans, the safer Svie would be.

"Can I help? What's going on now?"

Stefan explained how the FBI and Kentucky state attorney requested a meeting with him and his older sister, Abigail. However, on the advice of counsel, the Baptiste family had discontinued communication with the authorities.

Jules listened impatiently before interjecting. "Where's Korlemo?"

"His highness is fine." Stefan swore again. "He expects me to drop everything to protect his family. Fortunately, our influence in Kentucky has prevented legal attention from following him. We persuaded the state attorney to close the case."

"Is Korlemo's new home secure?" Jules prodded delicately.

"Nothing's wrong with the place. He's simply upset that the accommodations lack the opulence of his Kentucky mansion," Stefan mumbled. "Like my father could accomplish a miracle in a week. A week! That's how long Korlemo gave my dad to move a family of vampires."

Disinterested in Stefan's tirade, Jules asked, "Where did you move the dragon?"

"Don't worry about it. Enu's handling their finances—for now. The zauber has become a real problem. According to Enu, she's gained an ascendancy over Korlemo."

"She's a witch, not a zauber."

"Witch, zauber." Stefan chuckled. "It reminds me of a joke. What's the difference between a witch and a sorceress?" He paused. "The shoes."

Jules frowned. "Korlemo never struck me as susceptible to another person's influence. Is she drugging him?"

"The millennial vampire is a glutton for flattery. I plan to speak with Dayo. See if she can get rid of the witch."

"I'm sorry about what you're going through—especially Abigail. Let me help. I know—"

"Forget it," Stefan interrupted. "Korlemo's in a prissy mood. Besides, he'll insist upon Sylvia returning the money."

Jules' shoulders stiffened. "Did he tell you that?"

"Listen. We've been friends since diapers." Stefan paused. "Don't deny Sylvia embezzled from the quorum. Fortunately for her, Korlemo remains ignorant of her defalcation."

"This isn't her fault. What happened to our fathers—"

"The mwindaji murdered our families."

"How do you know? I read the authorities blamed local gang members." *Friends of Jackie.*

Stefan guffawed. "The police swallowed that garbage, but we know the truth. Gangs kill for drugs or money."

"Or revenge."

"Thugs don't use silver bullets, and nothing was stolen. If Jackie pissed off a biker gang, they would've assassinated her outside the bar."

True. But Herman bore some responsibility for what transpired. Though Jules held Herman responsible for the massacre, he needed Stefan's help to protect Svie. For the moment, he would consent to Stefan's perception of events.

"We should meet."

"Abigail asked me to invite you over, but now isn't the time. Once the police surveillance ends, we'll call."

"Okay, Stef. But soon. We need to discuss what to do next."

"Right. Later." Stefan hung up.

For several minutes, Jules stared at the phone. Eventually, he placed it on the coffee table and walked over to the windows. He considered arriving unexpectedly at the New Jersey estate. Abigail wouldn't be offended, but Stefan would, especially since he specifically advised Jules to stay away.

Perhaps he should've gone before calling Stefan. *Too late now.*

There would be heightened security around the estate. An angry Stefan had the ability to order his childhood friend's elimination—quite easily in fact.

The Baptistes have provided security, not simply for Korlemo, but other influential people—bindimèn and ajabu alike.

While Jules and the other Senegals focused on finance and technology, the Baptistes made their fortune from security services and armaments. A war between the two families would not end well for the Senegals.

He must tread softly. Mentally, he created a to-do list with Svie as priority one.

As the two remaining children of their father, he would ensure one of them survived. Much depended on it—for them and countless others.

Chapter 8

A S THE SUN CRESTED over the treetops, Makeda inhaled and leaned against the deck railing. The splintered boards wobbled.

"I need to fix this deck next."

In the distance, leaves on the majestic oak tree bristled, fluttering in the cool evening breeze. She wiped her forehead and sauntered over to the tree.

Makeda sat on the ground, admiring the oak tree for a full minute. She leaned over and pulled up a stray piece of kudzu.

"Thought I removed all of you yesterday."

Over the next hour, she lit a small fire in the backyard and burned any remaining kudzu. When she admired the old oak tree this time, it appeared more erect. Its leaves shone proudly. Makeda hugged the tree and kissed its trunk.

"Feels liberating with no kudzu choking you, right?"

Returning to the house, she spied a tabby cat perched on the deck.

'Yewande. Where have you been?'

The cat glared at her, then scrutinized the yard.

'What have you done?'

Makeda frowned. 'I cleaned up like you told me to.' She sauntered over to the herb garden.

'Look. I removed the weeds and replanted herbs.' Makeda removed a stake from the ground. 'I labeled them for easy identification.'

With a strut, the cat joined her beside the herb garden.

A moment of peace descended before in a frenzied whirlwind, the tabby tore up the plantings.

Makeda gawked and chased after the cat. 'Stop it! What are you doing?'

Spryly evading Makeda's grasp, the tabby leaped onto the deck. 'The point wasn't to acquire a green thumb. It was an opportunity to use sorcery.'

'What difference does it make? I replanted the herbs. Now you can teach me how to make potions and healing salves.' She pointed to the majestic oak tree. 'I even removed the kudzu.'

Instantly the cat morphed into a snarling pit bull.

Shocked, Makeda bolted backward and tumbled off the deck.

'I don't care about those stupid trees,' the dog growled, its teething chomping in the air.

Yewande resumed the form of a cat and shook her coat. 'Sorry. Sometimes, I lose my temper.'

Swishing its tail, the cat sat. 'You were supposed to practice sorcery, not waste time gardening.'

'I didn't waste time.' Makeda sulked. She dusted debris from her bottom and rested on the edge of the deck. She stared into the woods.

The cat gazed up at her. 'I don't remember you being this foolish.'

'And I don't remember you being so mean.'

Laying a paw on Makeda's thigh, the cat replied, 'I'm trying to protect you.'

'From what? You won't even explain why a demon wants to kill me.'

'Who do you think killed me?'

She gaped. 'I-I'm sorry.' Regarding the cat, she asked, 'But why me?'

'Because you're my great-granddaughter, and I love you. Zorulo will destroy anything—anyone—associated with me.'

Makeda shivered and surveyed the yard. 'Is it safe here?'

Stretching its back, the cat nodded. 'Yes. I've taken precautions.'

'Like what?'

'Doesn't matter.'

'And home? Are Mom and Dad safe?'

'They're fine.'

She rose, dusting off her shorts. 'How did he find out about me?'

'When you contacted me, he heard you.'

'Mom told me to be careful. Why didn't you reach out to me sooner?'

The cat strolled around the deck. 'Judith made you repeat a *go-mani dufa*, a binding spell. I had to wait to be invited back.'

Makeda frowned. 'From where? And if I had to invite you, how can this demon—'

'Too many questions.' The cat pointed with its paw. 'Remove these plantings.'

'You can't be serious.'

'I am. Do it now.'

She searched the ground, looking for the hoe.

The cat scampered over to her. 'What are you waiting for?'

'A hoe. I need something to pull them up with.'

Lowering its head, the cat meowed. 'Silly child. You're a zauber. Pull them up with maji.'

Makeda grimaced. 'How? You didn't show me—'

'I taught you spells and incantations. Use them.'

'But not about gardening.'

The cat scratched Makeda's shoe.

'Watch it.'

'Do it. Now!'

Following a quick glare at Yewande, Makeda walked over to the herb garden. She knelt down and touched the soil. For a moment, she gazed at the simpering pile of leaves, kudzu, and branches. Her fingers dove into the soil as Makeda considered the various spells Yewande shared over the past two weeks. She closed her eyes and mumbled an incantation.

Opening her eyes, Makeda found the garden remained unchanged. In fact, a tiny cardinal perched on one of the stakes. The cat flew into the herb garden and chased the bird away.

'Pull them up!' Yewande shrieked.

This time, Makeda kept her eyes open. Seconds passed. Nothing changed. A full minute elapsed. Her shoulders slumped.

'Sorry, I can't.'

With a piercing meow, the cat bounded onto her hand and scratched Makeda's wrist.

"Ouch!" She cradled her wrist. "That hurt."

'Now!' The cat glowered.

Her jaw clenched. Makeda slammed her hands into the earth. *Ubumi.* Herbs, plants, and flowers fluttered.

She concentrated on the garden, picturing it in her mind. Clutching the soil, Makeda yelled, "Ubumi!"

Suddenly, the ground trembled. Plantings spewed upward like an erupting volcano. All around vegetation littered the earth.

Tilting its head, the cat said, 'See. You did it.'

'Did you have to scratch me?' Makeda examined the slightly oozing cut on her wrist.

'Apparently, I did. You've wasted weeks playing farmer.'

'Why are you acting like this?'

'I'm trying to save your life!'

Kicking the soil with the toe of her boot, Makeda meandered around the yard. 'Maybe it's not worth saving.'

For the first time, Makeda reconsidered her desire to become a zauber, especially with Yewande as a teacher. She had been a proud mwindaji for most of her life. Why did she need to become a zauber?

As a mwindaji, she fought vampires and werewolves. Did she want to tussle with demons?

Besides, Mom warned her about Yewande. Perhaps for once Mom had been correct.

The cat trotted onto the deck. 'Oh, child. I've left you for too long. You've become weak.'

Tears streamed down Makeda's face. 'You don't understand.'

'Doesn't matter. I can't stay here and play nursemaid.'

'Where are you going?'

'My powers here are weak.'

'Why? What happened—'

'Dammit. Stop with the questions.'

Makeda's mouth snapped shut.

Circling the deck, Yewande replied, 'I'm sending you to a friend.'

'Who?'

'Eldridge. He'll train you.'

'Why?'

'If you practiced as much as you inquire, you'd be a magnificent zauber.'

Makeda frowned. What happened to the warm, supportive great-grandmother she once loved? *Had Yewande always been this fierce?*

That wasn't it. She worried Makeda wouldn't be strong enough to defeat the demon.

Or Mom had been right. She hoped not.

As Yewande gave directions about contacting Eldridge, Makeda considered her options. *Become a zauber or remain a mwindaji.*

Could she learn maji while maintaining her mwindaji fighting skills? *Why not?*

Her shoulders shrank. She shouldn't have to choose.

Inspecting her cut wrist, Makeda hoped Tennessee held answers and less risk of injury.

Chapter 9

T HE PAST WINTER HAD Michael on the verge of returning to Georgia. He'd never been so cold or seen so much snow. Thankfully, he found May in Ramsey more tolerable.

In the morning, he had picked up the department's canine trainee, Daisy. The German shepherd lived at the sheriff's station since none of his deputies would home the dog. Poor dog didn't even have a name until he christened her Daisy.

One morning, Michael had arrived at the station to let the shepherd out to relieve herself. As the dog bounded through the grass and rolled around, a daisy became stuck under her collar. Instantly, Michael named her Daisy.

Naming an animal capable of killing a human being after a delicate flower amused him, and the German shepherd answered to the name. In time, as expected, he had become de facto owner of the dog. But he hadn't taken Daisy home.

The department dispatcher, Carlotta, fed the dog, but permanent accommodations had to be arranged—and soon. Yesterday, the shepherd chewed up a box of old case files.

Since pseudo-adopting Daisy, Michael exercised more. He smiled, knowing Makeda would appreciate his toned physique. Like most mornings, he and Daisy hit the jogging trails adjacent to Cumberland Highway west of downtown Ramsey.

Trucks raced up and down the road all morning. Michael stayed vigilant. Though no longer a puppy, Daisy's curiosity often brought her near the roadway. This morning, while he tied a loose shoestring, Daisy wandered close to the road following a scent.

In the distance, a semi barreled down the highway.

With a whistle, Michael yelled, "Daisy, come here!"

The shepherd's tail wagged, and her head raised. After one long inhale, she trotted to his side. He retrieved her, reattaching the leash as a semi roared by. For a moment, he regarded the traffic.

Pulling on the lead, Daisy sniffed grass.

Michael's cellphone pinged. An alert reminded him about his phone date with Makeda. How long had it been since he'd seen her? How long until their next date?

Michael headed toward the trail when an older model RV towing a battered pickup truck sped down the road. Although it lacked any distinguishing features, Michael recognized it without recalling from where. As the vehicles approached, he focused on identifying the driver.

A dark-skinned man with dreadlocks zoomed past, instantly triggering a memory—one Michael would not soon forget. Visions of a refrigerator and dissected animal and human body parts flashed across his mind.

Pressure built up inside his chest. Michael rubbed his sternum in a useless attempt to push aside his fears. Because if Zeke had returned to Ramsey, the mwindaji would have returned too. And if the mwindaji returned...

His hand trembled.

"Come on." Yanking Daisy's leash, he returned to the trail.

On the jog home, he recalled what Makeda taught him about werewolves. His hand absently grazed his waist. Not finding his gun, he began sprinting, suddenly anxious to return home.

Chapter 10

P ETER GLANCED AT THE speedometer, checking Zeke's speed. In the rear of the RV, Raymond and Thomas cleaned weapons while watching a movie.

"Careful," Peter said. "There's a speed trap right before you enter Ramsey."

"No problem." Zeke increased the volume on the tape deck as *Get Up Stand Up* by Bob Marley belted out from the speakers.

Peter detected a decrease in the RV's speed and extended his neck along the headrest. His thoughts flowed to Brenda and their upcoming wedding. Once he returned home, he and his future bride needed to find an apartment. Newlyweds shouldn't live with their parents.

"Listen," Zeke said, giving him a side glance and interrupting his fantasies about the honeymoon. "I want to talk to you about Uncle J."

Peter sat up straight, scrutinizing Zeke's profile. "What do you mean?"

Instantly, conversations in the rear of the RV ceased. Peter had the distinct impression everyone was focused on their conversation.

"Man, we've been friends—brothers—since childhood," Zeke spoke without taking his attention off the road. "Uncle J's obsession with Korlemo..."

Heat burned inside Peter's stomach. He struggled not to reply harshly. "Dad's not obsessed."

"Dude, seriously?" Zeke peeked across the RV at him. "We'd be sitting at home twiddling our thumbs if Carolyn and I hadn't insisted on making this trip."

"Dad wanted us to lay low until the incident in Ramsey cooled off."

"Korlemo is not the only monster out there. We spend too much time chasing him."

Peter didn't reply because internally he agreed. But loyalty to his dad mattered and took precedence.

"He leads this crew. We follow his direction."

"To what end?"

Quiet engulfed the camper. Minutes elapsed before the mwindaji in the rear returned to their prior occupations.

Removing a flick knife from his pocket, Peter flipped the blade repeatedly, mulling over Zeke's comments. He stared out the side window, observing tall pines whizzing by.

Up ahead, he spied a man and a dog jogging along a trail. Peter remembered searching those woods for clues to Korlemo's whereabouts. At the time, he had no idea the ancient vampire worked in the hospital along with his sister, Makeda.

As the jogger came into view, Peter taxed his memory. Although Zeke zipped past in seconds, he had enough time to recognize Sheriff Michael Wilson. A tingle thrilled along his spine. Seeing Ramsey's sheriff signaled a bad omen.

As the RV traveled down the highway, the flick knife in Peter's hand rotated faster.

On the eastern side of Ramsey, closer to Edmonton, a cellphone rang. Peter pivoted in the seat, watching Carolyn speaking on the phone.

"I understand," she said, nodding her head. "Give me the address."

Once the call ended, Zeke asked, "Problem?"

"A job."

A mile up the road, Zeke pulled the RV over at an abandoned gas station.

Raymond rose. "I'm going for a walk."

"You mean a smoke." Thomas chuckled and stretched his back. "I'll come too. I need some air."

"Then don't stand next to Raymond," Peter said, unbuckling the seat belt and joining Carolyn in the back of the RV.

After Zeke set the emergency brake, they gathered around a table.

"Okay, Sis," Zeke said, "spill it."

"Anonymous call about a vampire in Ramsey."

"Shit," Zeke said, scratching his head.

"Not again," Peter said.

"Why are you surprised?" Carolyn asked. "The place was infested. No way one hit would cleanse Ramsey."

"Exactly," Zeke said. "Infested. We can't take on all those monsters. This time they'll be prepared."

"And we don't have the whole team, only five of us."

Carolyn exhaled. "Fine. We eliminate this one vampire."

"What if the vampire isn't alone and we knock over a beehive for a second time?" Zeke asked.

"We should call Dad," Peter said. "He can poll the mwindaji and make the decision."

"Do you call your dad to take a crap?" Carolyn asked, grimacing.

"I respect protocol," Peter said, considering their options. He recalled the hospital conference room filled with a horde of vampires and werewolves.

Last time, they were lucky. The element of surprise gave them a tremendous advantage. Korlemo had fled before they arrived at the vampire's estate. *Or had he?*

"This isn't about protocols. It's about making a simple decision without asking daddy," Carolyn said with a sour face.

What if the leech never left? What if this call concerned Korlemo?

Peter removed his knife and began carving along the table's edge.

"Dad should be informed, in case something happens, and we need help."

Zeke placed a hand on Carolyn's shoulder. "Peter's right. We'll call it in. That's what teams do."

Thomas reentered the RV and prepared lunch as Peter called Dad in North Carolina.

"We don't have any intel other than the vampire's location," Peter said in response to Dad's questions.

On the conference call, Dad asked the group, "So what do y'all think?"

After a hurried vote, the mwindaji decided the team should eliminate this one vampire.

Dad said, "Call *before* you need help."

"Will do." Peter hung up.

As he chewed on a sandwich, Zeke said, "We aren't far outside Ramsey. We can head back this evening."

Peter wiped his forehead and asked Carolyn, "You have the details?"

"Yeah, I'll plot the assault. In the meantime, I suggest we rest."

Smarting from Carolyn's earlier comment and unsure about their mission, Peter settled in the passenger's seat. Though his eyes closed, Peter's mind raced. The flick knife remained in his clenched hand.

At sunset, Peter hopped in the driver's seat.

"What's up?" Zeke asked, holding a cup of coffee. "I can drive."

Peter adjusted the seat belt. "It'll give me something to do. Get my mind off the mission." He pushed aside flashbacks from their last assault in Ramsey.

Aware of Zeke's scrutiny, Peter focused on the road. He executed a three-point turn and pointed the RV west toward Ramsey. Zeke road shotgun.

As night descended across Kentucky, Peter reviewed their plan. He needed to focus on killing one vampire and not the festering tension inside the camper. A glance in the rearview mirror showed Carolyn observing him. He glared at her, and she glared right back.

Chapter 11

A SHORT BEEP PRECEDED the hospital intercom announcement. "The summer ACLS class has been rescheduled until after the Fourth of July. Contact medical staff services for specific details."

Dr. Wilton glanced up at the ER wall clock. Another hour before her shift ended. Her stomach growled. *Should have eaten this morning.*

She smiled and entered bay three to examine a patient. Thirty minutes later, she completed her final patient note.

"Are you finished with the Dictaphone?" a nurse asked. "I need to use it."

"You're welcome to it. I'm heading out."

Propping sunglasses on top of her classic black bob, Dr. Wilton exited the hospital. Night had fully enveloped Ramsey. Her sliver-thin lips whistled a tune as she crossed the employee parking lot and hopped in her car. Despite having a difficult last patient, her mood lightened. Her housekeeper was preparing a special dinner.

Dr. Wilton pulled into her garage. In the mudroom, she exchanged a medical coat and dress shoes for a silk robe and slippers.

"That you, Doc?" Felicia asked from inside the kitchen.

"You expecting anyone else?"

"I don't know. There's been weird noises around the house all day."

"Probably those raccoons. I told you to place a heavy rock on those trash cans."

"A rock ain't gonna stop a raccoon."

Felicia handed her a glass of wine.

Seated at the dining room table, Dr. Wilton sipped wine and settled into a cushioned chair. "Mmm. Smells delicious." She licked her lips. "Did you follow my instructions about the meal?"

"Of course." Felicia placed a covered platter on the dining room table. "I've fixed this dish before."

"I know, but I had a taste for something different. The recipe called for pork, but protein is protein."

"Well, bon appétit." Felicia grinned and returned to the kitchen.

Dr. Wilton removed the lid and inhaled vinegary scents. On the platter, surrounded by garnish and doused in olive oil and spices, wriggled a sleeping infant.

"Excellent," Dr. Wilton said as her pointy incisors elongated. She reached for the baby. "Wait. Where's the hot sauce?"

No reply.

"Felicia, I told you to leave hot sauce on the table."

From the kitchen came only silence.

Chair legs scrapped along the wood floor as the doctor headed for the kitchen.

"How many times do I have to tell you—"

She pushed the kitchen door aside and hissed.

Chapter 12

B LOOD DRIPPED OFF PETER's knife onto the tiled floor. He wiped it on a kitchen towel and motioned to Zeke. The latter positioned himself on the left side of the kitchen doorway while Carolyn took a position on the right.

Thomas tossed him a tarp. They prepared to wrap up the bloody body strewn across the floor when a heavy-set woman with a black bob entered.

At the sight of them, she hissed. Her height increased and her fingers extended. The vampire shrieked and leaped at Peter. Clawed hands reached forward, less than a foot away from his face. As she pounced, a spear ripped through her back and thrust out of her left breast. With a roar, the vampire grasped the spear in an attempt to remove it.

Carolyn thrust and twisted the implement. The bloodsucker swiped backward at Carolyn's head but missed. Her fight proved futile.

A whimper escaped the vampire's mouth as its clawed fingers retracted. She disintegrated into a pile of dust as Zeke left the kitchen.

Peter looked up from where he and Thomas were wrapping the other woman's body in a tarp.

"How much money does it take for a human being to feed another human to a vampire?" he asked.

"I've never understood that either," Carolyn said, gazing down at the dead woman. "Anyone who helps a monster deserves what they get."

Thomas said, "Me—"

"Ah, hell!"

Peter glanced up at Carolyn. Before he could stand, the kitchen door crashed open.

"Look," Zeke said, carrying a squiggling baby in his hands.

Peter's gaze widened. "What the—"

The infant started crying, and its wriggling increased. It slipped from Zeke's hands. Carolyn swooped in and caught the baby before it hit the ground.

"Careful," she said, swaddling the baby to her chest.

Scents of garlic and basil filled the kitchen.

She sniffed the baby. "This was supposed to be dinner."

Thomas handed her a towel, and Carolyn wiped the baby's face. She rocked the infant until it simpered and quieted.

For a moment, everyone stared at the baby.

"What do we do with it?" Thomas asked, touching the baby's cheek.

"I have an idea," Peter said. "Come on, Thomas. Help me with this. We'll toss the body into the caverns after we make a quick stop."

He and Thomas removed the corpse while Carolyn and Zeke checked the rest of the house.

Back in the RV, Peter looked up a number. He didn't want to make this call. He'd hoped not to speak to this person ever again. The baby belonged with her mother though, and this person knew how to make it happen.

Chapter 13

MICHAEL GRUMBLED AND ROLLED over in bed as the shrill ringing of his cellphone ended his dream. A second prior, he snuggled in a mountain cabin with Makeda.

The screen read unlisted. He didn't appreciate anonymous calls at any time but especially not in the middle of a dream about Makeda. He sat up in bed and glanced down at the floor. Daisy lifted her head momentarily, then returned to sleep.

"Lucky dog. Don't get comfortable. This is temporary."

On the fifth ring, he answered.

"Hello."

"Michael?" the voice asked. "Sheriff Michael Wilson?"

"Yes. Who is—"

"Peter. Meet me at the abandoned shopping center across from the hospital."

"Why?"

The call ended.

He rubbed sleep from his eyes and stumbled out of bed, careful not to step on Daisy. A thought crossed his mind, and Michael quickly dressed. If Peter called him instead of Makeda... *This couldn't be good.*

Michael and Daisy jumped in the cruiser and headed toward the hospital. A glance at the passenger's seat confirmed he had brought both guns and extra silver bullets.

As he passed Lebanon Memorial Hospital on the right, Michael spied an RV idling in the abandoned shopping center down the street. Next to the RV sat an older model pickup truck. The same truck he had spotted earlier that morning while jogging along Cumberland Highway. Michael recognized Zeke by the dreadlocks and thick black framed glasses. Peter waited beside the truck.

Zeke might have spotted him and told Peter. *But why would they want to catch up late at night in an abandoned shopping center?*

Michael recalled the prior icy reception he had received from Peter when the mwindaji eliminated Ramsey's monsters. Something bad must have happened for Peter to contact him. Silently, he prayed it didn't concern Makeda. Before he left home, he called her but only reached voicemail.

Bringing the cruiser alongside the truck, Michael stepped outside. Zeke rolled down the RV window and gave him a salute. With a brief nod, he acknowledged Zeke.

He said to no one in particular, "I know you guys operate at night, but this is a curious time to socialize."

Before Peter replied, a tall, muscular woman exited the RV and approached him with a package wrapped in a fluffy blanket.

"We need your help," Peter said as the truck idled.

"What's up?" Michael cracked the window for Daisy but left her inside the cruiser.

The woman said, "Makeda told us to trust you." Without explanation, she placed the package in his arms, then returned inside the RV.

Frowning, Michael accepted it and pulled aside the covers. He gasped. "A baby?" His head shook. "I almost don't want to know."

Peter said, "This afternoon we received an anonymous call about a vampire in Ramsey. We killed it before the baby became dinner."

"Are you saying—"

"The vampire intended to drain this child."

"Who made the call?"

"I said anonymous." Peter frowned.

"Damn."

"We searched the house. Apparently, the vampire had been working at the hospital," the woman said, speaking from the RV door.

"Here." Peter handed him several items. "We found a doctor's coat and a name tag."

By this time, Zeke had exited the RV and joined them. "Bro, you still have a pest problem."

The baby cried. Michael tried to quiet it without success.

"Guys, we need to go!" the women shouted from the RV.

Peter said, "Give us a minute. We just handed him a baby."

The woman rolled her eyes.

"Are the mwindaji coming back?" Michael asked.

"No," Zeke said, "we have other assignments. Besides, monsters are endemic here. Y'all have an internal problem. Someone *wants* these monsters here."

The RV horn beeped.

"Gotta go. Sorry for dumping this on you." Peter jumped in the truck.

Zeke jogged back to the RV.

Speaking out the open truck window, Peter said, "Ramsey has a systemic problem. Look for someone with deep pockets and authority. Korlemo's gone, but you have another mastermind. Ramsey has become a haven for monsters."

Michael nodded but didn't answer. By the time he had secured the baby into the cruiser, the truck and RV had disappeared, heading west toward Mammoth Caves National Park.

Driving four hundred yards across the road to the hospital, Michael parked and stared down the empty street, wishing the mwindaji would return. Not simply because he missed Makeda, but because he feared fighting vampires and werewolves alone.

But he had allies. Well, one. Dr. Bones had helped eliminate the monsters. But if this vampire had been employed at the hospital...

From the rear seat, Daisy sniffed the new occupant, whining to enter the passenger seat.

"That's not a toy," he said, rubbing his throbbing temples.

Woof.

Michael realized he'd been lied to by the one person in Ramsey he had trusted.

First, he had to look after the baby. On cue, the baby cried. Daisy whined louder.

Cradling the infant, and with Daisy at his side, Michael entered the ER. Later, he'd get answers from the person at the center of this tragedy.

Chapter 14

TOWERING TREES SURROUNDED THE spacious estate, providing desirable privacy. An hour into the hike, a panting Zainabu scanned the area. Her eyes gradually adjusted to the night. Dense woods made travel difficult, but she no longer saw the mansion—which meant her activities should remain private.

Far enough from the mansion and confident of isolation, Zainabu relaxed her shoulders and recited an incantation. *"Nani dufa"*.

In Baoumali, she repeated the incantations, summoning the demon.

"Nani dufa."

Leaves rustled. A woodland animal trudged nearby. Zorulo failed to materialize.

Tired from the hike, Zainabu rested on a diseased tree stump. Mushrooms and wild berries thrived in the foliage. A lemony scent wafted on the breeze. She studied the vegetation and picked a few items.

"These herbs might be useful." She had forgotten the exact ingredients for a drowning spell. Once she returned to the estate, she'd review the book of enchantments her grandmother had compiled.

Before fleeing Kondoro, the largest city near her village, she had stolen the book. Against her aunts' wishes, Zainabu learned maji. Studying from her grandmother's book, she gained knowledge beyond her expectations.

Zainabu managed to deliver an invitation spell and contact Zorulo. With his assistance, she obtained a commission from a powerful vampire. Immediately, her fortunes soared.

Presently, she lived in a mansion and controlled a vast estate. Money, power, and influence beyond what a child of farmers expected for her future.

Though her lineage included centuries of zaubers, that privilege had not been bestowed upon her, according to her aunts. However, Zainabu desired a life beyond predicting the weather and cursing disobedient children and wayward spouses. The cost had been significant but the rewards boundless.

She selected a half dozen plantings.

A couple meters ahead, a gaseous form materialized. Gradually, it coalesced into the shape of a bindimèn from the waist up. It hovered above the ground and spoke in a deep baritone.

"It's been too long." The gaseous face snarled. "Much too long."

Deep breath. If she managed a millennial vampire, she could deceive a *dubwana* like Zorulo.

"It's not been easy. Korlemo's on edge."

"Well, you suggested he flee Kentucky."

"And it salvaged our plans. Otherwise, Korlemo would have faced the mwindaji, and we would've lost our advantage."

The form enlarged as it approached her. "Perhaps that would've been wiser. The mwindaji might have accomplished what you have not."

Zainabu's shoulders stiffened. "I'm gaining his trust."

"I need him dead and returned to *duka mali*," Zorulo's face loomed over her. "Hell awaits his talents."

Sweat beaded along her forehead. "I understand, but it requires time."

"You're out of time." The cloud retracted but continued glowering.

"It will be done. But if you want it to be quick, I'll need your assistance."

"Then you are not the witch I presumed."

Clenching her hands inside her pockets, Zainabu said, "I am above a witch."

The demon snickered. "You wish to be."

Her jaw clenched. *Patience.*

She needed Zorulo to kill Korlemo. *But how will I eliminate the demon?*

Five meters to the right, two deer foraged in the woods. Their sleek heads turned and observed her a moment before they scampered away. On the ground, a foot away from where they grazed, a plant with blue flowers and silver-tipped petals materialized.

"Steep the leaves in water to create a solution or compound the leaves into a paste. It is flavorless and will render the taker unconscious for an hour," Zorulo said.

Zainabu carefully plucked the plant from the ground and laid it in her satchel.

"Remember, you must complete the gomani dufa incantation before he wakes. The binding spell will render him unconscious, and you can slay him with the enchanted *poni* I provided."

"A simple dagger will kill him?"

"This dagger has been enchanted with a spell I acquired centuries ago. Remember to strike him in the heart."

"Why can't I simply kill him myself?"

Zorulo cackled. "Clearly, you are dumber than you look. If you could defeat Korlemo, little witch, would you be in my debt?"

Zainabu's fingers dug into her palms. She gazed distantly, counting the various ways she'd like to execute this demon.

"By using the gomani dufa with the poni, you will assume tremendous maji. Enough to subdue and then kill Korlemo."

Pouting, Zainabu said, "I should receive more compensation considering the work involved."

"Do you believe I have been unfair?"

A shiver crept along Zainabu's spine. She braced for a lashing.

Instead, the demon grinned. The gaseous cloud descended, resting a meter in front of her.

"Okay. I have a proposition for you. Kill Korlemo this week and I'll let you keep the rings."

Her brow wrinkled. "What rings?"

"How can you be so ignorant? Surely, you've heard of the Ibori rings."

Zainabu had never heard about any special rings. She frowned in thought.

In answer to her unspoken expression, Zorulo said, "The Ibori possess three magical rings. One belonged to Lumisi, one to Tau, and the other to Lumisi's father. Each ring contains three jewels. Three *rare* jewels."

A smile lit up Zainabu's face. "How rare?"

"Produced by ancient craftsmen. None like them exist today."

"Valuable?"

"What cost can one place on such stones?"

The gaseous form developed into an entire bindimèn. It walked forward and held Zainabu's hands. "They possess unique powers. Maji gifted by Sharik to whoever wears them."

"The goddess of *kuru buni*," she gasped.

"Yes. The goddess of the sky." He waved his hand upward. "How do you believe Korlemo managed to live for over a thousand years?"

She contemplated the value of such a ring. Monetarily, it would be priceless.

"One ring gives longevity. But three rings would bring the bearer boundless strength and wealth."

Zainabu's eyes twinkled, imagining the possibilities.

With the rings I could easily remove the vampire and the demon. But why would Zorulo share them if they contain such power?

"Deliver Korlemo to me this week and they are yours."

Her eyes narrowed. "Why give them to me? Why not use them yourself?"

"I cannot. A demon cannot harness the power inside the rings. But with you indebted to me, it will be the same."

Not if I eliminate you. Zainabu struggled to contain her excitement.

"Consider them a tip for services rendered."

The gaseous cloud darkened. "But if you delay, I'll claim them myself and gift them to another, more worthy witch."

She considered. "And Korlemo has all three rings?"

"He has one as does his brother. The last ring belonged to Lumisi's grandfather. He likely passed it down to a relative. With guile, you can discover its location."

Studying Zorulo, she weighed the veracity of his story. It must be verified.

Would one ring carry any significant power?

Korlemo had survived a millennium and maintained an opulent lifestyle. Once she eliminated him, she'd acquire his ring. Obtaining Enu's ring should be simple.

How can I discover the location of the third?

"Do we have a deal?" Zorulo extended his hand.

"Of course." Zainabu shook the hand, which instantly dissolved into a gas along with the remaining demonic form.

Before leaving, Zainabu made sure the demon had completely disappeared. Standing alone in the forest, she considered whether the rings were worth the risk.

It would explain Korlemo's success.

She checked the satchel and examined the plant Zorulo provided. If the potion worked as promised, she'd kill Korlemo, seize the rings, and eliminate Zorulo in quick succession.

On her fingers, Zainabu counted off the items required to complete these tasks. The ostrich feathers she had brought from home would come in handy. Bird eggshells would be easy to acquire.

"Hmm. I need lizard tongue, mushrooms, mold, squirrel feet."

To kill Korlemo, obtain the rings, and remove Zorulo from her life would be the perfect trifecta. There would be significant danger but an immense reward. However, the timeline had suddenly shortened.

Zorulo had lost patience, and now, she had, too.

Smiling, Zainabu scanned the forest floor in search of mushrooms.

Chapter 15

MICHAEL CROSSED THE EMPTY ER waiting room in three long strides. He motioned to the clerk, who buzzed him into the rear without question. The bundle in his arms squirmed. He repositioned his tiny package, clutching it tightly to his chest.

Noisy beeping machines and intense white overhead lighting greeted him. He stood there, searching in vain for assistance. Then, from a locked side room, a man emerged wearing pale green scrubs and rubbing a groggy, solemn face.

"Can I help you, Sheriff?" he asked.

"Where's everyone?" Michael asked, scanning the abandoned nursing station.

"Sleeping or eating. We rarely get a break, so we take advantage of any opportunity."

Michael unwrapped his bundle and handed it to the nurse. "I found this baby abandoned in the shopping center across the street.

The man's eyes enlarged, and a switch seemed to go off in his head. He hurried inside the nursing station and made an overhead announcement.

In under a minute, three people rushed through electronic doors separating the ER from the rest of the hospital. Staff swooped the infant from Michael's arms and carried it to a separate room.

They took vitals and placed the baby girl on a warming blanket. A nurse inserted an IV and drew blood. Someone provided a much-needed diaper change and bathed the infant.

Standing at the nursing station countertop, Michael watched the medical professionals in action.

Once the infant had been weighed, washed, and fed, a physician approached. "So, Sheriff, what's the story?"

He provided a brief fallacious story to satisfy the medical team. A nurse helped Michael complete a report for social services.

"We'll contact a social worker when they open at nine," the doctor said. "They'll need to speak with you."

"I understand."

Michael remained in the ER until the staff reassured him of the baby's condition. As he departed, the ER clock read 8:27 a.m. In the hospital lobby, a steady stream of employees entered and headed for their appointed destinations.

Furious and in need of answers, Michael decided to start with the medical director, Dr. Neil Bones. After a brief stop in the cafeteria for a much-needed cup of coffee and breakfast, Michael headed for the pathology department.

In addition to being the medical director, Dr. Bones served as head of pathology. Often, his friend could be found inside the morgue dissecting a corpse.

Michael tossed a strip of bacon to Daisy, who trotted along at his side. He sipped coffee to steady his nerves and wake himself up.

The morgue remained his nemesis. As sheriff, he'd seen plenty of dead bodies. But seeing dead bodies displayed on cold metal tables, flayed open for inspection disturbed him.

Besides, the last time he'd been in the morgue a hulking werewolf tried to kill him. In fact, it had sliced a deep gash in his chest before Makeda intervened. He hated morgues—this one especially.

With a deep breath, he pushed aside the swinging door and entered. Nauseated by the reeking antiseptic and formaldehyde, Michael tossed the coffee cup into a trashcan. The room's low light cast shadows along two empty gurneys. Empty.

After a quick peek across the hall into the pathology department, he and Daisy returned to the lobby and rode the elevator up to administration on the fifth floor.

With a nod, he greeted the administration staff. Daisy relished the attention, whimpering as people scratched behind her ears and patted her head. Michael gave her another bacon strip.

"Behave."

She licked his hand, and he gave her the final piece of bacon.

One brief knock preceded his entry into the medical director's outer office. The doctor's assistant hadn't arrived yet. The door to the medical director's private office sat ajar. Michael pushed it aside.

Neil glanced up from a computer screen. "Morning, Mike. A bit early for you. Give me a second to finish this note."

Removing his hat, Michael sat in one of two chairs positioned in front of the doctor's desk. His fingers circled the hat's brim, twirling it slowly as he contemplated the upcoming discussion.

"Hello, Daisy. You guys been out jogging already?"

"Busy morning. No time to run."

A slight frown creased the doctor's forehead. He tossed down the pen and leaned back in his leather chair. "Tell me. How can I help you?"

"A mutual friend called me last night. They rescued an infant before she became a vampire's dinner." Michael paused, regarding Neil.

The doctor held his gaze. Neither spoke.

Daisy yawned.

"One of your vampire doctors had an appetite for underdeveloped humans." He tossed the dead vampire's hospital name tag onto Neil's desk. Getting no response, Michael asked, "Did you know?"

Neil broke eye contact and stared at the wall over Michael's shoulder.

"Don't lie to me."

"I'm not going to." The doctor removed his glasses and cleaned them with a small square cloth. "You have to understand—"

"*Understand what?*" Michael shouted.

"Do you want me to answer your question, or do you want to shout at me?"

Michael reclined in the chair. They glared at each other.

"I struggled with the decision," Neil said, wiping his glasses before placing them on his head.

"Not employing monsters seems simple to me."

"With the hospital struggling financially, we don't have money to pay staff. If they're willing to work—"

"For what? What's the deal now?"

"Stop interrupting and listen!" Veins stretched taut in Neil's neck.

Daisy raised an ear and tilted her head.

"Fine." Michael hung the hat on his knee.

"You're judging me without appreciating my dilemma. I had to find a way to deliver medical services to the community. Ramsey depends upon Lebanon Memorial as does the surrounding counties. It may not be a perfect system, but we're making it work."

"Exactly how?"

"We have strict rules."

"Did those rules include eating babies?"

"Of course not." Neil rose. "I had no idea."

"You can't trust monsters. They have their own rules."

"My staff isn't like that. It's not their fault. Most of them want to live in peace like we do."

"They survive off human flesh and blood. How does your system work?"

"We use a blood bank to obtain human—"

"Neil, have you forgotten the refrigerator?"

A red bloom suffused the doctor's face and neck. He strode over to the coffee machine, gazing at the floor.

"Things have changed. We've put safety measures in place. They take a pledge. No unauthorized feeding."

"Well, your vampire missed the memo." Michael stood, slamming the hat onto his head. "Making a deal with the devil always turns out badly."

"It's different. I carefully select each staff member."

"I have news for you. Those security measures aren't working. If our friends hadn't received that tip, a baby girl would be dead."

At the door, Michael swung around. Daisy jaunted to his side.

"This is a mistake. You can't control them. Stop before the situation spirals out of control *again.*"

Outside, in his cruiser, Michael checked in with dispatch. As he placed his hat on the passenger seat, he popped open the glove box and retrieved the Bible his mom gave him when he graduated from the police academy. Fingering the pages, he noted a highlighted passage in the book of Luke.

When an evil spirit comes out of a man, it goes through arid places seeking rest and does not find it. Then it says, 'I will return to the house I left.' When it arrives, it finds the house swept clean and put in order. Then it goes and takes seven other spirits more wicked than itself, and they go in and live there. And the final condition of that man is worse than the first. Luke 11:24-26.

After a short prayer, he returned the Bible to the glove box and drove off.

What next? Request the mwindaji return.

Zeke had negated that possibility. Makeda refused to step foot in Ramsey. He couldn't rely on the mwindaji this time.

Enlist his deputies? First, he'd have to explain how vampires and werewolves lived and worked alongside them in Ramsey. It sounded insane.

Most wouldn't believe him. He had proof though. Actually, maybe his deputies were involved?

He was a Georgia transplant. Born and raised in Kentucky, his deputies might already be aware of the situation. *But were they complicit in it?*

From inside the cruiser, he phoned the courthouse. "May I speak with Councilman Holkum?"

"Hello, Sheriff. Let me check," the receptionist said. A moment later, she explained the councilman had a meeting.

Sure, he does.

"I can take a message."

"No, thank you." Michael hung up.

Since the incident at the hospital, city officials avoided him. District Attorney Walter Beaufort hadn't appreciated Michael's threat to expose the hospital's illegal operations—and the DA's complicity. With the state attorney general investigating the embezzlement at Lebanon Memorial Hospital and multiple homicides involving the hospital's CFO, Beaufort had reluctantly, temporarily, bowed to Michael's demands.

However, due to Beaufort's influence, Michael had consequently been ostracized. His position as sheriff remained precarious. He feared after the next election, his career in law enforcement would end—at least in Ramsey. The Beaufort family had enormous political influence in the tri-county area.

Michael had few allies in Ramsey. In fact, he just lost his strongest one. Dr. Bones now sided with the district attorney. Alone, would he be able to protect the citizens of Ramsey?

Fatigued and hungry, Michael drove home. He showered and fed himself and Daisy. Once refreshed, he returned to the sheriff's station but didn't go inside. Instead, he and Daisy walked down the street to the courthouse.

As hoped, Michael spotted Councilman Holkum leaving the courthouse with District Attorney Beaufort. He jogged up to the men.

Beaufort frowned. "Sheriff, I hope that's your dog."

"Actually, Daisy belongs to the department. Since we don't have a kennel, she's staying with me."

Mr. Holkum chuckled. "Daisy. What a name for a beast that can rip your hand off."

"Speaking about beasts," Michael lowered his voice, "I need to speak with you both for a moment."

"Not now," Beaufort said, circling around Michael and heading toward a Volvo parked at the curb. "We have an important meeting."

"Make time." Michael's jaw clenched.

"I'm getting tired of your attitude."

"Screw my attitude. Are you condoning the situation at the hospital?"

No one spoke. Mr. Holkum side-eyed the district attorney. Pedestrians walked by on the sidewalk. Several exchanged greetings with

Councilman Holkum and Michael. Once the pedestrian traffic lessened, Beaufort again headed for his car.

"This isn't a topic to discuss in public."

"When can we talk?" Michael asked, jutting between Beaufort and the car. "After they murder another baby? Or did they promise to only eat vagrants—again?"

Mr. Holkum's voice jostled. "What...What are you talking about?"

Pointing at the councilman, Michael asked, "Did you know Lebanon Memorial Hospital still employs vampires and werewolves?"

"Uh..." Mr. Holkum averted his gaze.

Beaufort's brows arched. "You don't understand how Ramsey works."

Michael leaned into his face. "Last night, one of your vampire doctors prepared a baby for dinner. Fortunately, I rescued the baby and brought her to the ER."

Mr. Holkum's face purpled. "That can't be. It's impossible. They prom—"

"Promised? A monster gave you their word and you believed them?" Michael took off his hat, wiped his forehead, then replaced the hat. "You relied on assurances from creatures who drink blood to survive?"

Mr. Holkum lowered his voice. "We made a deal to keep the hospital open. Do you know how many rural hospitals have closed in this country—in the next two counties over? All of them. We're the only medical facility available in a hundred-mile radius."

Beaufort straightened his tie. "They don't bother the citizens, and we look the other way,"

"Yeah? Well, they breached their contract. What next?" Michael glared at both men in turn. Since neither man replied, he stormed off.

Inside the sheriff's station, Carlotta was filling out a burglary report. "Hey, Sheriff."

Michael grumbled a reply and strode past her without making eye contact.

"The city council didn't approve our request for a canine unit," she said.

Another deputy said, "Guess she's all yours."

Laughter followed Michael into his office. He shut the door. Inside, Daisy curled up on the floor beside the desk.

"Guess you're not wanted here either," he said, glancing over at the German shepherd.

He sat there, staring at his hat. Reclined in the chair, Micheal allowed thoughts to scroll across his mind. *Does Ramsey want to be protected?*

Not everyone in Ramsey knew about the monsters at the hospital. But the city government those citizens elected did. Michael felt like he stood alone against the town's entire bureaucracy.

Once the mwindaji left in April, Michael hadn't wanted anything to do with monsters or the mwindaji. Aside from Makeda, he didn't care to see any of them again. In his mind, Michael had equated monsters with mwindaji. If the mwindaji left, the monster problem vanished.

But he'd been wrong. The mwindaji provided a solution. Without them...

Okay, set aside the monster problem for the moment. What about my job?

Initially, the town had eagerly recruited him for the position. Their prior sheriff had left. In truth, the man had disappeared. Interesting how Michael hadn't been curious about his predecessor's disappearance until now.

Had the prior sheriff retired to parts unknown, or had the man been disposed of like others who had disagreed with the operations in Ramsey?

Makeda explained how the psychiatric floor had operated as a detention facility. In order to keep Ramsey's nefarious acts secret, the district attorney had even imprisoned his own brother.

Since the state attorney closed investigations into the homicides associated with the hospital, Michael lost any leverage he had against the DA. The attention from the Kentucky Bureau of Investigations and FBI had restricted Beaufort's activities. Now that the state and national attention waned, did anyone care about what occurred in Ramsey?

Michael didn't want to disappear like his predecessor. He truly wished to help Ramsey.

With one gun and no backup, what the hell can I do?

He weighed the choices: stay and look for allies or leave and put this behind him. If the citizens voted these individuals into office, perhaps they didn't care about monsters as long as their lives were peaceful.

Michael sighed.

His family wanted him to return to Georgia. Even before he learned about the monster situation, Michael had considered leaving. Law enforcement hadn't turned out to be the career he envisioned. Besides, he wanted to be with Makeda, and she refused to return to Ramsey.

Eventually, Michael removed his revolver from its holster and placed it on the desk. Deftly, he typed a one-page letter, folded it, and secured it inside an envelope which he addressed to the city council. Once completed, he exited the office with the letter. In the open office space, Michael cleared his throat.

"May I have your attention?"

Carlotta completed her report, and another deputy hung up his phone. Michael raised his hands.

"Excuse me, guys. This will only take a moment." He paused and glanced at the envelope in his hands. "I wanted you to be the first to know. I'm resigning as sheriff, effective at the end of the month."

Over the objections of his staff, Michael apologized for the sudden decision.

"I'll talk with the city council and make arrangements for an interim replacement."

From the corner of his eye, he spied two of his deputies exchanging a nod with each other. Well, one of his suspicions had been correct.

"But, Sheriff," Carlotta said, rising and approaching him, "what're we gonna do without you?"

"You'll be fine." He patted her on the shoulder. "In fact, I'm going to recommend they appoint you as sheriff until the next election."

"Seriously?" Carlotta squealed and gave him a bear hug.

Michael spied the glower from those same two deputies. Inwardly, he relaxed. At least he upset their plans.

How deep did the conspiracy to keep the monsters in Ramsey extend? Would Carlotta be safe?

Her family ties ran as deep throughout Ramsey as Beaufort's, though less affluent. Should he warn her about the monsters? It required thought.

For the rest of the day, he completed outstanding reports and miscellaneous projects. Though he would officially remain sheriff until the end of May, he would hand over duties to Carlotta immediately, guiding her into the responsibilities associated with the position.

Ignorance of vampires and werewolves might be a blessing. Before he discovered the hospital's heinous activities, he had appreciated Ramsey's quaint hospitality. Nescience proved protective.

Later that evening, he exited the sheriff station carrying a box of family photos, a nameplate, and his academy diploma. Setting the box in the rear of his double-wide truck, he allowed Daisy inside the cab. She stuck her head out the window.

"I guess you're mine now."

She panted and licked his face. He patted her head and drove away.

On the way home, he considered what to do next. What would happen to Ramsey, and did he care?

Chapter 16

Evening rush hour choked the interstate as Makeda arrived in Memphis. She had left home early that morning, telling her parents she had a temporary hospital assignment in the birthplace of rock & roll. The drive west along Interstate 40 had been uneventful. She hoped her stay in Memphis would be likewise.

Feeling a twinge, she inspected the cat scratch on her hand. Yewande hadn't communicated with her since their argument about the garden. Given her great-grandmother's temper, Makeda appreciated the silence. Had she misjudged their relationship?

She had barely started grade school when Yewande mysteriously died. In her sorrow, Makeda possibly created the great-grandmother of her dreams. Instead, reality delivered a hawkish, demanding matriarch. What would she endure to become a zauber?

Her cellphone pinged. With one eye on traffic, she glanced at the screen. *Michael.*

The gas tank light flashed yellow. She merged onto Highway 79, searching for a gas station. While filling the tank, she phoned Michael.

"Damn, voicemail."

Inside the station, Makeda purchased soda and snacks. Before re-entering the freeway, she reviewed Yewande's directions.

Why did she send me to Memphis? Why couldn't Yewande train me?

Makeda hadn't practiced maji in nearly twenty years.

She should be more understanding.

Whether from age or dying, Yewande had changed.

Death would make anyone irritable, not to mention being murdered by a demon.

"What was Yewande anyway—a ghost or spirit?"

Next time they talked, Makeda planned to ask. Whether her great-grandmother would answer her questions remained doubtful.

Why didn't Yewande trust her? Did she worry Makeda would share the information with the mwindaji? And why this enduring schism between the mwindaji and zaubers?

She wanted to be a zauber *and* a mwindaji. There had to be a way to embrace both.

Sunlight waned as she navigated the city streets of Memphis searching for the home of her next teacher. Supposedly, an old acquaintance of her great-grandmother. Gray clouds gathered above.

Down a narrow peaceful street of a well-established neighborhood, she found the correct address and parked in front of a two-story home in the classical early twentieth-century structure.

First-floor windows sported gingerbread wood trim. Someone painted the front door light violet. Unusual, but it somehow worked with the lovely flower plantings. A miniature sloping yard framed five steps leading up to the entrance.

Makeda swooned. Dizzy, she rested her head on the steering wheel.

Must be tired. But the drive hadn't been excessive.

Once the giddiness abated, Makeda gathered her cellphone and overnight bag before tromping up to the door.

Don't take your anger out on them. It's not their fault Yewande sent me here.

With a deep exhale, she released her frustration and knocked.

A gray-haired gentleman opened the door. Dressed in a tan sweater and wearing a bowtie, he scrutinized her. He glanced quickly left and right before noticing her car parked along the street.

"Makeda Crawford, I presume."

"Yes, sir," she said, shifting her weight between her aching legs.

"We didn't expect you this early."

"Traffic was light."

"Humph." He stepped aside. "Come in."

Inside the wide foyer, Makeda noticed a hallway extended the length of the home to a rear door. Two wide doorways on each side of the hall gave way to spacious rooms. Her host invited her to the front room on the left.

"I'm Samuel. Wait here and I'll get Eldridge."

Square and richly appointed, the room contained a fireplace centered on the far outside wall and a grand piano in the corner beside a front window.

Makeda rested on a richly upholstered couch facing the front yard. While she waited, no cars or pedestrians passed by. Restless, she appraised pictures along the hallway. Mostly landscapes, though not representative of Tennessee. Their scenery appeared wildly beautiful and unmolested, harkening back to a bygone era.

In the front room, few personal photos adorned the walls or shelves, and none featured Yewande. Two pictured Samuel and another man, whom she presumed to be her host. The photos yellowed with age. Clothing the men wore bespoke of another time. Footsteps near the doorway made her start. Makeda spun around, and her eyes widened.

Next to Samuel, a man supported by elbow crutches scrutinized her. In a lumbering gait, he entered the room and sat in a chair facing the sofa. The crutches and his atrophied legs made her consider if he had cerebral palsy or suffered from a neuromuscular disorder.

Unsure whether to sit or stand, Makeda remained beside the fireplace.

Once the man sat, Samuel left the room and quickly returned with a tea tray.

"Be seated," Samuel said, pouring steaming liquid into delicate china teacups. He handed Makeda a cup and plate of sandwiches. "These will satisfy you while I prepare dinner. Hope you're hungry."

She inhaled the peppery-scented tea, and her stomach rumbled. "Thank you."

Peripherally, Makeda noticed the other man's piercing gaze. She sipped tea and slowly chewed on a sandwich, growing uncomfortable by each moment.

If he doesn't speak, I'll ask—

"So, you're Yewande's great-granddaughter." He repositioned himself in the seat, placing a pillow at his lower back. "I don't see a resemblance."

Samuel chuckled. "That's to your credit, my dear."

She smiled.

"I'm Eldridge."

Makeda rose and shook the hand he extended, surprised by the strength in his grip. His muscular arms showed no signs of atrophy. Wide slacks prevented her from examining his legs.

"Yewande—poor dear—never was a beauty."

"An absolute beast," Samuel said snidely before rising and leaving the room.

Eldridge frowned, watching his friend depart.

Were the men friends, married, or partners? Makeda didn't know, and proper manners prevented her from asking. She reached for another sandwich, then, remembering her upbringing, refrained.

Her host smiled. "Eat as much as you like. Samuel boasts about his cooking. Did you enjoy the tea?"

"Yes, thank you," she said before helping herself to another sandwich. Mayonnaise from the egg sandwich dribbled down her lip. Makeda licked it away. "I've never appreciated coffee, though that's what most people offer."

Reclining into his seat, Eldridge nodded. "Fads come and go. At one time, everyone served tea. Then, sometime early last century, coffee became the social beverage."

With a frown, Makeda appraised her host, curious about his age. A pity proper rearing prevented her from inquiring.

He grinned. "Now, you're wondering how old I am."

She blushed, squirming under his scrutiny. *He's peering inside my head.*

As a zauber, he could. Makeda closed her mind, blocking access. Uncomfortable with the quiet, she blurted out, "I'm here to learn about sorcery."

Eldridge made a dismissive action with his right hand. "No, my dear. You are not."

Her shoulders stiffened.

"You want to understand what it means to be a zauber."

"Are you a zauber?"

"Yes."

"And Samuel?"

"Question him directly." Eldridge sat up straight.

"How do you know Yewande?"

"Wrong question."

Makeda glared. "And the correct one?"

He leaned forward. "How to protect yourself from a demon?"

Her hand trembled. "You know about that?"

"Lesson one," he said, holding up a finger. "Determine your skill level."

She considered. "I can—"

With a slight movement of his right hand, Eldridge slapped her left cheek without leaving the armchair.

Half rising, Makeda tenderly palpated her face. "What did you do that for?"

A second after her question, he slapped her again. She gaped. Then another slap.

Her chest heaving, Makeda threw up her hand, blocking her right cheek. But this time, Eldridge slapped the other side.

Makeda's hands clenched. "Stop it."

"You stop it."

Glaring at Eldridge, Makeda studied his dark eyes. Another slap to her right cheek caused her eyes to water. She gritted her teeth.

Air swirled near her jaw. Alerted her to another assault, Makeda's hand shot up, not beside her face, but directed at Etheridge. Her movement pushed the older man back into the seat.

"Good." Eldridge readjusted himself in the armchair. "I wondered how long it would take."

Bristling, Makeda glowered.

"Oh, I see you are offended. Learn not to let your guard down and always be prepared. Always."

Samuel re-entered the room. "Dinner will be ready in ten minutes. I'll show our guest to her room."

Makeda gathered her belongings and followed Samuel upstairs. The layout resembled the entry level with four square rooms centered around the staircase in an open floor plan.

"I gave you a room facing the rear. It provides privacy."

"Thank you, Samuel. Where's the restroom? I need to wash up."

He opened a door with an old-fashioned key lock. Rose and lavender flooded her nose. Her shoulders relaxed. Inside, the room contained an enormous poster bed with plush coverings.

"Each bedroom has its own bath." He lowered his voice conspiratorially. "No one wants to share a bathroom with a stranger."

She smiled at his quip and thanked him.

"Don't be late. I prepared souffles." He shut the door after departing.

Once she washed her face and hands, Makeda found the dining room positioned in the rear corner of the home facing a substantial backyard. Enticing yeasty aromas of freshly baked bread calmed her nerves.

She stiffened at seeing Eldridge seated at the head of the table. Opposite him, Samuel stood. Once she sat down, he did likewise. On an antique victrola, Billie Holiday's *Strange Fruit* whispered in the background.

"How are the accommodations?" Samuel asked, handing her a tureen filled with soup.

"Lovely," she said, ladling soup into a bowl. "I appreciate what you're doing for me—both of you." With effort, she glanced at Eldridge.

"So all is forgiven?" he asked, helping himself to the soup tureen.

She ignored his question. "I've forgotten most of what Yewande taught me as a child. For the past two weeks, she's been teaching me spells and incantations. She sent me here because she became frustrated with my progress."

"Patience is not one of her virtues."

"Does she have any virtues?" Samuel asked, cutting a glimpse at Etheridge.

The latter turned toward Makeda.

"It will not be easy. Generally, a zauber must be taught before adolescence. An older mind is less accepting of education."

"I understand. Yewande's worried about my safety." Makeda noticed both men shared a quick glance. *What's going on?*

"Anything you teach me will be invaluable."

"Less talk," Samuel said, "more eating."

Dinner proceeded with discussions around current events. Makeda devoured the sumptuous meal. Samuel promised to teach her how to make souffles.

"Don't waste your time. I rarely cook."

He grimaced. His opinion of her—she believed—slightly diminished.

They retired to the living room. Makeda studied wall paintings.

"Who created these?" she asked no one in particular.

"You like them?" Samuel asked.

"They're lovely, but I can't figure out the locale."

Eldridge hobbled over to where she stood, pointing out a signature in the lower right corner.

Makeda had to squint to read it. "You?"

He smiled. "A hobby."

"Like decorating. E does our home décor."

She smiled. "You're an artist."

"A craftsman." Eldridge returned to his seat. "Artists starve."

As she pivoted toward a chair, a pressure tightened around her throat. Makeda choked as Eldridge's pinched fingers pointed at her throat.

Samuel placed a hand on his shoulders. "Careful. Not too much."

"She has to learn," Eldridge said, studying her.

While they politely conversed with each other, Makeda choked, flailing because she couldn't reach Eldridge. Noises sputtered from her mouth. Her eyes fluttered. She stumbled to the floor and felt unconsciousness gaining ascendency.

"E," Samuel said, "she's not ready."

"Yewande wants this. We don't have a lot of time."

Makeda struggled, trying to understand their words and search for a command to stop Eldridge.

She garbled, "*Chekate*."

The room started to spin and blur. She would faint soon. Summoning all her strength, she screamed, "Chekate!"

Eldridge's grip didn't lessen.

Her pulse soared, pounding in her head. With fisted hands, Makeda slammed the floor repeating a command for him to release her. *Sulami muni!*

Pictures on the walls teetered. Photo frames along the mantel crashed to the floor. Furniture slid around. Eldridge's chair swayed, knocking him onto the ground. The entire house trembled.

"Enough," Samuel said.

In an instant, the strangle-hold released from Makeda's throat. Her chest lifted and filled with air. She lay on the ground sputtering and coughing.

Samuel assisted Eldridge from the floor. He attempted to help her, too, but Makeda waved him away. Eventually, she rose from the ground. She wiped her forehead and climbed onto the couch.

"Was that necessary?" she asked, coughing between each word.

"Yes," Eldridge said, settling into the chair. "For some reason, you will not use maji unless pushed to the extremes. That must change."

"And you thought strangling me would help?"

"On-the-job training."

She grimaced. "I'm afraid to ask what comes next."

"Witchcraft revolves around the earth—understanding herbs and plants. Magic is supernatural, concerning the unseen. Sorcery and maji are elemental, incorporating space and dimension."

Samuel tidied the room as Makeda conversed with Eldridge. She wondered about the dynamic between the two men, and what she had committed to do.

"I want to learn. If it isn't too painful," she said, massaging her throat.

"We have much information to cover. I will share what I know, but you must listen and follow my directions."

Her shoulders slumped. "I don't understand why a demon would be after me."

Samuel shot Eldridge a quick glance. Neither man spoke but she perceived a sly exchange between them.

They're communicating in kasi kasi.

Makeda returned to her bedroom.

What is going on, and what has Yewande signed me up for?

Chapter 17

A SLIVER OF MORNING light penetrated the partially opened curtains in the study. Enu rose as three men entered the room. Two of the men appeared to be in their mid-twenties. They stood together, whispering and pointing at various objects around the room.

The older, distinguished gentleman with a square jaw and keloidal scar on his chin preceded them. He strode up to Enu, and they exchanged a brief hug.

"Hello, friend. Are you well?"

Enu said, "Stefan. Thank you for coming. Please, have a seat."

Stefan introduced the other two men to Enu.

"I am happy to welcome you and your family. Help yourselves." He directed them to a table laden with coffee and food. Enu guided Stefan slightly aside.

"Accept my sympathies about Herman. Any part my brother's actions played in your father's death... Well, please accept my deepest sympathies." Enu paused and lowered his head. "We all mourn Herman's death. A tragedy for everyone."

"Thank you." Stefan accepted a cup of coffee from a servant. "Have you discovered who butchered my family?"

"Unfortunately, I have been preoccupied with our relocation to Michigan. I assure you Korlemo—"

"Humph," Stefan grunted. "He won't lift a finger to search for the assassins."

"You are mistaken. My brother worries about the events that transpired in Kentucky." Enu sat on the leather couch while maintaining a neutral countenance. Unaccustomed to deception, he feared Stefan perceived his lie.

"Only in how those events will affect him."

The study's double doors flew open. Korlemo, wearing a sports coat and slacks, momentarily paused on the threshold before entering.

"Stefan." He charged forward with an outstretched hand. "About time." He glanced at the other men. "I presume you hired these men to protect my family?"

Stefan barely accepted Korlemo's handshake and said, "Wrong, they are my cousins."

"But surely, they—along with yourself—will stay and guard me."

Stefan's jaw clenched. "They will remain until you make other arrangements."

Korlemo frowned. "There will be no other arrangements. As Herman's son, duty as my protector becomes your responsibility."

Enu stood. "Brother—"

"No," Korlemo interrupted. "I have been inconvenienced long enough."

"Inconvenienced?" Stefan's brows rose.

Pacing around the study, Korlemo said, "Why Herman brought me to such a desolate area is unimaginable. No entertainment, freezing nights. Utterly unsuitable for hunting."

While Korlemo rambled on about his disdain for Michigan, Enu noticed Stefan's weighty glance at Zainabu, who, having entered behind Korlemo, perched on the corner of an immense oval desk.

Why is the witch present?

Enu said, "You do not understand the situation."

"Immaterial," Korlemo snapped. "I wish to leave immediately." He stopped near the fireplace and regarded Stefan. "You will secure a new house for—"

"Are you insane?" Stefan asked. "My father and brothers were murdered, and you're pouting about the weather."

Korlemo's back straightened. "How dare you address me in that manner."

Veins bulged along Stefan's temples. "Get this straight, I'm here as a courtesy, out of respect for my father's friendship with the Ibori. I'm not staying to protect you or your precious family."

"If you refuse, assign one of your brothers."

"I have no brothers. The mwindaji murdered them all!" Stefan's nostrils flared.

His cousins rose, standing beside him like pillars.

Silence descended heavily across the room as Stefan and Korlemo glowered at each other. Enu approached his brother.

"Conditions have changed. Alliances—"

"Ridiculous. Nothing has—"

"Stop interrupting and listen," Enu said.

Korlemo gripped the fireplace mantel.

"We must accept our situation. Stefan has other priorities. I have interviewed several security contractors, but we cannot relocate for several months."

"Unacceptable." Korlemo marched away from the fireplace and rested in a sizable leather chair behind the ornate desk. "Stefan, as Herman's remaining son, the responsibility for my needs falls to you."

One of the young men laughed, turned aside, and whispered to his companion.

"You mock me?" Korlemo snarled.

Stefan said, "We aren't your children, and I'm under no obligation to protect you. My cousins agreed to temporarily assist the Ibori given your present circumstances. If that's not acceptable, we can leave."

In a flash, Korlemo vaulted out of the chair and ran up to Stefan and the men.

"I am your father. If not for my sacrifice, none of you would exist," he said, taking a measure of each of them in turn.

On Stefan's left, the young man snickered, "Old fool."

Suddenly, Korlemo's arm shot forward, clenching the man's throat. At the same time, his height increased, and he morphed into a vampire. He lifted Stefan's cousin several feet off the ground.

The young man transformed into a werewolf and sliced Korlemo's arm. He thrashed about, striking Korlemo about the face and shoulder to no avail.

"Release him!" Stefan shouted, stepping forward as his cousin's lips turned blue.

Before Enu could intervene, Stefan's other cousin mutated into a werewolf and attacked Korlemo. With his free arm, the vampire swatted him in the chest, propelling the young werewolf into a bookcase alongside the fireplace. Books and assorted bric-a-brac rained down upon the werewolf's head. Breaking glass, tousling, and shouts of obscenities filled the study.

Though desirous of protecting his guests, Enu had no appetite for violence. He obeyed Korlemo due to filial obligation and practicality. Physically, Korlemo and the werewolves outmatched his strength. Despite those concerns, Enu sprinted across the room to assist the young werewolf off of the floor.

Increasing his grasp around the other cousin's throat, Korlemo said, "I see you no longer find me humorous."

"Enough, Brother." After situating the werewolf against the wall, Enu rushed to Korlemo's side. "This is not productive."

With a side glance at Enu, Korlemo tossed the werewolf onto the couch. "They must learn respect." His frame retracted to its prior state, and he returned behind the desk.

Enu surveyed the damage, carefully avoiding glass, books, and other scattered debris.

During the exchange, Zainabu retained her seat. At her direction, a trembling servant inched slowly around the fireplace clearing away debris. Enu studied her demeanor, unnerved by her apparent disinterest, except for a slight upturn in her lips.

Did she take pleasure in Korlemo's aggression? She demanded closer attention and should absolutely not be underestimated.

Korlemo adjusted his sports coat. "I demand Baptiste's family honor the ka'trete. Werewolves protect vampires. It has been law for ages."

Stefan's cousins composed themselves and huddled together near the fireplace.

"We came here to help," Stefan said, "and you treat us this way. Find your own security."

The three men prepared to leave.

Waving his hands, Enu intercepted them. "Please, Stefan, accept my sincere apologies. Korlemo misunderstood your situation. He is a little prickly at the moment."

Stefan glared at the vampire, who calmly read documents on the desk, oblivious to their conversation. "Forget it, Enu."

Gazing lazily up from the papers, Korlemo said, "The ka'trete remains in effect."

"No one cares about an outdated agreement forged during an ancient time of paternalistic traditions," one of the cousins said.

"Stupid child." Korlemo rose. "Perhaps you need another lesson in discipline."

Both of Stefan's cousins reverted to their werewolf state. Their jaws elongated, displaying a crooked jumble of teeth. "Come on, Grandpa. Let's go for it."

As Korlemo proceeded from behind the desk, his arms lengthened and his fingers sharpened.

Stefan bolted in front of his cousins. "Don't bother. Let's go." All three headed for the study door.

"I expect you will make arrangements for my protection in your absence." Korlemo regained his seat.

Stefan's mouth opened and closed without speaking. He addressed Enu. "I'm sorry, but this isn't going to work."

Enu's voice lowered. "Let me speak with you a moment."

"I appreciate what you're trying to do but forget it." Stefan glanced once at Korlemo, then said, "That monster is your problem now."

Precipitately, Stefan and his cousins departed. Enu followed, pleading for another opportunity. Stefan shook him off. The three men stormed outside and into a waiting limousine.

Once he returned inside the study, Enu ordered the servant to leave before shutting the doors.

"Brother, we must speak." Enu walked over to the desk.

Korlemo shrugged. "Then talk."

Glaring at Zainabu, he said, "Alone."

"What do you have to say which she cannot hear?"

"Leave," Enu addressed Zainabu, who in turn glanced at Korlemo. "Did you not hear me?"

Zainabu watched Korlemo for a moment before departing. Not until the doors shut did Enu speak.

"Why antagonize Stefan?"

"Youth today have no respect."

"How many times must I explain to you about the changing customs? Those young men have no interest in the ka'trete."

Korlemo pushed a stack of papers aside. "I honor it and expect others to do so. Vampires and werewolves have lived together peaceably for a thousand years. Why change things now?"

Enu rubbed his head and collapsed on a couch. "You cannot force people to serve you."

"Of course, I can." Korlemo smirked. "Do you believe servitude does not exist in this illustrious country? They simply wrap it up in technicalities, cleansing away disgusting titles. One can do anything with power and money."

"This again." Enu stomped around the room, waving his hands. "Not everyone considers you as important as you believe you are. Additionally, your finances are not bottomless."

"As to my finances, have you retrieved the stolen money?"

"I have not reviewed the accountant's report yet."

"My intel confirms Dr. Sylvia Senegal is the thief."

"What intel? The witch?"

"Zauber."

Enu sighed and paused near the bookcase. "How do you expect me to accomplish all these tasks? You want me to find another home, find an embezzler—"

"Sylvia Senegal."

"Hire security and employ servants who will consent to your abusive treatment. I cannot meet these demands."

Korlemo slammed his hands onto the desk. "I will not tolerate excuses."

Enu watched his brother's tantrum. While Korlemo detailed his position as leader of their clan, Enu reflected upon his tenure as attendant to the braggadocio vampire.

Did Mother have any idea what conscripting me to Korlemo would entail? Unless something changes, this will continue indefinitely.

"Zainabu will help," Korlemo said.

"I will not work with a witch."

"A zauber."

"Whatever she may call herself, she is not trustworthy."

"I trust her implicitly."

The door crept open, and Dayo entered. "You trust whom, my love?"

Korlemo greeted his wife with a kiss on each cheek. "Nothing to concern you, mere security arrangements."

"We were discussing Zainabu," Enu said. "I do not trust her."

"Nor should you." Dayo rested on a couch facing the three windows and crossed her legs. She smiled up at Korlemo. "That witch has her own agenda."

Palming her hand, Korlemo said, "Now, my sweet, jealously is pointless."

"And foolishness is fatal." She withdrew her hand. "Do you believe she would give you a moment's notice if you weren't rich and powerful?"

"Exactly." Korlemo grinned. "Her intentions are obvious. In exchange for money, she does my bidding." He turned toward Enu. "As I said before, money can accomplish anything."

Enu's jaw stiffened.

"Well, if we are listing household needs. Who will do our hunting?" She glanced first at him before Korlemo. "Abioye inquired after his family's needs."

Korlemo chortled. "Perhaps my brother and his family should hunt for themselves. It would hone their skills."

"New arrangements will be made," Enu said, addressing Dayo.

She rose. "And soon I hope." At the door, she pivoted around. "While I have no problem hunting for myself, others have lost their abilities." Dayo exited the room, leaving the door ajar.

"Brother, you cannot treat people with contempt and expect loyalty."

Korlemo perused documents on the desk. "I simply expect to be treated according to my station. Besides, once the servants get here, we *can* make sure they never leave."

"This is not Kentucky."

"Nor do I want it to be. Kentucky held a certain charm, but I want to live near a larger metropolis. A place with an active nightlife where we can hunt in the city instead of the woods." Korlemo straightened the papers on his desk and rose. "Since you are overwhelmed, I will entrust the security services to Zainabu. This will give you time to find the money Sylvia stole and secure a new estate—not in Michigan."

As he spoke those last words, Korlemo departed.

Staring at the fireplace, Enu considered the possibilities. He glanced over at the desk. Korlemo would not allow anyone to embezzle money without seeking retribution, even the daughter of a longtime associate.

Enu retrieved the financial ledger, read it, and dropped it back on the desk.

Where to begin?

He massaged his temples, and his head drooped. Enu's thoughts returned to Nintoubo, the land of their ancestors.

When his mother ordered him to obey Korlemo, he never imagined living in a foreign land far from Africa. A thousand years later on the shores of a country which did not even exist at the time of his birth. Over a hundred lifetimes had passed. He doubted the sacrifices had been advantageous for his family. Everything he had suffered, endured at the whims of Korlemo, had been for what ultimate purpose?

Restrictions had been placed on his wife and children. He had committed terrible acts in obeisance to his brother. Destroyed lives. Entire tribes had decimated. Dreams abandoned. One decision a thousand years earlier had sealed his fate and determined the destiny of their clan.

Had his position at birth led to all this destruction? If Korlemo had been the second born, how would their destinies have been altered?

As second son, Enu received whatever leftovers his brother discarded. However, Korlemo's appetite for everything had been—and remained—voracious. Enu received little attention from his father or grandfather, and a pittance of affection from his mother. Still, he had promised her to completely submit to Korlemo, to maintain Ibori tradition and honor.

And what had he received in return? What about his family?

His family deserved better.

In Nintoubo, he had limited options, no choice but to submit to Korlemo. As second born son, his choices included humble trades-man or farmer. Either would have provided a modest household.

Would Nambi have been satisfied?

She deserved more, exceeding what he would have been able to provide. As Korlemo's brother, Enu provided Nambi with a pro-longed, privileged life. The alternative paled in comparison.

Yet, Nambi lived simply. Perhaps he had misjudged her needs. Could he undo his mistake?

In 2010, he had choices. Obey his mother's dying plea, or—for once—place himself and his family first. Fatou longed for inde-pendence from his overbearing, selfish uncle. But did Enu have the courage to support his son's aspirations?

He lacked the physical strength to oppose Korlemo. Cockiness, however, limited Korlemo's insight. Enu possessed patience and in-telligence. He must uncover a path forward beyond this suffocating life.

Can I do it?

Enu sauntered over to the windows and cautiously pulled the curtains aside. As sunlight spilled across the wooden floors, an idea blossomed in his mind.

Chapter 18

A BEEPING HORN DREW Makeda's attention outside. Rain pattered against the window. An older model car cruised down the street, disappearing around a distant corner. Only the second vehicle she'd seen on this street since arriving in Memphis.

She figured the city of rhythm and blues would be a noisy, congested place bustling with activity. This peaceful, isolated street seemed incongruous with that assumption—unnervingly so.

Makeda returned to reading her book with little enthusiasm. Unable to sleep, she awoke before dawn and investigated the library while Eldridge and Samuel remained quietly in their room—or rooms. She still hadn't discovered the nature of their relationship.

Over the past week, Eldridge taught her while Samuel fed her. Neither man shared details regarding their personal lives. Though constrained by her upbringing, Makeda was determined to gather information about her hosts.

Across from the living room, and of similar size, the library had floor-to-ceiling bookshelves overflowing with books, artworks, and other assorted items. Makeda spent hours exploring the room. A plush reclining settee occupied the central space. The room included one high-back chair with a side table and a club chair with a footstool.

In a drawer of the side table, Makeda located a folder with miscellaneous newspaper clippings. Articles dating back to the 1800s documented the history of Memphis. Hearing light footfall on the staircase, she scooped up the articles and returned them to the folder as Eldridge entered.

"An early riser," he said, leaning on his elbow crutches. "I would think maji lessons left you fatigued."

"Simply curious."

"About what?"

She slid the folder across an oval glass table in front of the settee. "You like history."

He shrugged. "Not exactly."

"But you collected these newspaper clippings."

"I saved them."

She frowned. "How old are you?"

With a smirk, Eldridge sat in the high back chair. "What happened to Southern manners."

"I apologize, but I'd like to know."

"Well, I would like to create a masterpiece worthy of the MOMA in New York City. However, we must contend with what we have received." He hobbled off the seat and prepared to exit the library.

"So, you won't tell me."

Speaking over his shoulder, he said, "Impress me with your maji lessons today and I will."

Makeda followed him into the dining room. Scents of fried meat tickled her nose and rumbled her stomach. Eldridge sat at the head of the table farthest from the entrance. Makeda sat on the right side of Samuel's chair.

"Bon appétit," Samuel said, placing a basket of bread covered with a towel on the dining room table. He poured out tea as Makeda heaped eggs and bacon on her plate.

"What are we doing today?" she asked Eldridge after thanking Samuel for breakfast.

Eldridge began eating before replying, "We have an appointment."

Samuel and Makeda stared at him. The former asked, "Are you sure it's wise? She's…"

The men stared at each other.

Kasi kasi again. Why are they being secretive?

Suddenly, her appetite waned.

Glancing at both men, she asked, "Ready for what?"

"These lessons are not helping," Eldridge said, buttering a piece of toast.

"Of course, they are. I've learned—"

"Nothing," he interrupted. "Repeating incantations and creating potions does not make someone a zauber." He splayed his fingers toward Makeda and formed a fist. "You need to absorb the knowledge. Let it soak into your bones until it becomes as natural as breathing."

Her brow arched. "And how do we accomplish that?"

"*We?*" He sipped tea. "We are not the problem. You only use sorcery under duress. Why do you resist?"

"I'm not resisting," Makeda said, pouting slightly.

Eldridge chuckled. Samuel grimaced.

"We will not argue the point," the former said. "Today will prove which of us is correct."

Eldridge completed breakfast while Makeda studied him.

Samuel said, "It will be dangerous."

"Danger is natural to a mwindaji." Tossing his napkin on the table, Eldridge said, "Today, we discover her potential as a zauber."

Makeda swallowed hard. *What does he have in mind?*

Under Eldridge's direction, Makeda drove across town to a suburb southeast of Memphis. Although she offered to drive her car, he insisted on using the vintage Cadillac.

Despite its age, the spotless interior sparkled with polished chrome fixtures and soft leather seating. He—or Samuel—adored this car and maintained it in peak condition. With difficulty, Makeda navigated the narrow rain-drenched Memphis streets in the spacious Cadillac.

In under an hour, they parked in the driveway of a suburban tract home. The home resembled an iconic American abode of a married couple with 2.5 kids and a Labradoodle, who attended church on Easter and Christmas. Every aspect of the home's exterior signaled typical Americana.

She waited at the foot of the walkway—getting pelted by rain—for Eldridge.

Crutches impeded his dexterity but didn't affect his sorcery, a lesson she'd painfully learned. He nodded for her to proceed to the front door. She knocked. Barely a second elapsed before the door flew open.

"I saw y'all park," a woman whispered, clutching a robe around her waist. "Come in."

Makeda squeezed inside because the woman barely opened the door wide enough for them to enter.

"How are you doing, Loretta?" Eldridge asked, taking the woman's hands in his.

Tears pooled in the woman's puffy eyes. A checkered scarf on her head covered pink hair rollers. "He's worse. I had to lie about being ill. Otherwise, he would've gone to work."

"We're here now," he said, glancing briefly at Makeda. "Where can we work in private?"

Loretta led them downstairs into a dimly lit, dank basement. It smelled moldy.

"Sorry, but this is the only place where...where no one will see you."

Along the basement walls, boxes stacked four feet high narrowed the space. Cobwebs caked each corner accompanied by a light dusting over each surface. An older washing machine rested against the far wall. A tiny window under a foot wide gave no light. Makeda's nose wrinkled as she stifled a sneeze.

"This will be fine." Eldridge laid a hand on Loretta's shoulder. "Wait three minutes, then bring your husband down."

"Okay." Loretta headed up the stairs.

"Oh," Eldridge said, catching hold of her hand, "and after Allen comes down, you return upstairs. And under no circumstances, open the basement door."

Chills thrilled up Makeda's spine. *What's going to happen to Allen?*

Once Loretta left, she asked, "Why are we here?"

He ignored her and removed his coat. After resting his crutches on a box, he removed a green satchel from a coat pocket. Eldridge spoke without looking at her, instead scanning the area as if searching for something.

"Listen to me and do *exactly* as I say."

"What are you looking for?" Makeda asked, frowning.

"Hiding places."

Words teetered on her lips, but before Makeda formed a question, the basement door creaked open. Slowly, a man descended the steps. Each step he took made the creaking grew. Makeda's shoulders tensed as he came nearer. A cryptic tone followed each step.

Dressed in jeans and a t-shirt for a state sports team, the thin man approached Eldridge. He merely glanced at Makeda.

"Hello, I'm Allen. My wife said you came to fix the furnace. I don't recall a problem with the heating."

When the basement door shut, Eldridge addressed Makeda. "Block the stairs. Do not let anything get past you."

The hairs on her arms raised, but Makeda obeyed. *What the hell does he mean by anything?* Her eyes darted around the room looking for danger.

Allen stepped toward her, then pivoted toward Eldridge. "What's going on? Why are you here?"

"Observe his eyes," Eldridge said.

Allen exclaimed, "*What the hell*? Who are you people?"

Because Allen faced away from her, Makeda couldn't see his eyes. Once Eldridge alerted her though, she waited for the man to turn around. Alongside Allen's dark irises, she easily appreciated lateral pale-yellow arcs framing the pupils.

"Those yellow arcs?"

"Exactly. They represent part of a koleo."

Makeda stammered. "A koleo?"

"Yewande warned you about them?"

"Yes," she said, studying Allen.

The basement temperature increased.

Eldridge removed a vial from the satchel. In a flat, matter-of-fact voice, he said, "There is a monster inside you, son, and we will excise it."

A mocking laugh exploded from Allen's mouth. "Ridiculous. Get the hell out of my house before I call the police."

He approached the staircase, but Makeda jumped in front of him.

"Move or I'll move you." Allen's fists rose.

"Try it." Makeda's stance widened.

He placed his hand on her arm, attempting to brush her aside. Makeda wrenched Allen's arm behind his back and kicked his legs from under his torso. He crashed to the ground.

"Shit! You stupid bitch." Sweat beaded along Allen's forehead. He reached for her legs.

Makeda stomped on his hand.

"Do not injure him," Eldridge said. "Remember, he is the victim."

"Oh, right. Sorry. I'm used to shooting monsters, not..." A thought suddenly occurred. "Wait. How do we remove a koleo?"

"Get off me," Allen cried, wriggling from under Makeda's grasp. "Loretta! Call for help!"

Makeda released his arm but continued blocking his egress. Perspiration trickled down her back as the temperature in the room increased.

With wild eyes, Allen swung around and addressed Eldridge. "Look. Just let me go and I won't report you to the police."

Eldridge flicked fluid from the vial onto Allen's face.

Howling and flinching, Allen's voice deepened. "Get out and leave me alone."

Makeda retreated a step, shocked by the commanding voice. To herself, she mumbled, "Is this some *Exorcist* crap?"

Sweat gathered under her armpits. The temperature became uncomfortable.

"Koleo, you have caused enough suffering," Eldridge said. "Time to depart."

"Leave me alone," Allen croaked. Veins popped along the surface of his skin like fissures erupting along his body.

Flinching, Makeda repositioned herself. Her voice wavered. "Um. Eldridge?"

"When the koleo erupts, burn it," he said.

"With what?" She grimaced as a yellow blob poked out of Allen's mouth.

"You are a zauber. Do it!"

Allen's eyes boggled. Blood and snot oozed from his nose. "Help me," he cried, reaching toward Makeda. His body seized.

She hurried to his side as a yellow mass poured from his mouth.

"Uh." Gawking, Makeda moved aside to avoid the material.

In a continuous stream, a yellow doughy substance spilled from Allen's mouth and onto the basement floor.

"Careful," Eldridge said. "And keep your mouth closed. The koleo will flee into any open orifice."

Makeda eyeballed Eldridge. His solemn countenance made her shut her gaping mouth as the yellow material from Allen's mouth coalesced into a tube-like form.

The elongated stringy creature slithered along the ground. It reared up at Makeda and fizzed.

She scooted backward and slipped onto her buttocks. The creature's droopy eyes and craggy mouth made her shiver.

It screeched at Eldridge, revealing a mouth with multiple layers of tiny pincer teeth. The koleo swayed like a cobra, then like a spring, flew directly at Makeda. She batted it away.

"Ahh!" she screamed. Where her arm struck the koleo, a linear, red blister pulsed.

"Burn it!" Eldridge yelled, flicking fluid on the koleo.

The monster soared onto the ceiling, observing them while circling the room.

"The koleo wants to escape."

"I don't have anything to kill it with," Makeda cried, regarding her scalded flesh.

"If it gets out the basement, another bindimèn will be attacked." Eldridge retreated toward the wall, watching the shrieking creature crawl along the ceiling.

"You should've let me bring my weapons."

"A machete will not destroy this creature."

"What about bullets?"

Curled up into a corner of the basement ceiling, the koleo crouched.

Eldridge said, "It is preparing another attack. If you do not kill it, it will reenter Allen—or one of us."

More likely her than him. Makeda bit her lip, racking her brain for a spell to create fire. "Eldridge, please."

"Important lesson. When a zauber fails, bindimèn die."

Incantations tumbled across her mind.

Fire is a form of combustion. Oxidation of chemicals. It requires an ignition point and oxygen for fuel.

Makeda rubbed her hands together and said, *"Loko."*

A tiny flame flickered in her palms but released little heat.

Like an arrow, the koleo lurched at Makeda. Instinctively, she held out her hands to block the assault. Because the tiny flame diminished, she blew on it and created a torch. Flames exploded from her hands. She shot the inferno at the koleo.

Drenched in flames, the creature howled. It writhed on the ground before scurrying to a corner of the basement behind boxes.

"Finish it," Eldridge ordered.

Makeda focused on the flame. She directed it forward while repeating loko, guiding flames toward the corner.

The koleo shrieked and slithered toward Allen, who lay unconscious on the basement floor. Somehow, Makeda had forgotten about him. Keeping one hand aflame, she grabbed Allen's foot and pulled him away from the koleo.

Doused with another lob of fire, the koleo's surface bubbled. It gradually shrank in size and scuttled toward Eldridge, who doused it with fluid. When it shriveled to about two feet in length, its yellow globe eyes enlarged. It bellowed pitifully and attempted to climb the walls. Sliding back onto the cement floor, it thrashed around in the flames. Makeda maintained a constant fire on its shriveling body.

Gradually, the koleo's movements ceased. Its charred body disintegrated, leaving a mustard-yellow ash behind. Once the flame was extinguished and the smoke dispersed, a small stone lay inside the pile of ash.

With the toe of her boot, Makeda examined the object. "What's that?"

Eldridge used a tong to retrieve the stone. He placed it inside a metal canister before sweeping the ash into a separate container. "These stones have value."

"For what?"

"Healing, spells, incantations. Which reminds me, we need to treat your burn before it becomes a nasty scar. First, we must attend to our patient."

Makeda hadn't considered Allen as a patient. This exceeded her usual nursing duties. But she kneeled beside Allen and checked his vital signs. Swollen and bruised, his jaw had become dislodged.

Shaking Allen's shoulders, Eldridge attempted to rouse the man. He handed Makeda a handkerchief. She cleaned Allen's face but really wanted to dab the sweat dripping down her neck.

"Why is it getting hotter?"

"Heat makes koleos uncomfortable. It helps to remove them from infected bindimèn." Eldridge lightly tapped Allen's cheek. "He's completely unconscious. Carry him upstairs."

"Me?"

"Come. His wife awaits."

With effort, Makeda lifted Allen over her shoulders.

At the top of the stairs, Eldridge glanced at her. "Maji would have been easier."

Makeda frowned. "Now you tell me."

"I had hoped the idea would have come to you naturally." He shook his head. "If you make maji a part of your life, no one will ever have to tell you anything."

In the living room, a crying Loretta awaited them. She rushed up to Makeda and held her husband's face.

"He needs to go to the hospital," Makeda said. "His jaw is broken."

"They will be suspicious." Eldridge instructed Loretta what to tell the doctors.

Crying, she asked, "Will it come back?"

"No, we removed all the koleo."

Loretta gave him a bear hug. "Thank you. What do I owe you?"

"Nothing." Eldridge patted her hand.

Makeda carried Allen to Loretta's car. Raindrops refreshed her sweaty skin.

Eldridge gave Loretta directions on caring for Allen after the ER wired his jaw. He promised to return the following day.

On their drive back to Eldridge's home, Makeda asked, "So, you help people?"

"Indeed."

She noticed him admiring the stone from the koleo.

"It will help you heal people?"

He screwed the lid on the container and deposited it inside his coat pocket. "It has many utilities. Medicinally, monetarily, and magically."

Makeda spied a glance at him before dodging a water-filled pothole. "And how will *you* use it?"

"Depends upon what is needed at the time."

"Why didn't you tell me what to expect?"

"I did." He gazed out the window. "The first day you arrived, I told you to be prepared for the unexpected."

Her shoulders tensed. Fatigued and unable to come up with a snappy retort, Makeda drove in silence. In fairness, he had told her to always be prepared.

What other surprises would training bring?

"Are you going to explain koleos?" she asked, sneaking a peek at him.

"You said Yewande told you about them."

"Only that they were dangerous—and scary."

He chuckled. "Yewande fears nothing."

Makeda frowned. "You speak of her in the present tense."

His head slightly tilted as he gazed at her. "You spoke with her. Do you consider her to be dead?"

"Well, no. I mean. If she's alive, where does she live? Where does she go when she's not here?"

Eldridge gazed out the side window. "You think like a bindimèn. *Ersu* has many planes."

"Ersu?"

He smiled. "What bindimèn call earth."

She shook her head. "There's a lot to learn."

"Yet, despite your age, you progress well."

"Thank you. I think."

"Lesson koleo. Gelatinous creatures that feast on the nervous system of animals to survive. They prefer bindimèn as a food source. They have been known to use other mammals in times of limited resources. With over a billion bindimèn on ersu, they have an abundance of food."

"And only fire kills them?"

"A clever zauber can capture them in a glass or metal container. Without a food source, they die within days."

"What about the stone they produce?"

"Ah, yes. Mature koleos create stones rich in minerals. A valuable resource for witches and zaubers."

"Will you teach me about this stone?"

Eldridge gave her a wide, toothy smile. "If you promise to exercise your maji, I will answer the millions of questions you ask me each day."

Makeda laughed. "Deal."

Chapter 19

ENU EXITED THE STUDY. A peace had settled around the estate. Korlemo had quit ranting and raving about the accommodations.

Zainabu negotiated with associates of the Baptiste family to provide security—though it came with a hefty fee. Fortunately, Korlemo's solid finances made it possible.

Before departing, he said, "Brother, please be reasonable with the security detail and staff. Everyone is strained."

Korlemo shrugged. "Not my concern. Zainabu's arrangements are satisfactory."

"But she is not." Without awaiting a reply, Enu retired to his apportioned section of the mansion.

Inside a gathering room, he approached his son, who sat on a long couch with his other children.

"Fatou, what are you working on?"

"Nothing, Father." He closed the folder and rose.

"What troubles you?"

Sighing loudly, Fatou said, "I'm tired of this life—we all are."

With a sullen expression, Enu regarded his children, two sons and a daughter—not including Fatou. They nodded in agreement. Enu's shoulders shrank.

Their move to Michigan had been hasty. Members of their extended family had been murdered. Others decided not to relocate with Korlemo, desiring their independence. Presently, individuals inside their blended household questioned continued allegiance to their Ibori leader.

Though many sympathized with Enu's position, they refused to be placated. Korlemo's absolute authority died in Kentucky. The mwindaji attack revealed the vampire's vulnerability.

Enu shared their concerns regarding Korlemo. Aware of his brother's temperament, Enu worried what would happen if those sentiments of discontent came to Korlemo's attention.

Importantly, he feared Zainabu's growing influence inside the household. He doubted the witch had entranced his brother.

Why does Korlemo trust her? More likely, Korlemo needs Zainabu, but for what?

In order to maintain peace, Korlemo had consented to remain isolated in his apportioned area of the mansion until the situation calmed. This precarious détente worried Enu. A slight disagreement might disrupt the entire household, and Korlemo severely lacked diplomacy. Enu needed to reassure his children and keep them safe until he completed preparations.

"Fatou, my children, have I not strived to provide for your needs?"

"We want our freedom, Father," one of his sons said, standing beside Fatou.

Enu frowned. "But you are not enslaved." He regarded his daughter. "Do you not remember how I saved you from a plantation? How that brutal overlord repeatedly assaulted your mother?"

A tear flowed down his daughter's cheek.

"He threatened to sell you to another slaveowner. Have I not provided a better life?"

"I remember, Father. And I am grateful." She slid across the couch, resting beside him. "But have I not traded one captivity for another?"

He hugged her as she softly wept.

Sitting on the opposite side of his sister, Fatou said, "We want to leave. Live independently. Make our own decisions."

"The world is dangerous for vampires," Enu said. "You have no money or connections."

"We have contacts. People who will help us."

"Without the ka'trete, what werewolf would protect you?"

Fatou grasped his hand. "We have saved. Made our own friends. We can survive without uncle's influence."

His daughter said, "Uncle Korlemo's position has declined. He has many enemies and few supporters."

His sons nodded in agreement.

Enu circled the room. "Do not take any action until I weigh the options."

Fatou laid an arm on his shoulder. "We won't wait long."

Deep in contemplation, Enu staggered from the room. He stumbled down the hall into his private quarters.

Holding a book, his wife rose from a divan. "Where have you been?" Taking his hand, she guided him to the divan.

He collapsed. "Nambi, I have failed."

She frowned, palming his chin in her petite hands. "How? You are a considerate father, an intelligent man, and a kind husband."

"No. I have failed our children. They desire independence, not security." Enu gazed deeply into her eyes. "Freedom and choice. Two items they have never had."

Nambi laid her head on his shoulders. "Our children's wants differ from others. They crave neither security nor wealth. We..."

She pulled slightly away to look into his ebony face. "At the time, we did our best with the knowledge we possessed. Do not regret the past. Go forward with this new information."

Enu gathered her hands together and brought them to his lips. "I wanted you to have everything you deserved."

Her bow-shaped lips blew him a kiss. "This life has exceeded my dreams." In an aside, she mumbled, "Beyond what I needed."

He frowned. "Would you have preferred a humble life as wife to Tau's second son?"

"Tau was a bully. Korlemo resembles his father."

"And I?" He braced for her reply.

"A quiet life with my gentle husband is all I ever desired."

"Children?" His brows rose in a question. "We could not naturally conceive. If not for our vampiric life, we would not have our four beautiful children."

"True." Nambi frowned. "I fear what their lives would have been without our intervention."

She ambled over to the window, peering into the night sky. "Did we exchange one hellish life for another?"

Enu joined her. The cool breeze from the open window brought them closer. He nuzzled her to his side.

"They wish to leave."

"I know," she said.

"We should assist them."

"Yes, we will."

Enu spun around, noticing a sparkle in Nambi's eye.

"Then you agree?"

"We would be negligent parents if we did not support our children."

"And us?"

Her gaze bore deeply into his. "I am tired. A thousand years on earth is too long."

"We will be together."

Nambi nodded. "An eternity forever."

In the moonlight, he kissed her passionately. Wrapping his arms around her waist, he said, "Timing matters. Fatou's impatience mirrors Korlemo's."

Nambi grinned. "I will explain to him the necessity of patience."

As his wife departed, Enu sank into the divan's cushions, considering how to proceed. Though not foolish, Korlemo's overconfidence could be manipulated. However, Zainabu...

Though crafty and suspicious, the witch must have weaknesses.

Enu's gaze drifted out the window as he reviewed options. "There's a way. Dayo would serve as a distraction."

Korlemo loved himself and his wife, in that order.

I must give my children an opportunity to escape.

If his children wanted to leave, Enu would ensure they departed with a hefty financial cushion. Stealing from Korlemo carried serious consequences. Failure would result in certain death for everyone involved.

Chapter 20

Sunlight created a wall of glittering prisms along the solarium's glass walls. A momentary relief from the heavy rains over the past week. Rosemary filled the air as Makeda pummeled leaves with a mortar and pestle.

June in Memphis sizzles hotter than Asheville.

Despite it being morning, Makeda wore a t-shirt and shorts. If she were alone, she'd wear even less. Her fingers trembled as she sifted minute granules of powder into a glass beaker. Last night, Eldridge taught her how to create a healing salve.

This will help the mwindaji.

Recalling the phone conversation with Michael, she wondered when to return home. Yewande hadn't told her how long to stay. Though she learned more from Samuel and Eldridge than from her great-grandmother, Makeda needed to work and earn a living.

Presently, she lived at home with her parents and two brothers. Peter would move out after his wedding. Thomas would never leave.

Makeda wanted her own place, which required money. Besides, the mwindaji had missions to complete, and she intended to join them.

The solarium door opened, and Eldridge entered.

"Samuel has breakfast ready. Tardiness will not be tolerated."

She laughed. "I'll be right there. I'm preparing a salve."

Eldridge walked over to the workbench where she had dried herbs and solutions laid out. He frowned. "What are you doing?"

"Mixing the components together."

"What I mean is, why do it like that?"

Makeda regarded him. "Isn't this how you showed me?"

"Did I use a dropper and a beaker?"

She studied him, unsure what he meant.

"Come. Breakfast awaits."

It took Makeda a moment to clean up and follow Eldridge into the house. Already, the sun had begun to retreat behind looming storm clouds.

Samuel gave her a weighty glare. "Biscuits should be eaten hot."

"Sorry." She accepted a plate of biscuits and slathered one in orange marmalade. "I got carried away in the solarium."

"Oh, what have you been up to?" Samuel asked.

"Mixing together a salve," she said, piling hashbrowns on her plate. Between bites, she appreciated a silent exchange between her hosts.

They're talking about me. What did I do wrong this time?

"Which salve did you compound?"

"A healing salve. I thought it would be helpful for the mwindaji."

Samuel grimaced and continued eating.

She addressed Eldridge. "What's wrong?"

He carefully set down his teacup. "Why waste time teaching if you refuse to use maji?"

"What do you mean? I am."

Sinewy tendons bulged along his neck. "No, you are not."

Makeda shook her head. "I don't understand."

"Why use your hands when with a command, the ingredients would come together."

"Do I have to use maji for everything?"

"Maji is not practiced. It should become who you are," Eldridge said.

"Does it look like I dust blinds or turn on a washing machine?" Samuel asked, straightening his bowtie.

Her eyes gaped.

"Exactly." He smiled.

"You've been here two weeks. Why not use sorcery instead of clumsily measuring items?" Eldridge asked.

"For everyday tasks?"

Eldridge squeezed her hand. "Witches mix chemicals to make potions—hell—even bindimèn can do that. For a zauber, maji is like breathing."

He flicked his finger, and the marmalade container moved to his side.

"We employ no servants, maids, or gardeners, but our home remains immaculate," Samuel said.

"Despite being a zauber, you toil like a bindimèn." Eldridge asked. "Why?"

Makeda glanced at both of them, then out a window giving onto the backyard. "I guess it's because I've always had to hide my abilities. My family..."

Her eyes brimmed with tears. "No one knows I'm a zauber except my mom. And she won't let me tell anyone—not even my brothers."

"You are not a child. She does not control your actions—or should not." Eldridge smirked.

"If the mwindaji discover I'm a zauber, they'll kick me out of the group."

"True."

"Is being a mwindaji important to you?" Samuel asked.

She shrugged. "It's all I know. Being an mwindaji is part of my culture."

"Are you sure?" Samuel asked.

Makeda studied him. "What do you mean?"

"Anyone can become an mwindaji. Pick up a gun and shoot a vampire. Bindimèn can practice witchcraft, create potions and salves. Zaubers, however, are innate."

"Can't I be both?" she asked, leaning forward at the edge of her chair.

"No." Eldridge refreshed their tea.

"Mwindaji have murdered zaubers. They make no distinction between us and vampires," Samuel said, rising and retiring to the kitchen.

Makeda's eyes watered as she watched his retreating back.

Knock, knock.

Yawning, Makeda sat up on the bed. "Come in."

"Get up," Eldridge said.

A clap of thunder shook the walls.

"We have work to do."

Without questioning him, Makeda dressed and slipped into sneakers. In a few minutes, she joined him downstairs.

Heavy rain with the occasional rumble of thunder followed them as they raced to the car.

"We must hurry," Eldridge said, hustling her into the Cadillac.

Samuel waited behind the wheel. "Are we ready?" He glanced at her in the rear seat.

"Yes." She slipped the seatbelt across her waist as the Cadillac jolted from the curb.

They sped down residential streets headed for Downtown Memphis. From the rear window, Makeda observed clouds racing across the horizon, unleashing torrents of rain. In the west, a thick cluster of clouds blew in with the gathering winds.

Eldridge said, "Much of the downtown area remains underwater from the floods. I hope those boots fit."

Makeda hadn't noticed a pair of black boots on the floorboard when she entered the car. She changed out of the sneakers.

"They're a little loose."

"Thirteen inches of rain. In one day." Samuel sighed. "Damn, shame. Even the old church became waterlogged."

"Well, unless you want us to join them, avoid…"

Their voices retreated as Makeda surveyed the water-damaged homes. The closer they approached downtown, the greater the devastation. A flashback brought her to Port-au-Prince following the earthquake. She recalled a gentle octogenarian with a tenacity for life. Nadege's kind words and prompt warning revived her desire to reclaim her zauber heritage. Samuel and Eldridge claimed she resisted maji and it interfered with her growth.

I'm not resisting. Am I?

She wanted to be mwindaji *and* zauber. The two shouldn't be mutually exclusive. In Kentucky, she had desired nothing more than to learn maji. Now, she had the opportunity but also a difficult decision. Could she practice sorcery without being a zauber?

Screw it. I'll find a way to be both.

"I can't get closer without submerging the car," Samuel said, parking the Cadillac next to a park.

Makeda glanced up at approaching gray clouds as the rain slackened.

"We can walk the rest of the way." Eldridge glanced at Makeda.

She grabbed her backpack and exited the car. An odor of mildew hung in the humid air. Using elbow crutches, Eldridge lumbered down the street. Makeda followed.

Flooding left many overhead streetlamps non-functional with only an occasional lit lamppost. Makeda checked alleyways, concerned about the increasingly darkening skies.

"Are you going to tell me where we're going?" she asked.

"Flooding has brought out pests," Eldridge said. "We received notification about creatures feeding on bindimèn."

She gave him a side glance. "Creatures?"

"*Nommo.*"

"No—What?" She stumbled over a gap in the sidewalk.

"Beware of your surroundings," he said, lurching over an overturned can.

"It's hard to see."

He shook his head. "You refuse to use maji. Despite my spastic legs, I traverse these roads easily. Are you not embarrassed, given your youth and strength?"

Makeda grimaced and concentrated on the street.

Beside a red brick building, an alleyway led them right and into a slightly widened rotunda behind an abandoned building.

Eldridge inhaled deeply. "Smell that?"

"It stinks," she said, surveying the trash bins and wooden pallets spilled haphazardly along the alleyway. "Like seaweed."

"Nommo exude a distinctive odor."

"And what exactly does—"

Makeda discerned movement near a pile of rags, left of center. Her focus sharpened.

"Eldridge," she whispered, inclining her head in the direction of the rags.

With a nod, he acknowledged her findings. "Get ready."

"Fire?"

"A nommo can be killed with fire or—"

In a flash, the pile of rags rose.

Makeda retreated behind a trashcan.

Toddling on flippers, like a beached fish, a speckled moss-green animal under three feet in length covered in scales and puffing gills, bustled forward.

Exhaling, Makeda knelt down. "Oh, it's simply a—"

"Watch out!" Eldridge hollered.

Before Makeda reacted, the animal struck, knocking her to the ground. It scampered onto her chest, but she somersaulted to her feet, slapping it away.

"Loko." Eldridge created a flame from the air between his hands, steering it toward the creature. He scorched the nommo. It howled and wriggled in the flames.

Makeda's pulse increased. Absently, she touched her backpack, confirming she had strapped on a machete and lance. She peered over at Eldridge, who kept the flame on the nommo until it burned into a charred skeleton.

Tapping the skeleton with the toe of her boot, she asked, "What happened?"

"Nommo resemble mudfish. To travel, they need water or a host."

"How did they get here?"

"Torrential rains have battered Memphis since the end of April, flooding downtown. Nommo are parasites. They take advantage of favorable conditions."

A noise from farther down the alley drew Makeda's attention. "Look." She pointed at a disheveled, stumbling man, who used the occasional dumpster for balance. His vacant stare made Makeda reach for her machete.

Eldridge dashed in front of her. "Brother, are you well?"

In reply, the man's mouth gaped like a fish searching for air. As Eldridge recited another incantation, three other people staggered behind the first man.

Makeda surveyed the scene. "This is straight out of *Night of the Living Dead*."

One guy preceded three others.

"Uh, Eldridge, we have company."

The older man dropped his elbow canes. "As I feared. Nommo have overrun downtown." His palms shot forward, releasing a torrent of flames dousing the man closest to them.

"Once a nommo has possessed a bindimèn, they cannot be saved. Kill them with fire or decapitation."

After a slight hesitation, the remaining three people surged forward with a horrific moan.

Makeda detached the machete hooked to her backpack. She collided with one of the nommo.

It charged forward grabbing at her with arms outstretched resembling a zombie.

She whipped the machete in a semi-circle, slicing off its head. Instead of blood, an amorphous green goo oozed from its neck. Watching where she stepped, Makeda gave the body a momentary glance before leaping over it and fighting the next nommo.

Smoke from charred nommo choked the air, imparting the foul odor of fish cooked in a microwave. Bouncing off the brick buildings, the nommo's moaning coalesced into a roar, preventing her from hearing anything.

A foot ahead of her, Eldridge smote the last nommo. Makeda surveyed the carnage as a crowd formed at the other end of the alleyway.

"They search for fresh food."

"Great. Nommo zombies."

The crowd surged forward.

Makeda raised the machete and pointed at the throng. Shouting over her shoulder, she screamed, "Eldridge, we need a plan! I'm not sure how long we can keep this up."

"I will call Samuel."

"*What?*"

Two nommo lurched forward. Instead of white conjunctiva, their eyes had a sea-green moss color. They attacked Makeda simultaneously.

Their incessant wailing made her head throb and concentration difficult. She walloped a male nommo in the abdomen with her boot, sending him into a nearby trashcan. In the interim, a female nommo seized her right arm. Makeda kicked its legs, dropping it to the ground before whacking off the head.

As the male nommo clambered off of the ground, Makeda thrust the lance into its chest. It grabbed the lance, and they tussled over the weapon.

Makeda wrestled the lance away and slashed the nommo's neck with the machete in her left hand. It shrieked and gasped until she lobbed off its head.

Pivoting around to address Eldridge, Makeda saw a nommo tackle him to the ground. A foaming substance spewed from its mouth and onto Eldridge's boot.

"Ah!" he screamed as goop melted through the rubber. Acrid smoke sizzled around his foot. Eldridge crawled along the ground, trying to flee.

"I'm coming." Makeda sprinted to his side.

With a swish, the machete sliced off the nommo's head. Avoiding the green foam, she attached the machete to her backpack and scooped Eldridge up and over her shoulder.

It began raining again.

Makeda fled from the gathering nommo. Bobbing up and down on her shoulder, Eldridge shot projectiles of fire at the nommo encircling them.

While adjusting his position, Makeda swiveled around. She raised her hands and faced the nommo. "Ubumi!"

A nommo on her right lifted off the ground. With a flick of her wrists, she slammed the creature against a nearby brick wall. Taking advantage of the distraction, Makeda again fled away from the growing herd of nommo.

As they exited the alleyway, a yellow Cadillac drew up to the curb.

"Hop in." Samuel unlocked the rear door.

Makeda dumped Eldridge on the rear seat. In one swift movement, she unattached her machete, pivoted around and chopped the heads off two attacking nommo. She jumped over her teacher's body and into the car.

The door barely closed before Samuel gunned the engine, and the Cadillac zoomed down the street, fleeing the alleyway.

Removing items from her backpack, Makeda treated Eldridge's foot.

"Don't worry, child," he said, waving her aside. "Samuel will heal my wounds when we return home."

Despite his assurances, Makeda cleansed the skin and wrapped his foot in gauze.

"Next time, give me a warning about these nommo."

"Did I not tell you on the first day to be prepared?"

She shook her head and reclined into the seat. "My fault for underestimating your advice."

He smiled tepidly. "Thank you. You did well." He passed out.

On a long settee, Eldridge reclined in a sea of pillows. Makeda assisted Samuel, who washed off the ointment she had applied in the car.

"This will interfere with my healing," he explained.

While he tended to Eldridge's wounds, Makeda admired the grand, opulent bedroom. A heady, musky cologne lingered in the air. An enormous bed with overhead draperies occupied the far wall. Gold enameled doorknobs and fixtures graced the bathroom. Though she viewed only a tiny portion from the cracked doorway, Makeda saw plush rugs covering the wide-planked hardwood bathroom floors.

"Those are Turkish," Eldridge murmured. His eyes partially opened. "A beautiful room, no?"

"It's gorgeous," she said, ogling the extravagance.

"My Samuel has refined tastes."

"Quiet, E. I need to remember the correct words."

Makeda studied Samuel as he closed his eyes. His lips moved though no words came forth.

"Surely, you are not surprised by our living arrangements."

She shrugged. "I wasn't sure."

"And too polite to ask?" He chuckled, then cried, "Ouch! Samuel. Careful."

"Stop talking. I'm trying to treat your foot. Slimy nommo shit ate right down to the bone."

Samuel continued his incantation while gently holding Eldridge's ankle. Singed, rotting tissue disappeared from the wound, replaced by pink healthy muscle.

Makeda held a compress around Eldridge's bleeding foot. "People interest me."

Eldridge regarded his partner. "We have been together for nearly fifty years,"

"And we'll remain together if you'll stop moving and let me finish."

"Is that why you became a nurse?" Eldridge asked.

"I was accepted to medical school, but I believed nursing worked better for a mwindaji—in addition to being less expensive and requiring less time."

Eldridge's smile preceded a whimper. "Samuel, try a numbing spell before you debride any more tissue."

"Wait." Makeda prepared a syringe from her backpack. "I know it's not maji, but it will alleviate your pain."

Since neither man objected, Makeda injected lidocaine around the torn skin and into the area near the exposed bone.

"See, being a mwindaji can work alongside maji."

Eldridge closed his eyes and laid back among the cushions. Samuel gave her a side-eye glance before continuing with his treatment.

Once Eldridge's foot had been treated, Makeda sipped tea beside the resting couple.

Samuel sat in a chair beside the settee.

Eldridge napped intermittently while she and Samuel snacked on crab cakes.

"What about the nommo?" she asked between bites. "That's a substantial infestation."

"Once the waters recede, they'll leave," Samuel said.

"But how many people will have died by then?" Eldridge readjusted his bandaged foot.

Samuel's brows raised. "Should I call in reinforcements?"

"In the morning," Eldridge said. "For the moment, there are no people downtown for the nommo to possess."

"The homeless?" Makeda asked.

"They will have sought higher ground." Eldridge snipped a piece of crab cake from his plate. "We will wait for reinforcements."

"Mwindaji?"

"We do not work with mwindaji." Eldridge reclined upon the pillows.

"Do many zaubers live around here?"

Her hosts exchanged glances.

Samuel asked, "Have you decided whether to embrace being a zauber or continue with the mwindaji?"

"Why must I choose between them?"

"Because mwindaji kill zaubers," Samuel said.

Eldridge propped himself up. "We cannot betray our friends by letting you work beside them."

In a shaky voice, Makeda asked, "Aren't I a friend?"

Patting her hand, Eldridge said, "A dear one. You saved my life."

"Perhaps we should repay such generosity." Samuel glared at his partner.

Ignoring him, Eldridge said, "Everyone must take a side. Simply knowing their existence carries great risk. Who do you decide to be?"

A stray tear dripped down her cheek. "I love my family."

"A long time ago, I had to choose between family and destiny."

"Did..." Makeda swallowed. "Do you regret your choice?"

"It would not matter if I did. Time lost cannot be regained." Eldridge gazed into her face. "But I do not. I made the proper choice."

Samuel smiled and placed his hand over Eldridge's. "And you, child?" the former asked. "What will you decide?"

Makeda wiped her eyes. "To help my family, I keep my sorcery secret."

"Denying who you are stifles your strength. That is why your maji only works under duress," Eldridge said.

"Hiding your true nature leads to unhappiness." Samuel touched her hand.

"Nothing I teach matters until you embrace your essence." Eldridge closed his eyes.

"I want to be both. They aren't mutually exclusive."

"No zauber will trust you if you associate with mwindaji," Samuel said.

"But you two trust me, right?" Her gaze bounced between them, but their faces remained flat.

Repositioning himself to face her, Eldridge said, "We do, but our friends will not."

"What happened between the mwindaji and zaubers?"

"Betrayal on a massive scale."

Her brow furrowed. "Unforgiveable?"

"More than one incident. It formed a culture of distrust."

Samuel shrugged. "Some people never forgive or forget."

"Perhaps it's time to rebuild confidences."

Samuel and Eldridge shared a glance.

"We are not the ones to begin those negotiations," Eldridge said.

"It's easier to repeat centuries of hatred than learn forgiveness." Samuel sipped tea.

She nodded and prepared to leave. "I understand."

"Makeda, wait." Samuel rose but Eldridge grabbed his arm.

"Let her go."

Because the two men stared at each other, Makeda presumed they were conversing in kasi kasi.

Samuel settled back on the chair.

Makeda departed.

Inside her bedroom, she packed.

I'm not going to abandon the mwindaji.

Samuel and Eldridge didn't trust her around other zaubers—at least Eldridge didn't. She believed Samuel wanted to.

Did he want to share something else? How do I pose a danger to other zaubers?

Makeda prepared to leave with more questions than when she had arrived.

Chapter 21

BRIAN GAZED OUT THE side window at the golden setting sun and clear sky. He glanced at his younger brother, Zeke, who drove while singing along with Bob Marley's *Three Little Birds*. He switched the station to a news broadcast.

"Hey," Zeke said, reaching for the radio dial.

Brian slapped his hand aside. "Focus on the car ahead. This is our one lead to Korlemo."

The radio forecaster reported, "Clouds expected to clear with temperatures in—"

"Shut that off," Raymond said, from the truck's rear seat. "They're always wrong."

Impressed by the luscious vegetation of Upstate New York, Brian said, "I haven't traveled to this part of New York before. It's not bad."

"Humph," Zeke huffed. "Wait 'til winter. They get a ton of snow."

"It's great for skiing," Raymond said between clicks on his hand-held gamer.

Zeke glanced in the rearview mirror at his brother. "How would you know? You don't ski."

"I read." Raymond returned to his game. "Bet it's fun. Probably expensive."

Brian observed the SUV two cars ahead. "Watch it, Zeke. They're signaling for the next exit."

"I see them." Zeke switched to the right exit lane behind a passenger van.

At the next exit, the SUV, passenger van, sedan, and their truck abandoned the expressway for a two-lane state road.

"Why are we following these guys?" Zeke asked.

"Because we can't hit the New Jersey estate with the FBI surveillance, but their associates might lead to us to other vampire dens."

"I hope so." Zeke switched the radio on. "I'm tired of chasing Korlemo."

"Daniel's intel led us to our biggest werewolf and vampire nest yet."

Zeke drummed his fingers along the steering wheel. "What good did it do? Ramsey remains infested with monsters."

"That's because the town invited them back," Brian said.

"Nothing we can do if people want to live with monsters." Raymond reclined along the rear seats.

"I doubt the citizens of Ramsey even know about them," Brian said.

"Well, they elected them fools into office. If you don't like your politicians, vote them out." Raymond closed his eyes.

"Thank you for the public service announcement. Now, can we focus on the road?" Zeke checked his side mirrors.

Raymond yawned. "We should've placed a tracker on the SUV."

"Woulda, coulda, didn't." Zeke overtook the passenger van to be one car behind the SUV.

"Careful," Brian said. "We don't want to be spotted."

Zeke chuckled. "What can they do? We're following them."

Brian admired the two-lane road surrounded by a canopy of trees. Leaves fluttered in the breeze. A piney scent enveloped the truck. While his brothers conversed, he appreciated the increasing cloud cover above. Trees swayed.

"Is a storm coming?" he asked no one in particular.

"Radio said clear skies and warm weather."

He frowned. "Then look outside."

Among the sky of overhanging tree limbs, a lone dark cloud gathered.

Focused on the road, Zeke asked, "What?"

"It..." Brian hesitated. "It looks like a cloud is following us."

The passenger van and sedan took a secondary road. Only they and the SUV remained on the state road.

"Um, Bro." Brian tapped Zeke's shoulder. "We should head back."

Raymond gazed out the rear window. "It's one cloud."

Thunder crackled above them. Sprinkles popped off of the windshield.

Zeke switched on the wipers and headlamps.

"We can handle a little rain," Raymond said in a shakier voice.

"I don't believe that's a cloud." Brian's eyes strained, following the strange weather phenomenon as they traveled the increasingly darkening road.

All three men glanced out of the windows. As if someone flipped a switch, the sunlight disappeared. Heaviness pressed around the truck, plunging them into complete darkness. Not a star shown above.

"Zeke." Brian squeezed the door handle while observing the cloud hovering directly above.

"Yeah, man. I feel it."

Raymond sat up straight and tightened his seatbelt. "I'm ready to go back anytime—"

Crash!

"Ah, hell!" Zeke yelled, swerving briefly into the opposite lane.

A fissure split across the entire front window.

"Something smashed into the window," Raymond said.

"Look!" Brian gawked, pointing at a dead bat lying on the hood of the truck. Its wing had become trapped between the windshield wipers.

Raymond gaped. "Oh, damn."

Brian rolled down the window.

"*What are you doing?*" Raymond asked.

"Getting it off the truck's window." Brian leaned outside, attempting to pry the bat free from the wipers.

"Skip this shit." Slamming on the brakes, Zeke spun the truck around, knocking Brian against the doorframe.

Ringing in his ears made Brian momentarily dizzy.

"Wait a minute." He managed to free the bat before Zeke charged back toward the expressway.

In the darkness surrounding the truck, Brian counted dozens of tiny yellow eyes. He rolled up the passenger side window moments before a wing struck it. He flinched.

"Damn. Another bat."

"They grow big ass bats here in New York," Raymond said. "Could they be vampires?"

"In daytime?" Zeke flipped on the high beams.

Brian focused on the bat. His mind raced with possibilities. "It's essentially night with all this tree cover and the mysterious cloud."

Should I contact the mwindaji? But their team was in North Carolina. *Wait.*

Using kasi kasi, he reached out to Makeda.

'You there?'

'Brian?'

'Yeah. We have a situation—'

'Are you in immediate threat of death?'

'Um, I'm not sure.'

'Well, I am. There's a horde of nommo—'

'No—What?'

'Later.'

Brian lost the connection. He needed to learn sorcery—quick.

"Raymond, snap a picture," he said.

"Oh, right."

As Raymond filmed the bats, Zeke raced back to the expressway, clocking a hundred miles per hour. When the next road sign read expressway two miles ahead, the cloud lifted.

Brian perceived the pressure lifting and took a deep breath.

The truck merged onto the freeway with the setting sun in the distance and a cloudless sky above. Brian and Zeke shared a glance. The former scrutinized the sky for clouds or bats.

Raymond asked, "Are we gonna pretend that didn't happen?"

"You think they ID'ed us?" Brian asked, smirking at his brother.

"Okay, fine." Zeke adjusted the rearview mirror. "Maybe they spotted us."

"How the hell did they command a cloud of bats?" Raymond searched his pockets. "I need a joint."

"You can get high when we get back home," Zeke said, eyeing him in the rearview mirror.

Brian regarded Zeke. "You still doubt this lead?"

"Shut up and watch out for bats."

"We thought the horde of monsters in Ramsey was bad." Brian stared at the passing tree from a side window. "There's something worse here in New York."

Gazing across at Zeke, Brian noticed his brother's hands clenching the steering wheel. They had uncovered something significant in Ramsey, and it extended well beyond the Bluegrass State.

Chapter 22

BESIDES THE OCCASIONAL SOFT patter of footsteps, the enormous mansion remained quiet. Zainabu suspected—no, she knew—many staff had defected.

Not as many people around as before.

Whether due to Korlemo's aggressive management style or the security staff's dereliction, people were leaving. This created an opportunity.

Chaos made Korlemo irritable and prone to mistakes. In addition, his desperation to establish order made him dependent upon her.

Delighted with the current situation, Zainabu carefully balanced the silver platter in her hand while trekking down the hallway. She worried about spilling the valuable beverage.

"Excuse me," a servant said, scampering past her and down the extended hallway.

The staff should wear uniforms. They blended in too well with the family. She'd speak with Korlemo about it. But, if this potion worked, it wouldn't be necessary. The ancient vampire would no longer be her problem—or anyone's.

Remember to grab the ring.

Using her hip, Zainabu pushed open the study door. As expected, Korlemo sat at the oblong desk reading reports.

"I have a treat for you." She entered and closed the door with her foot. "The chef was busy, so I brought it myself."

Grunting, Korlemo gave her a slight glance before returning to the papers.

"Come." She slid the platter closer. "You work too hard. Enu should attend to such affairs."

Zainabu perched on a corner of the desk, observing the three-jeweled ring on his right index finger.

How did I miss it?

"I arranged the security services. What has he done? The servants strut around here like they're part of the family."

Korlemo sipped from the foaming tankard while sampling breaded meats. "Enu has become lazy, distracted. He worries too much about what these bindimèn feel."

"I suppose I'll have to address that problem, too." She sighed.

Korlemo smirked. "I am fortunate to have you attending to my needs."

Zainabu simpered. "Anything for you. I'm happy to—"

"To what?" Dayo strutted into the study and up to the desk. She glared at Zainabu. "What are you promising my husband now? Ass-kissing early this evening, aren't you?"

Zainabu retreated from the desk.

"Dayo." Korlemo laid a hand on his wife's wrist. "Such hostilities are unnecessary."

"Oh." Dayo sat on the arm of Korlemo's chair. "Am I to watch in silence as this common witch seduces you?"

Korlemo guffawed. "You imagine a tryst where none exists. Zainabu merely brought me a snack from our new chef." He handed her the tray. "Try some."

Zainabu grimaced. *There's no more potion. I can't waste it on Dayo.*

"No, thank you." Dayo rested in the leather chair Korlemo vacated. "My stomach aches."

"Because last night you fed on intoxicated bindimèn." He retrieved a book from a shelf near the fireplace.

"I was hungry."

"Reckless."

"They are easier to capture."

"But the alcohol goes straight to their blood. It makes me nauseated." Korlemo shooed her out of his chair. "You will heal in time."

Dayo leaned against the desk and rubbed her stomach.

"If you prefer, Zainabu can prepare a healing tea."

"That witch." Dayo sneered. "I would not trust my health to her."

Zainabu's shoulders stiffened.

"Be nice," Korlemo said.

"I am." Dayo regarded Zainabu. "There are nastier words I have for your new pet."

"Here. I can smell the yeast." Korlemo handed Dayo the tankard. "It will settle your stomach."

Hurrying forward, Zainabu lightly extracted the tankard from Korlemo's grasp. "But I prepared this treat for you. I would be happy to create something special for Dayo."

Placing the tankard on the tray, Zainabu began to depart.

"Give me that." Dayo pulled on the tray, spilling a sizeable portion of the liquid.

"This will irritate your stomach," she said. "I'll make you a different drink."

"If this would satisfy Korlemo, I can drink it, too."

Zainabu refused to yield. "I insist."

"How dare you." Dayo lifted the tankard while releasing the tray, causing Zainabu to stumble. "Now get out of here before I show you why I am mistress of this mansion." Dayo flashed her pointed canines.

Korlemo stood between them, waving Zainabu aside. "We will discuss staffing later. Leave."

Reluctantly, she departed.

Damn. I need to get that—

A cry made her burst inside the study.

Dayo had collapsed on the ground, clutching her abdomen. Korlemo hurried to her side, delicately lifting her in his arms.

He softly tapped his wife's face. "Dayo, Dayo."

Zainabu rushed up to them. "Let me." She raised unconscious Dayo's eyelids and saw the vampire's chest rise and fall like waves.

Well, at least I discovered the potion works. Zorulo will not be pleased.

"What should we do?" Korlemo asked, his voice trembling while he tenderly cradled his wife. His eyes teared up and his mouth drooped.

The vampire did care for someone.

Surprised, Zainabu stuttered, "We, uh… Take her to the bedroom."

With alacrity, Korlemo flew from the room and bolted up the stairs. Zainabu ran to keep up with him.

Halfway up the staircase, they encountered Enu. "I heard a scream. What happened?"

"Dayo's stomach." Korlemo delicately placed his wife on an enormous bed, settling her head on plush pink pillows. Enu helped settle Dayo, checking her pulse and feeling her sweaty forehead.

"She has a fever," Enu said. "We should call a doctor."

"We do not have a doctor here in Michigan." Korlemo rubbed his wife's hand as he peered eagerly into her face.

"Well, it is time to find one." Enu glared at Zainabu. "Make yourself useful and call a doctor."

As she exited the room, the two men sat on opposite sides of the bed hovering over Dayo.

"Please, my love," Korlemo said, kissing Dayo's head.

Rolling her eyes, Zainabu left the room. Downstairs, she located the head of security in the kitchen. "Mr. Sherman."

"Yes, ma'am." He stood and set down his coffee cup. "How can I help?"

"Call a doctor. Dayo's ill."

"Right away." He rushed out of the kitchen, speaking over a walkie-talkie.

For the moment, staff hurried around the mansion, answering summons from Korlemo to comfort Dayo. He demanded a cool towel for her forehead and herbal tea. Zainabu ordered the staff around to satisfy her boss, meanwhile, waiting for an opportunity to retrieve the tankard.

At the foot of the staircase, Zainabu watched the hallway that led to the study. She needed to dispose of the potion and cleanse the tankard. If they analyzed the contents, Korlemo would kill her. No, torture her then kill her.

Get that tankard.

Time passed. With the staff occupied, she scurried into the study and gathered the tray and tankard. In seconds, she had returned to the kitchen and began washing the items.

Enu entered.

She froze.

With electric speed, he dashed over to the sink and grasped her wrist.

"Ouch." Zainabu reflexively dropped the tankard into the sink of soapy water.

"What are you doing?" Enu asked, eyeing her.

"Washing dishes." Her chin jutted forward.

"Is that one of your new duties?"

She inched away from him, avoiding his gaze. "I wanted to help."

"How can washing dishes help Dayo?"

Zainabu started to depart. "There's nothing to do for her until the doctor arrives."

"True." Enu zipped up to the doorway, blocking her departure. "Because you poured the poison down the drain."

Her hands tingled. Zainabu forced herself not to move. Hurling a spell at Enu would not improve her situation. "I did no such thing."

He inhaled deeply. "I smell your sweat, your fear. Not a convincing liar—yet."

Stepping cautiously away, Zainabu scanned the kitchen.

"Are you afraid?" His head tilted slightly.

"You can't touch me. Korlemo won't allow it."

His dark eyes bore into hers. "If Dayo dies, so do you."

She detected a pull. He was trying to entrance her. Zainabu tore her eyes away and rushed from the room. Not until securely inside her bedroom did she exhale. Reclined against the wall, she panted from the sprint.

"Shit. You messed up big."

Zorulo would be pissed, and Korlemo would be suspicious.

I have to retain Korlemo's trust and appease Zorulo.

She sat on the bedroom floor thinking. Noises from the garden made her glance out of the window. Sherman escorted someone inside. Zainabu exhaled deeply.

At least Dayo wouldn't die.

Zainabu hated the reality that her life depended on a diva vampire's survival.

"Stupid vamp wouldn't be sick if she had listened to me," Zainabu mumbled.

Peeking out the bedroom door, she watched as the doctor entered Dayo's bedroom. Before slipping back inside, Zainabu caught Enu spying on her. She hurriedly slammed the door.

Inside the bedroom closet, Zainabu removed a trunk hidden behind suitcases. Using a talisman around her neck, she opened it and removed a thick book covered in weathered leather.

The book had been in her family for ages. Her grandmother had updated the spells. When Zainabu escaped from her village, she stole it from her aunt, a zauber who refused to mentor her in sorcery.

With the book on her lap, she repeated an incantation. A short click preceded the cover flying open. Pages fluttered as her fingers stirred the air above them. She located the chapter on binding demons. Careful not to touch the delicate—and toxic—pages, Zainabu located the desired section.

For the rest of the evening, she carefully studied the information. Already, she had gathered most of the items required.

Hoping to kill Korlemo tonight, she'd hesitated in using the spell. But since she hadn't subdued the vampire as Zorulo ordered, killing the demon became imperative. Because as much as she feared Korlemo, Zorulo could chase her to the ends of the earth—not to mention holding her to their bargain and dragging her soul to hell.

Sitting cross-legged on the floor, Zainabu committed the incantations to memory. She studied spells and developed backup plans in case the original spell failed. Tomorrow, she would need everything she ever learned about witchcraft and sorcery.

"Damn, Dayo," she said.

The vampire's foolishness forced Zainabu's hand. She hadn't wanted to eliminate Zorulo until she had sealed Korlemo's fate. If she removed Zorulo, how would she kill Korlemo? The likelihood of being able to poison him now sank to zero.

Sleepy, Zainabu locked the book and secreted it away. She collapsed on the bed as her heavy eyelids drooped. Between her, Korlemo, and Zorulo, someone would not survive the week.

Chapter 23

Heavy footfalls proceeded in her direction. Frazzled, Zainabu straightened the desktop restoring the spreadsheets to their original location.

Get this right.

Two days had passed since Dayo accidentally drank the sedative intended for Korlemo. The household had remained tense, terrified of Korlemo's reaction if Dayo had died.

Stupid tramp.

All Zainabu's plans had to be readjusted because an Elvira wannabe decided to show off. If Korlemo suspected—

"Why are you here?" The millennial vampire stormed up to the desk, glowering over Zainabu. His eyes blazed hell fire-red.

Relax. Don't show fear.

"I have a surprise for you," she said, struggling to moderate her voice.

"Dayo believes you tried to poison her." He snarled, his teeth gnashing. "Explain what happened to my wife or I will allow her to rip you apart and feed you to the staff."

Concerned about her trembling hand, Zainabu commanded the paper to float over to Korlemo.

He snatched the note and began to crumple it.

"Wait," she said, holding up a hand. "You're going to want to speak with this person."

Korlemo read the note, which simply included a phone number. His brows raised in question.

"If you want to get back the money Dr. Senegal embezzled, I suggest you call that number."

His red pupils shifted to black. Korlemo walked past Zainabu and sat behind the oblong desk. His fingers formed a steeple, and he grinned.

"Outstanding. Be seated."

Cautiously, Zainabu settled in front of the desk. Her tense shoulders made her neck ache. Not until she restored Korlemo's trust could she relax. This information should satisfy him or at least distract him from her attempted coup d'état. It required a sizeable sum, but she'd been able to convince—

The study door crashed open and slammed against the adjacent wall. Dayo blasted into the room and up to the desk.

Before Zainabu could rise, Dayo transformed into full vampiric form. The vamp snatched her out of the chair by the neck.

Zainabu choked, barely able to breathe. Murmuring a spell, she blew a noxious cloud into Dayo's face.

Coughing and spluttering, Dayo's grip loosened, and Zainabu escaped her clutches. But she tripped over a chair and crashed beside the desk.

Dayo smacked her head into the side of Korlemo's desk. Zainabu's head ricocheted off the wood, causing her vision to blur. Blood from biting her lip trickled down her throat.

Grabbing a handful of microbraids, Dayo swung Zainabu around the room and into a wall causing an enormous dent.

With raised hands, Zainabu cast a spell, hurling Dayo into the stone fireplace. Books tumbled across the floor.

Both women glared at each other a moment before they leaped forward.

Korlemo bolted in between them.

Because she stopped suddenly, Zainabu slid on the carpet and into a couch centered before the fireplace. She bumped her shin against a coffee table.

Dayo lashed out. With elongated fingers and dagger-shaped nails, she thrashed around Korlemo attempting to slash Zainabu. Korlemo wrestled his wife into a far corner.

Transformed to about eight feet tall, he bellowed, "Enough!"

Panting, Zainabu shouted, "She started it!"

"I want that witch dead!" Dayo roared. "She tried to kill me!"

"Ridiculous. You became sick from drinking alcoholic bindimèn blood."

"Liar." Dayo soared at Zainabu, but Korlemo grabbed her arm and jerked her backward.

"Sucking trash made you ill," Zainabu said, snidely.

"And what of my husband's have you been sucking since you arrived?" Dayo asked, slapping back. She faced Korlemo. "That slick witch has created a wedge between us."

"Jealousy clouds your mind," he said.

"And you like having a young skank kiss your derrière."

"Who are you calling—"

"Shut up!" Korlemo growled.

Both women quieted but continued glowering at each other.

Korlemo placed Dayo on the couch.

Zainabu retreated to a chair beside the desk.

Regaining his normal stature, Korlemo said, "Dayo, love, this will make you happy." He presented the note Zainabu gave him with the phone number. "Zainabu located the person who stole from us."

Disregarding the note, Dayo stormed toward the study door. "What do I care about money when I will die in my own home." On the threshold, she said, "And by the hands of a tramp with a cheap weave."

"Your stomach hurt before you drank from the tankard. And, if you remember correctly, I told you not to drink it. I offered to prepare something specifically for you."

"True. She did, my sweet." Korlemo joined her at the door, kissing her hands.

"Humph." Over his shoulder, Dayo's gaze bore into Zainabu's. "That witch will be the death of us all."

She departed.

Zainabu started to reply but smartly refrained. Reminding Korlemo she had advised Dayo not to drink the beverage scored points.

Go slow.

Clearly, the dragon adored his wife—a weakness she would exploit.

She straightened her braids, then repositioned the chair. Sitting up studiously, she asked, "Would you like me to phone?"

"No. This call I must make."

Korlemo sat behind the desk and read the number. Dialing, he said, "Later, you will tell me how you found her."

Not if I don't have to.

The phone rang twice.

"Hello?" a woman asked.

Korlemo switched the call to the speaker. "This is Senegal, Mangus, and Cortland," he said.

"Oh, yes. Do you have a message from my brother?"

Perfect. Zainabu exhaled, relieved the information had been accurate.

In a smooth solicitous voice, Korlemo asked, "Sylvia, my child. How are you?"

The intake of Sylvia's breath made him beam. "My condolences on the tragedy that befell your family. I wanted to reach out and offer my support."

Reclined in the seat, Zainabu realized the doctor would wonder how Korlemo found her. But he hadn't, she had. Or at least her contact in Stefan's organization had.

Money destroyed allegiances. What happened next didn't concern her, but if it won points with Korlemo, Zainabu would deliver Dr. Sylvia Senegal alive or dead.

"Korlemo, what can I do for you?"

"I miss you. Herman is deceased, and I need a financial advisor."

"Oh." Sylvia's voice quivered.

"Come back and I will forgive all."

No reply.

"I will even allow you to keep the money you stole."

Silence.

"Our families have traversed continents together for a millennium. We belong together."

"I don't know." Sylvia hesitated. "I have to think about it."

Korlemo grimaced. "Time is fleeting. Of course, if I do not hear from you, I will have to contact your brother."

Zainabu looked up, and Korlemo snickered.

"He lives in Manhattan, correct? A penthouse with an enchanting view of the park, if I recall."

"I'll call back—soon."

"I know you will."

The call disconnected. Korlemo replaced the receiver.

He rose and lightly cradled Zainabu's hand. "You have made me a happy man." He peered deeply into her eyes. "Now, what do you desire?"

Her shoulders relaxed. Zainabu snuck a quick glance at the ring on his finger.

If you only knew.

"Your trust."

"Granted but come." He escorted her to the couch. "I am sure you would appreciate other compensation."

She smiled. "I'm curious about your ring. I've never seen anything like it before."

"And you will not." He slipped the ring off his finger and handed it to her.

The cool gold metal weighed more than she suspected. Light glistened off the ruby. Tanzanite twinkled with a trichrome of blue hues, overshadowing a modest emerald in comparison. Zainabu examined each angle of the jewels.

"Craftsmen from Nintoubo selected each stone specifically for my great-grandfather. Tanzanite is rare, especially back then as it came from East African caravans." He accepted the ring from her and replaced it on his finger.

"Three identical rings were commissioned. My father gave Enu his ring and my grandfather's ring to his dear friend."

"That must have been a very close friend."

Resting on cushions, Korlemo snapped his fingers, signaling Zainabu to prepare him a drink. She returned to the couch with a goblet of bourbon. He sipped the liquid and continued his story.

"In the time of our ancestors, we valued friends like family. Alliances were forged on battlefields. Frederic—Herman's father—descended from a noble lineage. Our ancestors shared blood. He gave the ring to his dear friend, Gerard Senegal, Sylvia's father."

Since Gerard Senegal died in the mwindaji Kentucky massacre, who now has the third ring?

Zainabu set the question aside for the moment.

"Have you been back?"

"To Nintoubo?"

She nodded.

"It no longer exists." He drank his liquor, gazing dreamily up at the ceiling. "After leaving Africa, we remained in Europe until the last world war."

"Do you miss it?"

He swallowed the remaining bourbon. "I care not where I live. Only *how* I live." He placed the goblet on the coffee table. "Other questions."

"No, Korlemo." Zainabu stood. "Thank you."

He rose. "Do not antagonize, Dayo. I would hate to lose you." Though Korlemo departed, his slanted grin remained imprinted on her brain.

Zainabu sank back onto the couch. Korlemo and Enu had rings. *Who had the third one?*

According to Korlemo, the last person in possession of the ring had been Gerard Senegal. Therefore, it most likely went to one of his two remaining children.

Stefan might know. She grinned.

Maybe I'll ask the source of the leak about Sylvia.

Chapter 24

BARBEQUE SMOKE BILLOWED ACROSS the rear porch deck and into the kitchen. Cooler than Memphis, Black Ridge, North Carolina had no koleos or nommos.

Ten days had passed since she returned from Tennessee. After a week of twelve-hour shifts in Durham, Makeda needed a break and proper food. Though she appreciated the money, travel nursing was exhausting. This weekend, she simply wanted to relax with family.

Delicious aromas stimulated her appetite. A pack of dogs, composed of various breeds salivated beside the rear door leading out to the rear porch.

"Chekate." She commanded the doors to open and the herd scrambled outside.

"Good morning."

Makeda startled and swung around. "Morning."

Damn, I hope she didn't see that.

Sniffing, Mom entered the kitchen carrying a bowl of roasted corn cobs. "What's that smell?"

A scorching odor itched Makeda's nose. "Oh, no."

She rushed to the oven and removed a casserole dish. "Sorry. I let the macaroni and cheese burn." Using a knife, she trimmed the edges of the dish. "Not too bad. Slightly crispy."

Peter entered with an aluminum tray overflowing with ribs. "Barbeque is almost done. Is someone going to help with the tables and chairs?"

"Where's Thomas?" Mom asked, tossing lettuce in a salad spinner.

"I'm here." Quickly pulling a shirt over his head, Thomas darted in from a rear hallway. "What do you need?"

Peter said. "Help setting up tables and chairs. I need to get back to the grill. People should be arriving soon."

"Brenda coming?" Thomas asked as they exited.

As their voices trailed away, Makeda peeled potatoes, slicing them into a wide bowl of water.

"So." Mom inched closer to her side. "Tell me about your young man."

Ding, dong.

"I'll get that." Makeda answered the door.

"Hey, Brian." They hugged.

She gazed past him at a truck and caravan. People spilled out of vehicles. A toy poodle jumped out of the caravan and ran in circles around the yard.

"Mom," Makeda said, shutting the front door, "the Hills are here."

Brian preceded her into the kitchen and kissed Mom on the cheek.

"Hello, Mrs. Crawford." He placed a sheet cake on the dining table.

"How have you been? Did you bring your little boy?" Mom asked.

Others entered and conversations filled the house. Makeda finished the potato salad and gathered dishes to carry outside.

"I can help." Brian carried a tray of bread and the macaroni and cheese. As they exited the house, he spoke telekinetically.

'We need to talk.'

She glared at him. 'Not here.'

'Why not? No one can—'

'Mom's a zauber and former teacher. Extremely suspicious by nature.'

He nodded and placed the food on one of three long folding tables situated in the backyard under tents.

With a slight turn, Makeda perceived Mom's prying gaze.

Zeke hooked up a music player. Vocals from Sly and the Family Stone's *Family Affair* crooned from two four-foot speakers seated on the flatbed of a pickup truck.

People exited the house carrying food, beverages, and dishes.

Flipping burgers on the grill, Peter waved to guests. "Y'all ready?"

"Almost." Makeda hurried inside, not simply to gather food for the picnic, but principally to avoid Mom.

Cars parked on the front and sides of the house, almost to the barn which sat about two hundred yards east of the house. The two-story barn functioned as a workplace where Dad and her brothers crafted furniture. Crawfords had designed wood crafts in western North Carolina for generations.

People circulated and conversed. Dogs raced around being chased by screeching children. Makeda greeted guests while bringing the remaining food out to the picnic tables.

"Come on guys," Dad said, inviting people to gather around the tables.

Using two fingers, Peter whistled. "Guys! Time to eat!"

Dad said, "First, let's pray."

"Hurry, Uncle James," Raymond said. "I'm hungry."

"That's what happens when you smoke weed," Aaron said.

People laughed.

"All right." Daddy prayed, "Heavenly Father…"

Zeke lowered the music's volume but continued fiddling with his tracks. Half the people closed their eyes with bowed heads. A couple of children snuck fruit off the table during the prayer.

A second after Dad said "Amen," Zeke blasted the music and people stirred.

Carolyn's toy poodle sprung off her lap and charged the larger dogs. Children raced over to a play structure in the rear yard. In time, people settled into groups.

Makeda noticed Mom resting on the screened back porch, sipping iced tea and talking with Aunt Mirlande.

After making a plate of food, Makeda joined Brian. He arranged two folding chairs in a shaded area beside the barn.

She placed her soda on the ground beside her foot. Holding the plate up near her mouth, she said, "Don't use kasi kasi around my mom."

"Why? Can she tell?" Brian watched the two women on the porch.

"I'm not sure, but if she detected our plans to practice maji..." Makeda shook her head. "I wouldn't hear the end of it."

He smiled. "Where's Michael?"

"I didn't invite him."

Brian's brow creased. "I thought y'all were dating."

She sighed. "Does everyone need to know my business?"

"Just curious."

"Well, don't be." Because his face clouded over, Makeda hurriedly said, "It's not that I mind, but Peter can be—"

"Difficult." Brian smirked. "I'm familiar with your brother."

Makeda ate her burger and reclined into the chair.

Brian leaned close to her ear. "So, you gonna help me?"

She studied his profile, opened her mouth to speak, but didn't. Once she finished her meal, Makeda set the plate on the ground and picked up her soda.

"I'm not sure I should."

Seeing his grimace, Makeda said, "It's not easy." She laid a hand on his forearm. "And not safe."

"I can handle it."

With her chin, she pointed toward Brian's son, who hung upside down with his legs wrapped around the playset's gym bar.

"What about him?"

Brian followed her gaze. His eyes misted. They sat silently watching the children play.

"He's my responsibility. I wouldn't do anything to risk his life."

"But we risk our lives all the time as mwindajis." She glanced over at him. "The risks may be greater for a zauber."

He nodded slightly and continued watching his son.

Stretching her back, she rose. "Give it some thought. I don't understand much about zaubers or maji, but if you're sure, I'll share what I do know."

"Agreed."

Makeda left him in the shade and walked around to the front porch and entered the house, desiring to avoid her mom. She opened the door.

Damn

Sitting in the living room, Mom looked up as she entered.

"I've been waiting for you."

"Oh." Makeda pivoted to the kitchen and deposited her dishes in the sink. "I wanted to take a nap."

"What were you and Brian talking about?"

Avoiding eye contact, Makeda said, "He asked about Michael."

"That's all?" Mom entered the kitchen.

Circling around the opposite end of the island, Makeda marched toward her bedroom. "Brian asked where Michael moved after Kentucky." Her hand touched the bedroom doorknob. "Well, I'm tired."

Mom pushed her inside the bedroom, snuck in behind her, and bolted the door.

"Why—"

"I know Brian is a zauber," Mom interrupted.

Makeda's jaw dropped. "How? He doesn't know any maji. He can barely kasi kasi."

"Zaubers sense each other." Mom sat on the bed. She tapped the area beside her, directing Makeda to sit. "It's like a zap, a tingle."

"I didn't know."

Squinting, Mom scrutinized her face. Makeda squirmed.

"Is this about Michael?"

"We'll talk about him later." Mom grasped Makeda's chin and tilted her face upward. "Have you contacted Yewande?"

Makeda transfixed her face into a stony expression. "No."

"You never lied well." Mom's glared intensified.

Her shoulder twitched.

"What have you been doing at Yewande's house?"

Continue bluffing or admit defeat and face the consequences? Neither great options.

Mom's grip on her chin increased. "The truth."

"She's teaching me maji."

Mom jumped off the bed. "Dammit!" She stormed around the room. "Didn't I warn you to stay away from her?"

"I wanted to find out for myself."

"Find out what? How selfish Yewande is?" Mom rushed over and snatched Makeda by the arm. "Have you taken any oaths for her? Tell me."

Wrenching her arm free, Makeda rubbed the tender area. "No, I haven't. But I've learned a lot."

"How to hurt people? How to get yourself killed?"

"I've learned maji! And not to be ashamed of my heritage!" Seeing Mom's hands clench, she quickly apologized.

"Sorry. I didn't mean to yell." She sighed. "I know you don't trust Yewande, and truthfully, I don't either."

Mom guided her to bed, and they sat. "After working with children for years, I should have realized the one thing denied is the one thing they desire."

She kissed Makeda's temple and hugged her to her side. "You're an adult. I have to let you make your own decisions."

Rising, Mom pivoted around at the door. "It took a lot for me to cast a spell strong enough to protect you from Yewande. This time, I won't be able to."

Makeda joined her at the door. "It won't come to that."

In a partial sobbing chuckle, Mom said, "Yewande is a sphinx."

"What does that mean?"

Mom shrugged. "Not sure. That's what my mom called Yewande."

Makeda frowned.

Teary eyed, Mom gave her a bear hug. "I don't want to lose you."

"I'll be all right. I can take care of myself."

"There are worse things than death." Mom opened the door, preparing to leave.

Barely audible, Makeda mumbled, "Like a demon."

Mom gasped and shut the door. "What?"

Why the hell did I say anything about the demon?

Shaking Makeda about the shoulders, Mom asked, "Did Yewande have you summon a dubwana?"

"Of course not." Makeda peeled Mom's hands away. "She's trying to protect me. That's why I visited her house."

Mom's head trembled. "A dubwana cannot attack someone unless that person summons them first."

"How do you know?" Makeda observed Mom's expression. "I thought you didn't know anything about zaubers."

"My maji is weak, but Yewande is—was—my grandmother. And my mother practiced sorcery." She grasped Makeda's hand. "I do know dubwanas are restricted to the underworld unless summoned by a bindimèn to the surface world."

"And we are where?"

"On the surface world, *tafa buni. Duka mali* is the underworld, or more colloquially known as hell."

"Why didn't you explain any of this before?"

"Because I didn't want you involved in sorcery."

"I'm going to be a zauber with or without your support."

"Perhaps you're more like Yewande than I thought." As Mom departed, she said, "If you want to be a zauber, don't follow her example."

The cellphone rang, and Makeda startled. She picked up on the second ring.

"Hello?"

"Hi, beautiful."

She envisioned Michael's smile by the tenor of his voice. "Everything okay?"

"Not sure. Are we—"

"Hey, got a minute?" Peter asked, craning his head around the open door.

"I'll call you later." Makeda hung up.

"Important?"

"No, it's fine." She sat on the bed. "What's up?"

He leaned against the doorframe. "Look, I didn't say anything to Mom or Dad, but I know you didn't have an assignment at any hospital in Memphis."

Makeda's lip slightly parted.

"Were you with Michael?"

"No," she insisted, hopping off the bed.

Peter crossed his arms over his chest. "You can trust me."

"I wasn't with Michael."

"Oh, with whom?"

She hesitated.

I can't tell the truth.

Her mom being upset about Yewande would be nothing compared to telling Peter she had been studying with zaubers.

"It's none of your business." Not original but functional.

"Everything you do is my business."

"Look—"

Peter raised his palm, cutting her off. "You're my baby sister, and I'm going to protect you no matter what. Remember the last bum you dated?"

A flush bloomed across her chest. "Don't throw that in my face again."

"If Thomas and I hadn't uncovered his marriage, you'd probably still be dating that jerk."

Makeda's shoulders trembled. "One mistake—"

"Can screw up your entire life." He came over and gave her a side hug. "Like it or not, I'm always going to protect you."

She buried her head on his chest. He kissed the top of her head. At the door, he turned around.

"And make sure he wears a condom." He laughed and dashed from the room as Makeda's shoe hit the door.

Chapter 25

S CENTED MEATS AND SPICES hung heavily in the humid summer air. Makeda returned outside with two Labradors at her heels. The pleasant summer afternoon made her sleepy. As Bob Marley's *One Love* crooned from speakers, Makeda stretched along an Adirondack chair on the front porch and napped.

Noises tugged at the recesses of her consciousness. A vision of her great-grandmother morphing into various animals flitted across her mind. Makeda forced them away.

She craved rest, to shut her mind down. Blackness engulfed her before oblivion.

A strong hand gripped her shoulder. Makeda struck out, punching the person in the ribs.

"Ouch. Wake up," Peter said, smacking her fist aside.

Groggy and unaware of the time, Makeda rubbed her eyes and sat up. "You shouldn't surprise people like that."

"Right. It's suspicious when your brother wakes you up at the family home."

Makeda saw people gathering around the living room. "Mwinda-ji?" she asked, regarding Peter.

"Meeting time."

She yawned and stretched, following him inside. Makeda scooped a pillow from the couch and rested on the floor beside the fireplace. Snippets of a dream danced around her head, reminding her to call Michael. With the dogs surrounding her, she laid down and watched.

"Everyone get something to eat or drink," Dad said, "and let's talk this out."

"Who's watching the kids?" someone asked.

Peter carried a chair in from the kitchen table. "Brenda."

Dad stood on the other side of the fireplace. "We have a quorum. Let's begin."

"We should leave this Korlemo mess alone," Aaron said, carefully wiping his mustache with a napkin. "From what Zeke reported, there's crazy shit going down in New York."

"Watch your language," Dad said.

"Sorry, Uncle James."

Dad shook his head. "No problem."

"If there's a horde of vampires in New York, we need to be there," Peter said, flicking open his pocketknife.

Zeke extended his legs forward. "Y'all didn't see those bats. Big as cats. And their wings—"

"They cracked the truck's front window," Brian said. He glanced at Makeda. Using kasi kasi, he asked, 'You okay?'

'Yes.'

'What's going on?'

'Sleepy.'

'That's all?'

'Mom knows you're a zauber.'

'How?'

'She's always known. Apparently, zaubers can detect each other.'

'Did you detect me?'

'No, but I'm just learning.'

'Yeah, and I know nothing.'

Repositioning herself among the dogs, Makeda focused on the conversation.

"Forget New York," Dad said. "It's time we hit the compound in New Jersey. Daniel said police surveillance lifted last Friday."

"Who's going?" Peter asked, whittling a piece of mahogany.

Zeke jumped up. "Y'all seriously aren't interested in New York?"

"Son—"

"Why focus on Korlemo?" Zeke interrupted his father, pacing around the room, gesticulating. "There's heavy shit going down in upstate New York. Mwindaji kill monsters. Let's go kill monsters."

Uncle John said, "Watch your language and calm down."

Zeke glanced at his dad and slowed his pace. "Sorry, but this is major."

His sister Carolyn stood. "Zeke's right. Other threats exist besides Korlemo. If there's a bigger problem somewhere else, why aren't we there?"

Dad rose. "Because I lead this group, and our goal is to kill Korlemo."

"Well, maybe it's time for another leader," Carolyn said before retreating toward the front door.

"Where're you going?" Uncle John asked.

"Outside. I need air." Carolyn and her toy poodle departed.

People murmured and milled around the living room. A few retired to the kitchen for food. Peter continued whittling an animal head from a piece of mahogany. Makeda prepared tea and communicated with Brian in kasi kasi.

'Were the bats large?'

'Huge.'

She frowned. 'And they simply descended out of the sky?'

He nodded. 'Someone—or something—signaled them.'

'A vampire?'

'Or a zauber.'

Makeda's brows lifted.

'Who else could command a cloud of bats?'

'We need to meet. I'm ready to share what I learned and hopefully teach you a thing or two.'

'Nice. I'll finally become a zauber.'

She smiled.

"It's getting late," Uncle John said, "and we need to hit the road. Charleston is a long drive."

Dad eyed each person in turn. "I know this has been a long battle, and it's not fair to place my personal burdens ahead of the team." Dragging his swollen foot, he sat on a rocking chair near the fire.

"My gout's acting up. I won't be on the next mission." He massaged his leg. "I'll leave it up to the group. New Jersey or New York?"

A beat passed before Peter asked, "Where in New York?" He gazed at Zeke, who raised his shoulders.

"I don't know."

Brian said, "We made it to the Finger Lakes area south of Rochester when the bats surrounded us."

"Nothing specific?" Peter wiped the knife blade over his jeans before closing it.

Zeke glowered. "We don't know where the bats came from."

"Then we hit New Jersey," Peter said. "There, we have a location."

"Figured you'd say that." Zeke crossed his arms over his chest and stomped to a far corner.

"He's right," Brian said, walking over to Zeke. "Besides, we learned about the New York lead from following associates of the Baptistes. The New Jersey mansion belongs to the Baptistes. We can search the place for information related to the Finger Lakes."

"Sure," Zeke huffed.

"You have a better idea?" Peter asked.

Zeke stared at Peter a moment and said, "No."

Peter scanned the room. "Anyone else?"

"If y'all done man-sculating," Nyesha said, "I'd like to work out arrangements. We don't live as far away as Charleston, but Jamestown is quite a drive."

"Fine." Peter flipped open the pocketknife. "When should we attack?"

"There's an order for a sofa set," Dad said, addressing Peter. "It's due next week. Our schedule should open in a few weeks."

"In Charlotte, banking slows down in August," Aaron said. "Bankers don't like to sweat."

People chuckled.

By the time they confirmed arrangements, the sun had begun to set.

Makeda followed her cousins outside, where people hugged and shared goodbyes.

Brian walked over to her. "My son starts kindergarten in September."

"I can't believe he's five," she said.

His brow creased. "I wish I could spend more time with him."

Her left brow arched.

"His mom." Brian's countenance darkened. "We're going through a divorce."

"I'm sorry." Makeda laid a hand on his shoulder. "I didn't know."

"Not the kind of thing you want to share."

"True."

Walking up behind her, Carolyn sniped, "Besides, y'all don't seem to care about anything but your own needs."

"What's that supposed to mean?" Makeda asked.

"Your daddy will kill us to satisfy his personal vendetta against a vampire."

"This isn't about Korlemo." Makeda squared off with Carolyn. "You don't believe my dad should lead this team."

Carolyn leaned into her face. "He shouldn't be leading mwindaji. He's not a natural mwindaji. He joined because my dad served with him in the military."

"My—"

"Enough," Uncle John said, coming between her and Carolyn. He laid a hand on his daughter's shoulder. "You're wrong."

Both Carolyn and Makeda looked at him.

"James leads this group because I asked him to." He gave each woman a stern glance before heading toward the RV.

Makeda and Carolyn quickly followed.

"What?" the latter asked. "Why didn't you tell us?

The older man's shoulders slumped. "Because I-I didn't want to admit I was afraid to lead the group." He wiped his brow. "'Nam showed me how incompetence can get soldiers killed. I'd rather follow into battle than give the order to charge."

His chin trembled, and Carolyn hugged him. Makeda rubbed his shoulder. In a second, he wiped his eyes and hopped into the RV.

"Let's go," he said. "Maybelline needs gas, and I want to get home in time to watch the game."

"The game's tomorrow," Carolyn said, climbing into the RV behind him.

Makeda didn't hear the reply as she'd retreated to allow them room to drive off.

"Wait up," Brian said, jogging up to the RV. Climbing on the running board, he said telekinetically, 'I'm available for zauber lessons until school begins.' He grinned and hopped into the rolling RV.

Makeda watched the guests depart before returning to her bedroom. She gathered a few items and tucked them neatly inside a backpack. Scrolling through her cellphone's contact list, she reflected on training Brian. He had a son, and maji carried serious responsibilities and dangers.

Besides, she had many unanswered questions. What prevented her from being a zauber and mwindaji? Who had greater power, a zauber or a demon? How did Yewande become involved with a demon?

She collapsed on the bed and stared up at the ceiling. Tonight, demons would have to wait. Makeda had another priority.

Chapter 26

The plastic window shades parted as Sylvia peeked outside, scanning the parking lot. It had been a week since Korlemo had called. He had located her.

How?

Who had given Korlemo her number? Stefan must have because Jules wouldn't.

Sylvia's packing commenced as soon as she hung up. In a whirlwind of activity, she quickly gathered items around the small New Jersey apartment. While tossing pants into a suitcase, Sylvia had reviewed her options and determined not to become Korlemo's pawn again.

A glance at the three-jeweled ring on her right index finger, a gift from her father after receiving her medical degree, made her pause. He had entrusted her with the ring because he believed she would protect their family.

She reflected on that horrible day in Kentucky when the mwindaji slaughtered her family. Her ears still rang with the sounds of mwindaji tramping through her childhood home, butchering anyone in sight.

Sylvia cried.

Her father had been a noble, sincere gentleman. The single flaw in his life had been blind obedience to a maniacal vampire. Countless times, she had warned him. Jules tried, too.

But no. To his dying day, her father's faith in Korlemo never faltered. Korlemo shared blame along with the mwindaji for the murder of her family.

Grabbing her luggage, Sylvia had fled. She hopped in a non-descript sedan purchased at a used car lot and headed west.

Sylvia had checked into a seedy hotel outside of Cincinnati. For the past week, she tried to contact Jules to warn him. Calls went straight to voicemail.

Where is he?

She feared reaching out to him in person. Before she had fled his Manhattan condo in April, they had established a sophisticated system to contact each other—because the ancient vampire wasn't their only enemy.

Korlemo's blatant threat against her brother worried Sylvia more than her own safety. She could fight. Jules tended to be an intellectual, believing knowledge could overcome any hurdle. Fortunately, she had learned that sometimes you simply had to kick ass and drop bodies.

The vampire's threat carried conviction. Korlemo would murder Jules—and not quickly.

The one thing that old bloodsucker relishes above money is revenge.

Sylvia scanned the contacts in her cellphone for someone trustworthy and not afraid of the Baptistes.

How can I protect Jules?

A furious and impatient Korlemo would dispatch Stefan's henchmen to physically enlist her cooperation. He wouldn't forget about the money she took.

Should've simply hung up.

Unsure if he had simply located her cellphone number or also her location, Sylvia had wasted no time in securing alternate accommodations. But now, she resided in a seedy motel with no contact from Jules.

While repeatedly checking her cellphone, Sylvia paraded up and down the room. The thread-bare carpet wore the markings of her energetic stride.

What about Abigail?

They weren't close, but Abigail wouldn't knowingly allow Stefan's thugs to assault her.

Does Stefan keep his business transactions hidden from his sister?

Sylvia wondered about Abigail's involvement with the Baptiste's business enterprises. Herman Baptiste certainly kept secrets, but he had paid for his sins.

How long would Korlemo wait for a reply?

Sylvia's cellphone pinged. The screen read *Jules.*

"Where have you been?" She collapsed on the bed.

"Why? What's wrong?"

"Korlemo called me."

"Shit. How did he get your number?"

"I don't know!" She sensed Jules digesting the information.

"It's a burner phone. The only people who know the number—"

"Are who?"

"Stefan—in case something happened to me."

"Would he tell anyone?"

"I don't know why he would."

"Did *you* tell anyone?"

"I keep a few burner phones in my office. My assistant buys them for me."

"Does your assistant know Korlemo?"

Jules chuckled. "Get real. Besides, why would he reveal your location to a vampire?"

"He's ajabu?"

"Lupasteri."

"He wouldn't be the first werewolf to betray his people."

"Not a chance. I vouch for him."

"Fine. What should I do?"

"Right now, we have to get you moved to a new hotel."

"I'm in a rat hole motel in Cincinnati." She glanced around the boxy room with its tired 1960's décor. "Jules, we should leave."

"To where?"

"Anywhere. We don't need to live in America."

"True."

Car headlights shined into the ground floor room. Sylvia rushed into the bathroom. Her voice lowered. "Please. I-I don't want to leave alone."

"Why are you whispering?"

"A car pulled into the lot. I thought… I'm worried about Stefan's goons."

"He isn't supplying Korlemo with security any longer?"

Tiptoeing up to the window, Sylvia peered across the parking lot. Seeing a couple enter a room at the end of the motel, her shoulders relaxed.

She sat on the bed. "What happened?"

"I'll tell you later. First, I need to make arrangements."

"Like what?"

"Svie, we'll need money."

"I have funds secured offshore."

"That won't be enough, not for a lifetime. Besides, we agreed to share the hospital money with the ajabu stranded in Kentucky."

"Money won't help if Korlemo executes us."

"He won't. Besides, there's our project in New York."

It took her a moment to understand his meaning. "We agreed not to support it any longer."

"Stefan and Abigail disagree."

"Shut it down."

"I can't, not completely. But I can make it impossible for them to continue without our input."

"Whatever it takes. Jules, it's dangerous."

"Yeah, I know. But the possible rewards are astronomical. And Stefan craves power like Korlemo."

Sylvia's leg jostled. Exercise calmed her nerves, so she circled the room. "If you're right, he'd sacrifice me to Korlemo for information to continue the project."

"They won't find it."

"This is a mistake. Let's go. We can fly out of Canada to Europe, then wherever."

"Not yet. I must speak with Stefan."

"Why?"

"Someone betrayed us."

"Forget it." Sylvia tossed the few unpacked items into a gym bag and zipped it up. "Now we know about the leak we can prepare. If you tell Stefan, the informant will be on their guard."

"Stefan is likely the informant."

"Another reason not to approach him."

"Herman Baptiste caused this problem. Our family died because of him. I'm not leaving until I get answers."

They argued for another minute. Sylvia stressed the futility of approaching the Baptistes on their estate.

"I'll be fine," Jules said.

"Nonsense. I'll go with you."

"Absolutely not. I'll hire associates from the office."

"Who?"

"Wait. I'll call our cousins in Philly. They won't mind."

"Are you sure? I can be there by tomorrow."

"I can't do this unless you're safe."

Exhausted and not interested in remaining in the fleabag motel, Sylvia conceded. "Fine. Where do you want to meet?"

He gave her directions which she memorized. Unable to convince Jules to avoid Stefan, she hung up.

When their call ended, Sylvia left the motel.

Chapter 27

MORNING DEW GLISTENED OFF tree leaves. Zainabu reclined against an enormous spruce. For her, the day had already been long. She scanned the tree line, confirming the distance from the mansion. After resting a moment, she hiked deeper into the woods.

She checked the time. The task needed to be completed before anyone became suspicious and searched for her.

Like a song on repeat, incantations played in her head. She had to get them right. Order mattered—and precision. She'd have one opportunity to send Zorulo back to hell. And if she failed...

Not an option. She had sacrificed too much to lose this early in the game.

The sun barely crested over the treetops when she reached a narrow clearing with a charred tree stump and a huge boulder. From a satchel, Zainabu removed a half dozen herbs and assorted items. With precision, she lined them in a neat row on the ground.

Digging a small well in the damp soil with a trowel, she formed a tower of branches and lit the pile. Puffs of smoke rose from the wet twigs but no fire. She blew on the branches, creating a continuous, smoky ribbon.

Zainabu repeated several spells, tossing a specific herb on the fireless pit after each. Once all the herbs had been added, she unrolled a desiccated lizard. On the pit. the amphibian's body crackled. A tiny flame sparked, then quickly smoldered.

Leaning over the pile, she breathed in the rising, yellow smoke. With one last deep inhale, her back arched causing her head to almost reach the ground. In a spasm, she lunged forward, slamming her hands onto the earth. She clutched the soil and screamed an incantation.

"To duka mali and the lands beneath ersu, I summon Zorulo. Answer my command dubwana and arise. *Juma koyi na.*"

She'd barely completed the incantation when ten meters to the south, a mist formed. Over seconds, it transformed into a grimacing face.

"Who orders me?" the face demanded.

Opening her eyes wide, Zainabu said, "I did."

Wrinkles of confusion crisscrossed the demon's gaseous face.

"Zainabu?" Zorulo frowned. "What have you done?"

She glanced down at her dirty, trembling hands. "Remove my obligation, demon, or feel my wrath."

Zorulo let out a loud, creepy cackle.

For a moment, Zainabu's confidence wavered. Her fingers trembled.

What if the spell didn't work?

Zorulo would torture her as an example before condemning her to duka mali. She had nothing to lose except her soul.

Make sure it succeeds.

"Ungrateful, silly bitch," Zorulo spit out. "I'll rip off your limbs and watch you bleed to death before I order you to hell."

Her legs shook. "I'll ask once more. Will you free me from my obligation?"

The gaseous form enlarged. It acquired definition as it approached, transforming into a gigantic, muscular bindimèn.

With a mocking leer, Zorulo said, "On second thought, I'll bring you to duka mali and teach you what hellish nightmare servitude can truly be."

When Zorulo came within a half meter, Zainabu recited a different incantation in Baoumali.

Zorulo snickered. "Stupid, witch. Do you believe any spell your dumb ass knows could touch me?"

Sweat trickled down her back. Zorulo inched closer. Her words came faster. Over and over, she chanted incantations from the book of her ancestors. The book she stole while escaping the village of her parents. For generations, zauber women from her tribe handed down this tome, guarding it with their lives.

Since arriving in America, Zainabu studied gomani dufa dubwana binding spells. Memorized them for this specific moment. Over several days, she collected the proper herbs and killed and prepared the necessary animals.

Did I make a mistake? Had my aunts been wrong about the incantation?

With limited options, Zainabu endlessly recited the spell.

Reaching a gigantic hand forward, Zorulo said, "Prepare to die, little witch."

She smelled his hot, putrid breath. Shaking and on the verge of tears, Zainabu shouted the spell at Zorulo and threw her hands forward, blasting him into a nearby tree.

The demon struggled off the ground. "How did you do that?"

Confident, Zainabu firmly set her feet and repeated, "Chekate."

This time she used her arms to manipulate the demon. She spun him upside down, battering his head on the ground.

Zorulo screamed and cursed. He thrashed beside the tree trunk, wrestling to free himself from her grip.

"How is this possible?"

Zainabu didn't respond.

His piercing cries shattered the evening sky. Trees shook. Zorulo howled and fought.

At the stomping of Zainabu's feet, the earth around him split apart, revealing a seemingly bottomless fiery pit.

"No!"

Tree bark shredded as he desperately clung to any object to halt his descent.

"I won't go. You can't do this."

"Oh, but I can." Zainabu beamed during a tiny pause in her spell.

"You'll regret this," the demon swore as only a small portion of his face remained above ground.

"Doubt it."

Dirt muffled his voice, but Zorulo vowed, "I'll make you—"

The earth consumed his words.

Grinning, Zainabu slammed her hands downward, thrusting the demon's form completely underground. Soil collapsed into the hole, sealing it tight.

Once his entire form had disappeared, Zainabu launched onto the patch of earth, stomping it with her feet. Singing the incantation like a popular hymn, her fists pounded the ground where Zorulo departed.

Her chest heaved. Zainabu rested on a boulder. She stared at the patch of freshly disturbed soil, the sole evidence of the demon's disappearance. Wiping her forehead with a shirt sleeve, she studied the base of the tree.

With a trowel, Zainabu gathered the remains from the tiny pit she had dug. She poured the ashes on the spot where Zorulo descended into the earth.

"One down, one to go."

Laughing, she tapped the spot with the tip of her shoe. "Guess we know who's smarter after all."

With a skip in her step, Zainabu trekked back to the house.

"Korlemo should be sleeping. He hunted late last night."

She hummed a song her aunts sang while they prepared potions and creams for villagers. At home, Zainabu detested the tune. It reminded her of the servile vocation zaubers performed in Kondoro.

"No more."

With Zorulo eliminated, her focus shifted to the vampire.

Korlemo trusted her. Now, Zainabu simply needed to find the right time to destroy him. Then there would be no limitations.

America, Europe. Her gifts would be in demand by the wealthy and influential. And using her grandmother's book of spells, the possibilities were enormous.

As she danced away, a wisp of cloud rose from the ashes.

A faded cloudy grimace spotted a tiny portion of herb dust clinging to Zainabu's shoe. The cloud smiled.

Chapter 28

Inside the kitchen pantry, Enu sat at a folding table review-ing spreadsheets. Conversations from the kitchen staff faded into white noise. He scribbled notes while reviewing data.

"There you are." Abioye slipped inside, quietly closing the door behind him.

Enu half rose, inviting Abioye to accept his chair. "Brother, what troubles you?"

Abioye waved aside the offer and stood beside a shelf. "Why hide in the kitchen?"

"I am not hiding." Enu sat and straightened the papers. "Appar-ently, no space could be found for my office."

"Yes. I heard Korlemo assigned that zauber the library."

"She is not a zauber," Enu huffed. "That witch has entranced Korlemo. He sided with her over Dayo."

"No."

Nodding, Enu returned to reviewing spreadsheets.

Abioye hovered at his side. "We must talk."

"About what?"

"Shh." Abioye glanced at the door.

Enu scanned the gap at the bottom of the door, noticing footsteps traipsing by. Off to the left, someone cast a shadow. He sniffed the air, certain he recognized—

"Zainabu." Speaking in their Ibori tongue, Abioye said, "She tells Korlemo everything."

"What can I do for you?" Enu asked, leaning back in the chair.

"I know Korlemo wishes to leave, but my family prefers to remain."

Shrugging, Enu said, "I can do nothing. Korlemo demands to leave. He will not be persuaded."

Abioye laid a heavy hand on Enu's shoulders. "We no longer care. I have four delicate daughters. They cannot forage in the woods like animals."

"Not my decision. I cannot disobey Korlemo's orders."

"Can't you?" Abioye raised his gray eyebrows suggestively.

Enu shook his head. "It is foolishness to disagree with Korlemo."

"Fatou wishes to leave." Abioye hesitated.

Avoiding his brother's invitation to expand on the topic of his son, Enu said, "It would be folly to cross Korlemo."

"If anyone could succeed against him, it would be you."

The men regarded each other for a tense moment before Abioye said, "We will speak on this later."

As his brother departed, Enu gathered the spreadsheets into a brown folder. His head throbbed. He needed rest. However, he had an appointment to keep.

A curtained patio deck hugged the right side of the mansion. It provided views over the front, side, and rear yards. Once they moved in, Enu directed servants to create shading to allow the Ibori to entertain on the deck protected from sunlight.

Enu glanced between the shades at the blossoming rose garden. A low wrought iron fence surrounded the property in the front and on the sides. In the rear, the property ended at a copse of trees that expanded into dense woods beyond. Rose hedges created a half-moon in front of the patio windows with a well-manicured lawn beyond.

Reclining in a rocking chair, Enu shut his eyes. He inhaled the rose-scented air, appreciating this moment of peace. The atmosphere reminded him of how much he missed sitting on freshly cut grass, warming his ebony skin in the intoxicating sun's rays. Picking flowers for Nambi. Playing sports. Activities he sacrificed for what?

A life of servitude to his older brother. Obeisance to a long-deceased mother, who in truth regarded him as less worthy than her first-born son.

For too long, he had abided by the customs of his tribe. Ibori rituals and mores confined a person's station in life based on their gender and birth order.

While he preferred security, his children cherished freedom and independence. But they had no idea what freedom cost. He simply wanted to live a peaceful existence with his wife. Folly.

Lives had been sacrificed and blood had been spilled. He had committed atrocities in fidelity to his kin. An ignorant coward, hiding behind tradition to condone his actions.

"Father."

Enu startled, and the manila folder slipped off his lap.

Fatou hurried to his side and helped him gather the papers together. Enu retrieved the folder and placed a sheet of paper with his scribbled notes on top.

A breeze fluttered the parted curtains. Movement near the entrance drew Enu's attention. Though he did not see anyone in the doorway, he discerned a presence. He sniffed the air, but the breeze obscured detection.

"I've been looking for you." Fatou handed over the papers he had retrieved.

"In the pantry, I reviewed your uncle's finances." As he observed the doorway, Enu handed his son the folder. His index finger stabbed at the top sheet.

"Such a lovely day. It is unfortunate Korlemo does not wish to remain. I believe Michigan would make a perfect home." As he spoke, Enu unfolded the sheet of paper. He stabbed at a note, directing his son to read it.

While reading the note, Fatou said, "Yes. The woods overflow with wildlife. But uncle worries about the winters."

The note read: house in California. ready in two months. Study banking information. Memorize access codes. Destroy note.

"They can be brutal." Enu glared at his son. "Death to anyone caught outside without protection."

Fatou nodded.

Confident his son understood the gravity of the situation, Enu exhaled. He collapsed in the rocking chair.

"I hope you and Mom will appreciate it while we remain here."

He shook his head. "Nambi does not care for change. She wearies of this life." Enu grasped his son's hand. "Youth desires adventure."

Tears gathered in Fatou's eyes. He wrapped his arm around Enu's shoulders.

Enu shook off his fatigue and rose. Remembering something, he jotted a quick note and handed the sheet of paper to Fatou.

Have you spoken with anyone about leaving?

The latter scribbled two letters.

No.

Aloud, Enu said, "Come, Son. Helping your uncle has left me weary, but I must acquaint him with these new arrangements."

"Oh?" Before Fatou followed him inside the mansion, he folded the notepaper into a small square and secured it inside his pants pocket. As they departed, the shadow made a precipitous retreat. Enu and Fatou shared a glance.

"Korlemo will be pleased. I located a home in Miami to meet his needs."

"Uncle does like water."

"And it has the nightlife Dayo craves. A tradition exists where college students vacation in South Florida. They should provide sufficient sustenance for our entire household."

"Father, are you talking about spring break?"

"I have no idea what titles these bindimèn give their holidays. There will be plenty of nourishment to satisfy your uncle's demands."

"The whole family will be pleased."

With a plastic smile, he led Fatou toward the study. "His finances are impeccable. We will join him and toast to his good fortune."

Though he provided his children with the information and assistance they would need to flee Korlemo, Enu worried. Moving money between banks would cover his trail for a time. But if his brother allowed Zainabu to employ an outside accountant, Enu's embezzlement would become apparent.

Time. His machinations required time. But how much did he have? Enu must keep Zainabu away from the bank records and Korlemo distracted.

As they reached the study door, Fatou asked, "So, we'll be leaving soon?"

"Once workers prepare the house we will leave."

"Thank you, Father."

"Remember always, I love you." He patted his son on the back while opening the study door.

"Brother," Enu said, "I have good news." He inhaled deeply and began the greatest performance of his life.

If I cannot deceive Korlemo, my family will surely die.

Chapter 29

LIKE A SEA OF green, the manicured lawn stretched from the gray wood barn to a gently flowing stream at the base of the property. July in Asheville had never been this beautiful. A perfect day for a wedding.

"Please move slightly to the left," the photographer asked.

Makeda did as requested, squeezing closer to her brother, Daniel's side.

"Now, let's get one of the groom and bride by the well." As the photographer herded Peter and Brenda away, followed by a small contingent of family and friends, Makeda retired inside the barn's reception hall.

Ornamental and no longer used for farming, the barn's wooden floors had been sanded and polished until they sparkled. Makeda slipped out of her heels and padded across the floor in bare feet.

The barn's ceiling had been cleansed and resurfaced. A perfect place for her brother to marry.

She laid the shoes on her assigned seat. Sipping water, she scrutinized the reception hall.

"What're you doing?" Meria asked, propping her purse on the tabletop.

"Making sure everything is perfect." Makeda guzzled the entire glass of water. "Weddings are exhausting."

Meria chuckled. "And this one isn't even yours."

"No, it's Peter's wedding, and I want it to be perfect."

"You're gonna miss him, aren't you?"

"He's moving out of the house, not away from Asheville."

Makeda rushed over to a table and rearranged the flatware. She instructed a server to replenish the water glasses and bring another entree.

"It's okay," Meria said, laying a hand on her shoulder. "I know how close you and Peter are."

Not wanting to explore her emotions, Makeda circled the hall, examining tables and arrangements. She marched up to a small podium where the DJ played.

"The bride requested no reggae."

"Who doesn't like reggae?"

"Zeke, it's not your wedding," Makeda said, crossing her hands over her chest.

"Fine." The music blended into Whitney Houston's *Saving All My Love for You.*

Makeda returned to her table and sat, massaging her feet. "I'm never going through this," she said, nibbling on an entrée.

"Famous last words." Meria pointed her chin toward the bar. "Have you told him that?"

Following her friend's gaze, Makeda noticed Michael at the bar speaking with Brian.

"It's not like that."

"Oh, sure."

Loud applause interrupted her reply. Zeke decreased the music as the announcer spoke.

"Welcome Mrs. Brenda and Mr. Peter Crawford."

Everyone stood as the bride and groom took their seats at a twenty-foot table at the head of the barn. A wide banner displayed above their heads included their names in bold block lettering with signatures of the attendees sprinkled throughout. Balloons and streamers in their wedding colors dripped from the ceiling in an artistic expression of the festivities.

The maid of honor and best man gave speeches. Brenda and Peter shared a slice of cake, and other desultory comments followed.

"Now, it's time to throw the bouquet." The announcer invited the bride toward the center of the room.

"I'm up." Meria scuttled from the chair. "Can't pass up any opportunities."

"Oh? Who do you have in mind?" Makeda asked coyly, aware of her best friend's long-simmering devotion to her youngest brother.

"Don't play with me. Daniel's here for the weekend, and I plan to take advantage of every possible moment."

As her best friend hurried away to catch the bouquet, Makeda sighed. Not only did her brother live thousands of miles away in California, but he acted completely ignorant of Meria's affection.

"Hey, beautiful."

Startled, Makeda hiccupped.

"Sorry," Michael said, taking Meria's seat and handing her a drink. She sniffed it.

"Only soda."

"Thank you." She drank and surveyed the festivities.

Brenda tossed a bouquet at a screaming horde of women. Meria knocked over three people and caught the flowers in a manner resembling a football player.

In a secluded corner of the hall, Zina tapped incessantly away on a cellphone.

At the long table in the front of the barn designated for VIPs, her mom and aunts conversed.

"I suppose that's too juvenile for you," Michael said, glancing at the bride.

"Much. Besides, my feet ache."

Scooting his chair back, Michael lifted her feet onto his lap and massaged them. "How's that?"

"Wonderful." Makeda's eyes closed. "Mmm. Nice."

"Imagine when we're alone." He smirked.

"It's been a while since we've had time for each other."

"I'm adjusting to Atlanta and my new job. And you've been traveling for work."

A herd of children rushed over to them.

"Auntie Makeda. Auntie Makeda."

In their excitement, talking simultaneously, she couldn't understand what they wanted.

Michael whistled. "Calm down. One at a time."

An older child said, "Aunt Carolyn's mad."

"At whom?" Makeda asked, slipping her feet off Michael's lap.

They all pointed at Michael.

"His dog."

Makeda and Michael hurried outside and discovered Daisy running around the parking lot chased by a toy poodle.

A sweaty Carolyn ran up to her. "Is that your boyfriend's dog?" She frowned. "Well…"

"What's wrong?" Michael asked. "She didn't bite anyone, did she?"

"No, but she's making a scene." Carolyn dashed after the poodle.

Michael hurried to the parking lot and called Daisy. The German shepherd immediately scampered to his side. A second later, the toy poodle followed.

Daisy circled around Michael's legs with the poodle giving chase.

"It looks like your poodle created the problem," Makeda said, joining Michael. She bent down and corralled Daisy. The shepherd cowed at her feet as the poodle snipped and barked.

"Come here, PooPoo." Carolyn tried to pick up the poodle, but the tiny dog scampered away, barking.

"What did Daisy do?" Michael asked.

"She riled up my dog." Carolyn hollered after the poodle.

Eventually, Carolyn managed to collect her dog. As she headed inside the barn, she addressed Michael. "Keep your mutt away from PooPoo."

As she spoke, the poodle barked and yapped at Daisy. The German shepherd barked but remained between Makeda and Michael.

He chuckled. "You misunderstand the problem. It looks like PoPo doesn't like Daisy."

Carolyn frowned. "It's PooPoo, not PoPo. What is she, a cop?"

The poodle attempted to jump out of Carolyn's embrace.

"Come. Let's get something to eat." Before leaving, she said, "And if that dog hurts PooPoo, it's your ass."

Michael gawked. "What is she, a prison guard?"

Makeda laughed. "No, she teaches preschool."

Together, they leashed Daisy and returned inside the barn.

Wearing headphones, Zeke played Atlantic Starr's *Always* as Peter and Brenda swayed together on the dance floor. The song concluded and other couples joined them on the dance floor.

"Want to dance?" Michael asked.

Without answering, Makeda shook her head.

"Sore feet?"

Her brows rose.

"Outside?"

He held out his hand. She accepted it, and they exited the barn with Daisy trotting at their side.

"Wait a minute."

Michael trotted over to his truck and removed a blanket. Eventually, he settled them under a shaded tree not thirty yards from the barn. Though close enough to hear the music, Makeda appreciated the modicum of privacy provided.

Starting at her calves, Michael massaged her legs.

She smiled. "You're a good boyfriend."

"Only good?" He grinned.

From the open barn doors, Makeda watched Peter and Brenda socializing with family and friends. The bucolic scene left her conflicted. Despite what she had said to Meria, she had strong feelings for Michael.

Marriage? No. But for a relationship? Absolutely.

Makeda placed her hand on his. "There's a lot I want to tell you."

"Then tell me."

"It's complicated."

"Ramsey complicated?"

She admired the grounds.

Simply appreciate the moment and beautiful scenery.

"Forget it." She rested against his side.

He kissed the top of her head. "I want to be a part of your life."

"I know you do."

They sat there, soaking up the atmosphere.

Daisy barked, and Makeda jerked awake. She wiped her face.

"How long did I sleep?"

"Almost an hour."

Sunset unleashed a rainbow of red and orange across the sky. People exited the barn, hugging and kissing the bride and groom.

"We should get going." Michael assisted Makeda to her feet.

"I wish we didn't have to." Makeda yawned and slipped into her heels.

Michael kissed her lightly on the lips. "Are we still meeting tonight?"

"It'll be late before I get there."

"Any time works for me."

Daisy rose and shook leaves and debris off her coat. The three of them ambled toward the barn.

Peter and Brenda slowly advanced to a limousine idling in the parking lot. They waved to guests. Makeda noticed Peter searching the crowd. She abandoned Michael's side and ran up to the limousine.

Peter noticed her approach and pulled her into a tight embrace.

Tears wet her cheeks. Words choked in her throat. "I... Have a nice trip."

Peter tugged on her loose curly hair. "Cry baby."

She smiled. "I don't know what to say."

Michael shook Peter's hand. "Congratulations. You're a lucky man."

Though he nodded in acknowledgement, Peter turned his attention to another guest. Meanwhile, Makeda hugged and kissed Brenda.

Once Peter assisted Brenda inside the limousine, he took Makeda by the shoulders and said, "Be smart."

"I am."

He winked.

Crying, Makeda hugged him about the neck. "I love you."

"I love you, too." He kissed her on the forehead. "And just because I'm not at the house, doesn't mean I won't know what you're up to." Peter shot Michael a glare. "Be safe."

"Always."

His eyes bore into hers. "I trust you."

Makeda's shoulders shuddered. She nodded, unable to speak without crying.

The limousine drove off as well-wishers followed behind. Gradually, guests returned to the barn or departed.

Makeda detected Michael at her side. Before turning around, she wiped her face.

He handed her a handkerchief. "You're gonna miss him."

"I'm glad he's gone. Less people in the house."

Michael hooked his arm around hers. "You're a terrible liar." He glanced at his watch. "I want to give Daisy a run before night."

"Okay. Talk later?"

"We'll do more than talk."

Makeda awoke surrounded by darkness and Michael's cologne. Heavy and cloudy, her head pounded. Last night, she hadn't drunk any alcohol. Makeda wanted to be fully in control of her faculties for her first sexual encounter with Michael.

Their relationship blossomed quickly, and she needed to confirm her emotions were genuine. The circumstances that brought them together had been tragic. Makeda wanted a clear mind to ascertain her true feelings.

One unfortunate affair was enough.

But why did her head feel like mush?

'Makeda, listen!'

She rolled to the edge of the king bed. 'Yewande?'

'Why did you leave Memphis?'

'I have a job. And Peter got married yesterday.'

'Do you *want* to be killed by a demon? I'm doing this for you. I begged my friends to train you, and you treat it like a damn vacation retreat.'

Makeda sat up, tossing aside the covers. 'You're not telling me the truth. I need—'

'You *need* to listen to me or you're gonna die.'

"Up already?" Michael asked, running his fingers along her spine.

Her head cleared. "Yes." Makeda collapsed onto the pillow, staring up at the ceiling. "Sleep okay?"

"Umm hmm." Michael pulled her across the bed to his side. He nuzzled her neck. "Hungry?"

"Not right now."

He smiled. "I didn't mean food." His hands explored her body as they shared a deep, passionate kiss.

Makeda twisted his hair playfully between her fingers. "I'm glad you let your afro grow out."

"Really?" He tickled her nipples with his tongue. "I'm getting a haircut next weekend."

"Why? Your hair is so soft. I like running my fingers through it while—"

"I do this." Michael parted her legs. While his fingers lightly explored, Makeda moaned and caressed his shoulders. Michael cupped her buttocks. He climbed on top of her pelvis when a whine wailed from the other side of the door.

They paused only a moment. When their lovemaking resumed, bellowing and scratching continued.

"Guess someone needs a walk," Makeda said, giving Michael a peck on the lips.

"We should've left her at your house." He climbed off the bed and into jeans.

"That wouldn't work with the lie I told my parents about you leaving town after the wedding."

"Is your family ever going to like me?"

She chuckled. "They'd like you more if you weren't dating their only daughter."

"Back in a few." Michael departed with Daisy.

Makeda rose and showered. While dressing, she considered what Yewande had said. But she knew her great-grandmother had lied at least once.

What else was she hiding? Were the answers in Memphis?

Samuel seemed inclined to help, but Eldridge either didn't trust her or didn't care about her welfare. She needed to understand Yewande's relationship with the two men.

While Makeda preferred to spend time with Michael, questions demanded solutions. Principally, why a demon wanted her dead.

In Ramsey, Makeda had a vision of two women. A man attacked the younger woman before an older woman of regal bearing with gray locks intervened. The latter had defeated the man.

Did this older woman represent her great-grandmother? Did the vision reveal how Yewande would save her?

Because Yewande appeared in the form of a familiar, Makeda had no idea what she looked like now. She'd been in grade school the last time she saw her great-grandmother in human form. It didn't make sense for a zauber to manifest as an animal.

Finished dressing, Makeda decided to cut her visit with Michael short. She started packing. Somehow, she had to convince Samuel and Eldridge to confide in her.

Peter had moved out and on with his life.

Daniel lived in California.

Thomas...

Dad suffered from gout, and Mom refused to use maji.

She wouldn't lead a demon to her family's doorstep.

Chapter 30

A DJUSTING THE CELLPHONE AGAINST her ear, Makeda observed traffic, preparing to exit the expressway.

"Mom, I told you, it was a last-minute decision."

"I don't see how a hospital can wait until the last moment to hire a nurse."

"Emergencies happen. People get sick."

According to the road sign, her exit was in two miles. She slowed down and pulled behind a semi-truck.

"Are you spending the week with your boyfriend?"

"No, Mom. Michael lives in Georgia. I'm in Tennessee."

"Hmm. Your daddy wants to drive over and check on you."

"Tell Dad, I'll send a picture of a Memphis newspaper with the date."

"You can buy a Memphis paper in Atlanta."

"I'll take a picture in front of the hospital."

"That works."

"Bye, Mom." Makeda tossed the cellphone on the passenger seat and concentrated on landmarks. Though she had an excellent sense of direction, it had been over a month since she'd visited the Memphis house.

Again, she reached out to Samuel *and* Eldridge with kasi kasi. Neither responded. Their maji dwarfed hers. If they didn't appreciate her visit, things could deteriorate fast.

Makeda circled the block twice before a parking spot cleared within a decent distance of the house. Approaching the house with gingerbread trim, a slight nausea made her pause.

This happened the last time.

Waiting until her stomach settled, Makeda grabbed her backpack and cellphone before knocking on the door.

The door flew open, and Eldridge glared. "It is not polite to visit unannounced."

"How can a person get an invitation if the host will not answer their summons?"

"Why have you returned?"

"To check on you two."

He studied her face. "Is that the true reason?"

"I tried to contact you right after I left, but neither of you responded."

Eldridge readjusted himself on the crutches. "Why should we? You made your decision."

"I decided—"

"Let her in," Samuel said, joining Eldridge at the door.

Makeda hurried inside before either man changed their mind.

Eldridge entered the library on the right. Samuel invited her to the living room on the left.

"We didn't expect to see you again."

She sat on the couch opposite his chair. "I hope it's not an unpleasant surprise."

Samuel glanced toward the library. "It presents complications."

Eldridge hobbled into the living room and glowered down upon her. "You should not have returned." After his pronouncement, he headed upstairs.

Conflicted, Makeda wavered between staying and leaving.

But what would Yewande say?

And she still needed to learn about this demon.

Hurriedly, Makeda said, "Yewande told me to return. She was upset I discontinued my lessons."

Mumbling, Samuel said, "I'm sure she was."

Makeda's brows raised but he didn't answer the unspoken question. Instead, he led her upstairs.

"I'm sure this will be satisfactory."

Before he departed, Makeda laid a hand on his arm. "If Eldridge wants me to leave, I will."

A cloud darkened Samuel's expression. "You don't understand. He wanted you to stay away for *your* safety."

Makeda gaped as he departed.

Morning brought a delightful scent of muffins. "Mmm, blueberry."

She rushed downstairs, recalling how Samuel detested any delay in consuming his freshly prepared meals. Maji cleaned the house, but Samuel took pride in preparing meals by hand.

Like kings on a chessboard, her hosts sat on opposite ends of the table. Samuel rose as she entered. Without speaking, he tapped his wristwatch.

"Sorry. It was a long drive."

"Excuses will not keep muffins warm."

Makeda slathered a muffin with butter and gobbled up the luscious pastry.

"Delicious. You should open a bakery."

"Missed opportunities." Samuel piled eggs, bacon, and hash-browns on his plate.

Eldridge sipped tea but did not eat. Makeda regarded the wrinkles zigzagging across his brow.

"I'm sorry Yewande imposed me upon you. I promise to learn quickly and leave as soon as possible."

As if she hadn't spoken, Eldridge continued gazing absently at the table and sipping tea.

She turned to Samuel.

He said, "We will resume lessons on potions and unguents. Finish your breakfast then join me in the garden."

The meal proceeded in silence.

In the solarium, Makeda watched Samuel dry herbs and crush chicken bones—hands free—using and mortar and pestle. Scents from rosemary and lavender gave a spring buoyancy to the air. She became dizzy.

Am I high from smelling herbs and flowers?

"Samuel, I don't feel well."

"Sit down."

She obeyed, holding onto the worktop for balance. "Each time I come here, I become nauseated and dizzy."

"It will pass in time. You're not accustomed to being around other zaubers."

"Is that it?"

"Zaubers sense each other, like a zap of electricity or a slight twinge. A zauber's maji determines the strength of the response."

"And you and Eldridge are powerful zaubers." She smiled.

He did not.

The dizziness abated, but her discomfort grew. "Please, tell me what's going on."

He side-eyed her. "I can't."

"Why not?" she asked, slipping closer to his side.

"She won't—"

"Samuel," Eldridge said entering the solarium, "finish the potions. I will instruct Makeda in her maji lessons."

"As you wish."

Eldridge exited the solarium. Makeda started to follow when Samuel grabbed her wrist.

He whispered, "Don't repeat any incantations."

Her eyes widened. "What?"

"Go. Hurry."

Samuel returned to his potions on the workbench.

Uncertain, Makeda hesitated between asking for clarification or joining Eldridge. When the latter yelled for her, she rushed out of the solarium. She had no idea what Samuel meant, but Makeda immediately decided not to trust Eldridge.

In the backyard, Eldridge requested she join him beside a magnolia tree.

"Lovely flowers." He plucked a white blossom off a low-lying branch and sniffed its light perfume.

Makeda duplicated his actions.

"Zaubers cannot create life or manipulate the seasons." He spoke an incantation and waved his hand over the flower. A tiny rain shower sprinkled over the petals. "We can, however, simulate both."

He closed his hand, and the shower stopped. "Repeat the incantation and water the flower."

Makeda waivered.

Samuel seemed sincere. What happens if I repeat the incantation?

Then she sensed a message.

'Instead, say this.' Telekinetically, Samuel recited a slightly different spell.

"Now," Eldridge insisted.

She repeated the spell Samuel dictated.

"No, no." Eldridge struck the ground with a crutch. "Listen carefully." He repeated it again.

Instead, Makeda recited what Samuel had dictated. After five iterations of this, Eldridge stormed off.

"Ridiculous. You refuse to listen. I cannot teach you. Yewande will have to accept you are not up to the task. Perhaps she overestimated your potential."

Makeda remained beside the tree until he entered the house. The moment the door closed, she sped into the solarium.

"Samuel—"

He held up a finger and pointed at the plantings. "Since you're incapable of maji today, help me with these herbs."

In kasi kasi, he telegraphed. 'I'll tell E I need to go shopping. Wait a short time, then leave the house. If he questions you, say you need to clear your head.'

'Where?'

He gave her the address.

Chapter 31

L IKE A MANTRA, MAKEDA repeated Samuel's directions. Fortunately, Eldridge hadn't questioned her about leaving. Maybe he thought she'd finally left for good.

She considered him a friend and believed he did likewise. After they slayed nommo together downtown, he expressed such sentiment. Clearly, he no longer wanted her around. His behavior remained barely polite and definitely not friendly.

'Where are you?' Samuel asked.

'Trying to find a place to park.'

In little time, Makeda found a garage and arrived at the designated deli. Samuel waved her over.

"I ordered."

She glanced at the menu, then pushed it aside. "I'm not hungry."

"It'll look strange if we sit here and don't eat and speak telekinetically." He waited as the server brought beverages.

Makeda tasted the iced tea and winced. "I don't like iced tea."

He smiled. "It's a Southern staple."

"Supposedly."

Once the server brought their entrees, Samuel scooted his chair closer to hers. Makeda tasted the curly fries and recognized her hunger.

"Please forgive E," he said.

"What's with him?" She wiped salt from her fingers. "I thought we were friends."

"You can't understand." Samuel placed his hand on hers.

She appreciated a slight tremor.

"He... Eldridge had to make a hard choice, between you and Yewande."

"What choice?" She leaned toward him. "Tell me what's going on."

"I am—will." He scanned the room.

"Would Eldridge follow us?"

"No, but Yewande has various means to track people."

She frowned, and he patted her hand. Again, Makeda detected a tremor.

"Yewande saved E's life. He's beholden to her."

Makeda's hunger evaporated. She clung to Samuel's words.

"Do you know what an *emi* is?"

"An angel?"

He chuckled. "Not a bad comparison." Samuel sat upright and straightened his tie. "History lesson one. In the beginning, *Mawu* created emis."

"Mawu?"

"God."

Her eyes ballooned.

"I don't have time for a full lesson, but zaubers descended from emis."

"Okay." Makeda wondered if she made the wrong decision in choosing Samuel as an ally over Eldridge.

"Bear with me. It sounds like nonsense, but it shouldn't to a young woman who practices maji and has killed nommo."

"Fair point." She leaned forward. "I'm with you."

"Read Genesis 6:4. Time and translation have distorted much of the truth, but even the Bible speaks of the creation of Nephilim, or giants."

"Zaubers descended from the giants of old?"

"In Baoumali, they are called *nefilimu*, and they were not physical giants but grand in their talents and abilities."

"Go on."

"Zaubers, nefilimu, descended from emi and bindimèn. Certain zaubers possess more emi DNA than bindimèn and consequently, they live extended lives."

"Yewande possesses a lot of emi DNA."

"Yes, as does E. He was born into slavery in the Deep South." He sipped tea and took a deep breath before continuing.

Makeda appreciated a slight slouch in his shoulders.

"Slaveowners had no use for an injured or disfigured slave. In the Antebellum South, they had no concept of cerebral palsy, nor interest in those afflicted. Eldridge's mother realized he would be killed. The master of the plantation wouldn't waste food on a slave unable to work in the fields."

"She escaped," Makeda said, helping the story along.

"Tried to. She escaped with E and his siblings, but she didn't have a plan or help."

"Yewande helped them."

"I'm sure she sensed E's maji potential. Yewande led them to the Underground Railroad, and they fled to Canada. She taught E maji and everything he knows about zaubers."

A noise by the front door made Samuel jump. Makeda surveyed the restaurant unsure of what to look for. There were no cats. But if Yewande could transform into an animal, what about an insect or a—

"E feels obligated to do whatever Yewande asks." He grimaced. "And believe me, he has repaid her a hundred times over."

"Doing what?"

Samuel ignored her question. "Yewande ordered E to teach you an invitation spell, a nani dufa."

"Why? What would—"

"Listen." Sweat erupted above Samuel's lip.

"Are you all right?"

"It doesn't matter. Let me finish." He dabbed perspiration from his lip and forehead with a handkerchief. "A dubwana, demon, cannot enter the surface world unless invited."

"Tafa buni."

His brow rose. "Impressive. You know more than you let on."

"Not really. Recently, my mom taught me about the different worlds."

Samuel grabbed her arm. "A demon cannot approach you unless invited."

Makeda gaped. "But why would Yewande want me to invite a demon to kill me?"

"She needs you to invite the demon to the surface world where you can kill it."

Her stomach gurgled. Makeda regretted eating the fries. "Yewande wants me to kill the demon—"

"Because she can't."

Tears teetered along her eyelashes. "She's using me."

Silence enveloped them. Makeda digested the information as Samuel scanned the restaurant.

"I have to go. E keeps asking when I'll be back."

Speaking to herself, Makeda said, "He encouraged me to recite an invitation spell."

Samuel's lips pursed. "Don't judge E harshly. He wanted to refuse. In fact, he became upset when you returned. If you hadn't returned, he had an excuse for not teaching you the spell."

"I see."

Her great-grandmother deceived her. A woman she idolized and revered manipulated her to kill a demon.

"Wait. Why would a demon try to kill Yewande?"

Samuel had already exited the restaurant. Makeda ran after him.

"Please. I have more questions."

He hopped in the car. "E will become suspicious. I have to go."

"Wait. I'll follow you. I have to get my stuff."

"No." His stern face glared. "Leave and don't come back to the house."

"But my bag."

"I'll mail it to you." He started the Cadillac. "E can't protect you from Yewande, and neither can I."

Because he drove away, Makeda communicated via kasi kasi.

'I want to discuss this demon and Yewande.'

Seconds passed. Minutes. Realizing she stood in the middle of a parking lot, Makeda hiked to her car and headed home.

At least Mom will be happy.

On the drive, questions circled in her head. Emis, zaubers, Mawu.

She was leaving Memphis more confused than when she had arrived. If Samuel and Eldridge wouldn't answer her questions, she had to rely on Yewande.

Mom had been right.

Her great-grandmother couldn't be trusted. Or perhaps Yewande simply needed help and didn't know how to ask.

Why hadn't she simply told the truth in the beginning?

"Hmm. In the beginning." Once she returned home, Makeda would read Genesis. Despite years of summer Bible school, she had forgotten more verses than she remembered.

She navigated around Downtown Memphis and caught the expressway east toward North Carolina. As she merged into traffic, Makeda wondered if the demon had killed her great-grandmother once, why do it again?

"Damn."

To get answers she would have to contact Yewande. Or...

How good is my Creole?

At the next rest stop, Makeda exited the expressway. Once she relieved her bladder, she reclined in the car seat. The few Haitian

Creole words she knew would have to suffice. She needed to verify what Samuel said about demons and confirm whether or not Yewande had lied.

'Hello, Nadege. It's Makeda.'

While concentrating on kasi kasi, she gazed out the window. A screen of trees secluded the rest area from the expressway, creating a quiet, relaxing atmosphere. She drifted off to sleep when a voice startled her awake.

'*Bonjou, timoun. Ou byen?*' Nadeje asked about how she was doing.

Makeda sat upright and rubbed sleep from her eyes. '*Pa vrèman. Mwen gen yon kesyon sou demon yo.*'

'*Poukisa?*'

'*Youn ap eseye touye m.*' Without becoming upset, Makeda tried to communicate that a demon wanted her dead.

'*Ou te rele yon demon?*'

Hurriedly, Makeda explained about Yewande and the demon. '*Non, men granmè mwen te di m yon demon vle touye m.*'

'*Sa pa posib.*'

A moment elapsed as Makeda lost focus. She realized Samuel told the truth.

Nadege asked, '*Ki moun fanm sa a? Bay non li?*'

'Yewande.' But she couldn't remember her great-grandmother's maiden name. Makeda cursed and searched her memory.

'*Mwen pa sonje... Ou te di Yewande?*'

'Yes.'

'*Yon zauber?*'

'Yes. My mom's maiden name was Sanford.'

'Oh, no.'

She clenched the steering wheel. '*Kisa?*'

'*Mwen pa konnen Yewande pèsonèlman, men gen rimè sou li.*'

'*Bon rimè?*' Her shoulders tensed when Nadege mentioned rumors surrounding Yewande.

'*Move.*'

'Evil. How? In what way, is Yewande evil?'

'*Makeda, kisa k ap pase? Ou pa an sekirite avèk li.*'

She struggled for the proper Creole words. '*Mwen pa ka eksplike an Kreyòl.*'

Nadege's reply exceeded Makeda's limited understanding.

"Damn. I need to learn Creole—or find an interpreter." Tamara refused to help anymore.

'*Bagay yo difisil isit la,*' Nadege continued, '*Pitit pran prekosyon.*'

'*Of course.*' Haitians were suffering due to the recent hurricane, not to mention their general dysfunctional government. How could she expect Nadege to have time for her personal dramas? '*Mèsi anpil.*'

'*Bondye avèk ou, timoun.*'

Their connection evaporated. Makeda's head flopped against the headrest.

"Well, I confirmed Samuel's information about the demon." She reversed out of the parking spot. "Now I have to figure out why Yewande lied to me."

Makeda chewed her bottom lip.

How do I find the answer without confronting Yewande?

It would be a long trip home to North Carolina.

Chapter 32

AROUND TEN IN THE morning, Makeda traveled down the dirt road leading to her family home in Black Ridge, North Carolina. She arrived in Asheville late last night but decided to crash at Meria's place. Her precipitous return home would lead to a confrontation with Mom, and Makeda preferred to have the conversation after a night's rest.

However, she slept poorly. Meria peppered her with questions and only reluctantly allowed Makeda to sleep after the latter threatened to inform Daniel of Meria's obsessive infatuation.

After parking the car, Makeda fed the dogs. She entered the house through the rear door which led directly into the kitchen.

"Morning."

Surprised, Makeda dropped her car keys.

"Hey, Mom."

Mom watched as she picked up the keys and headed for the bedrooms located on the opposite side of the house.

"You're back early."

She noticed an upturn in Mom's lips and braced herself.

"What happened to the 'nursing job'?"

"There was no job."

"Meeting up with your boyfriend. I'm not surprised. What happened? Did you two have a fight?"

Makeda hurried inside her bedroom, but Mom skirted inside before she shut and locked the door.

"Well, are you going to tell me? I know it's hard for kids to date nowadays, but—"

"Mom, please." Makeda sat on the bed and cradled her aching head. "It's not like that."

"Then what?" Mom stared down at her. "Did you get fired? Don't tell me you did something to lose your job."

"No, Mom. I didn't lose the job." Gesticulating, she said, "No job, no boyfriend."

Frowning, Mom slowly lowered herself onto the bed. "Then what?"

After a deep breath, Makeda said, "I was training with two zaubers."

"*You what?*" Mom scowled. "Are you insane? How many times have I warned you about associating with zaubers. It's bad enough contacting Yewande. Now, exposing yourself to zaubers. They—"

"Mom, stop!"

Both women stared at each other. A crease formed along Mom's brow. Makeda quickly apologized.

"I'm sorry for shouting. Truly. I-I want to talk with you—explain what's going on—but you need to listen. I made a mistake, but I'm going to fix it."

I hope.

Mom's temples pulsed. Placing her hands on her lap, Mom raised her chin. "Fine. Explain."

Makeda said, "I trust these zaubers. They've taught me maji and zauber history."

"You can't be a zauber and a mwindaji."

"I can, and I will." With a deviant glance, Makeda asserted her position while remaining at a safe distance.

I seriously need my own place.

"Then why did you return so soon?" Mom's head tilted to the side. "Did you already graduate from zauber training?"

Sarcasm. Great. This isn't going well.

"Yewande sent me to learn an invitation spell."

Mom leaped off the bed. "Oh, Lord. You didn't recite it did you?"

She hurried over to the bed. "No. One of the zaubers alerted me, and I left."

Mom's shoulders shrank. "Good." She rose and headed for the door. "Now, you understand how dangerous maji is."

"Maji is like any weapon. It depends upon the user."

With her eyes widening, Mom asked, "You're going to continue learning maji?"

"This doesn't change how I feel. I'm a zauber. Maji is my birthright."

"What in the world did I do to deserve such a hard-headed child?" she asked, shaking her head. "You're determined to kill yourself."

"Do you believe I'm at a higher risk of dying from sorcery than from a vampire?"

With her hand on the doorknob, Mom again started to leave.

"Wait." Makeda touched her arm. "I need to know how you kept Yewande away."

"Why?"

"I want to protect you, our home."

Smiling and ruffling Makeda's thick, black curly hair, Mom said, "Don't worry. I cast a *zamba dufa*, a protection spell, around this house long ago. Yewande can't touch us here."

"But what about other places?" At the moment, Makeda didn't want to discuss plans to get her own apartment. But she wanted to know how to protect any future homes.

"You mean like when you're on a mission?"

"Yeah, sure."

Mom's brows knitted in thought. "You have to use a personal item belonging to the victim." Her lips pursed. "I don't have anything here belonging to Yewande."

Makeda's face brightened. "The house. I can find something belonging to her there."

"Stay away from that house. It's dangerous."

"The zaubers in Memphis said Yewande wanted me to summon a demon. Probably the same one that killed her."

"I saw Yewande's dead, mutilated body." She clutched Makeda's chin and lifted her face. "That demon tortured your great-grandmother before killing her."

Shivering, Makeda stepped backward and out of Mom's grasp. They regarded each other.

Knock, knock.

On the other side of the door, Thomas said, "Makeda, there's a mwindaji meeting. We're planning the New Jersey mission."

"Not now," Makeda said.

"Dad said—"

"Thomas, we'll be out in a moment." Mom pulled Makeda forward into a bear hug. "I shouldn't have kept maji from you." Her chin trembled. "I don't want to lose you." Mom rushed from the room.

Makeda's chest sank. She meandered toward the bed, weighing how much maji meant to her and why. It claimed her grandmother *and* great-grandmother. Perhaps for their family, sorcery was a curse.

"Makeda!" Dad yelled.

She hopped off the bed. Maji had to wait. Right now, she had to put on her mwindaji hat and help her dad find Korlemo.

Chapter 33

WHIRLING TIRES AND THE swaying RV lulled Makeda into a light slumber. Seven hours in an RV with her cousins made her more determined to get her own apartment when she returned home.

Conversations barely reached her consciousness. Though she reached out, Samuel ignored her kasi kasi messages.

I hope Yewande hasn't bothered him.

Makeda wanted to make sure he and Eldridge were fine, and Yewande hadn't retaliated because they failed to get her to issue the invitation spell.

'What's wrong?' Brian asked.

'Nothing. Just tired.'

'Right.'

"Hurry up, Carolyn," Peter called from the back of the camper.

"You want to drive this bus?" Carolyn asked, increasing the windshield wiper speed. "Rain's decreasing, but these wipers need to be replaced."

"Don't insult Maybelline," Uncle John said. "This RV has gotten us through a lot."

"Yes, and it's time to buy something new." Carolyn squinted into a darkening sky.

"We can't afford it," Zeke said, checking weapons. "Besides, we're here."

"In New Jersey but not our destination," Peter said. He joined Carolyn and Zeke up front and gazed out the window. "You can slow down though. I remember a tiny clearing about a quarter mile from the house."

"That far?" Carolyn scanned the road for the turnoff Peter mentioned.

"It's an exclusive neighborhood of million-dollar homes," he said. "A rat-trap—"

"Watch it," Uncle John cautioned.

"Maybelline will stick out like a wart on a model's face."

Zeke chuckled. "Nice save."

A half hour elapsed before Carolyn drove the RV into a small grove surrounded by austere trees and shrubbery.

"What now?" she said, placing the RV in Park.

"We wait. Aaron shouldn't be far behind." Over a cellphone, he gave directions to their location.

Fifteen passed before a longer, newer, RV pulled up beside them towing a pick-up truck. Peter and Zeke exited Maybelline and approached the second RV.

Peter entered the RV's side door. "Where y'all been?"

Aaron, seated in the driver's seat, swiveled around. "We stopped for gas at a discount station off the state road."

"Why didn't you call?"

"I did, but the line was busy."

"Talking to Brenda?" Aaron asked, grinning.

Peter frowned, blushing at the mention of his new bride. "Daniel gave instructions on how to—"

"What's the holdup?" Carolyn asked abruptly entering from the RV's passenger door. "We ready?"

"We're working out the logistics." Peter inspected weapons stowed underneath seat cushions.

Makeda entered the RV, slipping on a black hoodie.

"Am I going in alone?" Zeke asked.

"No." Peter removed his flick knife, twirling it between his fingers. "Zeke, Makeda, Thomas, and Carolyn will go in first." Pointing to Zeke, he said, "You'll take care of the electrical and security while we search the property."

"What about Dad?" Brian asked.

"Back up," Peter said. "Uncle John will drive the RV and drop us off close to the property. He'll wait here for our call."

Carolyn said, "I hope we're taking this RV because Maybelline's slow."

Peter grinned. "Sure."

"Ammo?" Aaron rose from the driver's seat and stretched.

"No bullets unless absolutely necessary," Peter said.

"What?" Aaron frowned. "You must be kidding."

"We can't afford attention on the mwindaji," Peter said.

"The FBI finally dropped their surveillance," Brian said, "but it'll look suspicious if we shoot up the place like in Ramsey."

"Besides, we're after intel on Korlemo," Peter said. "We have no issue with these people."

"But they're werewolves," Aaron said. "We kill werewolves."

"True, but we're on shaky ground." Peter twirled the flick knife once before stowing it in a pocket. "And we don't want the FBI looking closely at the attack. In fact, if we can get in and out without killing anyone, it would be a successful operation."

Carolyn strapped a rifle over her shoulder. "Unless they give us no choice."

"Kill them if they resist," Aaron said.

"Safety takes priority," Peter said, strapping a rifle over each shoulder.

"At least try the tranquilizer guns before killing anyone," Zeke said. "And use a machete or lance before bullets. Silver is expensive, and we need to watch costs."

"Also, silver bullets signal mwindaji," Brian said. "And we want this operation on radio silence—even from other mwindaji." He nodded at Peter, who gave a thumbs up.

Makeda sat on the sofa while Peter detailed the operation and layout of the home. No maji. Here, she became mwindaji. If the team discovered she practiced sorcery...

Don't create problems.

"Questions?" Peter asked while adjusting his face mask.

"What about me?" Raymond asked, setting aside his game controller.

"Stay with Dad," Zeke said.

Raymond gave a thumbs up and returned to his gamer.

A couple of people shook their heads, but no one spoke. They donned the traditional mwindaji assault garb of black outfits and face masks with slits for their eyes. Makeda finished braiding her hair and fastening the braids underneath her cap.

She glanced around the RV. "Did I miss anything?"

"Nope," Zeke said, "you're with me."

Uncle John jumped in the driver's seat. "This piece of shit ain't nothin' compared to Maybelline."

"Daddy, please," Carolyn said, riding shotgun.

The RV inched out of the grove and onto the secluded street. In under ten minutes, they arrived outside a huge, private, gated estate.

"Everybody out." Uncle John slowed the RV as the mwindaji scrambled out of the moving vehicle. "Call when the job's done." He drove away.

Chapter 34

PETER HOPPED OUT OF the RV, ran up to a wrought iron fence, and hurled a package wrapped in cheesecloth over it. By the time he scurried behind a row of hedges, the RV had departed and the mwindaji hid in various locations around the property's perimeter.

Seconds later, jingling chains approached the fence. Though not barking, guard dogs sniffed around the perimeter. They quickly located the cheesecloth package and devoured it.

Makeda's brows raised in a question.

"A sedative," Peter said, consulting his watch. "Give it ten minutes."

"That long?" Zeke asked.

"We're not going to scale the fence here," he said, crouching low while scurrying to the south side of the property. "It'll take time to get to a section closest to the house."

"Are you sure about the layout?" Aaron asked, delicately wiping his mustache before lowering his face mask.

"Yeah," Nyesha said, following directly behind Peter. "You haven't been inside since spring."

Because Peter stopped abruptly, Nyesha careened into his backside.

"I doubt they've changed the footprint of the house since then," Peter said. "It's been months, not years. Besides, Daniel reviewed the property specifications the builder filed with the county."

"Those aren't always accurate," Aaron said. "I worked with this banker—"

"Shush," Peter said, glaring at the team. "Get in position." He tapped Zeke's shoulder. "You guys get going."

Zeke led Makeda and the other mwindaji around an oak tree on the north side of the estate.

As she departed with Zeke's team, Makeda heard Peter giving orders.

"Ready guys?" Peter asked his team.

"I thought you said it takes ten minutes for the sedative to take effect?" Brian asked, observing the pack of Dobermans consuming the tainted meats.

"Don't worry. This'll work."

Hope so.

Before she lost sight of Peter and his team, Makeda spotted a Rolls Royce drive up to the front gate.

Chapter 35

JULES BARELY KNOCKED ON the massive wooden metal framed doors when a servant opened them. A tall, cadaverous man stepped aside, allowing Jules and his two cousins to enter.

Off white marble floors dazzled in light streaming down from a chandelier mounted on the twenty-foot-high ceiling. Decorated in minimalist art deco with bright white walls, Jules detected Abigail's influence in the mansion's impeccable interior design aesthetic. If the Baptiste family didn't shun publicity, their home would easily grace the covers of architectural and design magazines. His leather-soled shoes clicked on the marble floors as Jules marched toward the study.

Untouched by Abigail's influence, Stefan's massive study exhibited an old-world atmosphere. Dark wood-paneled walls, subdued lighting, a massive wood fireplace, and dark heavy leather furniture defined the room.

Animal heads dotted the walls between the floor-to-ceiling bookcases. Before the bookcases, a grand oriental rug draped the flooring away from the hearth. Jules and his cousins entered and found Stefan and several associates present and occupying chairs distributed around the room.

Stefan rose as they entered but did not offer a greeting.

A dramatic departure from their usual interactions.

Jules's shoulders tensed. Raised liked brothers—as their fathers had been—this recent estrangement was startling, though understandable.

The schism arose because Jules blamed his family's execution on Jackie Baptiste, Stefan's younger sister. Whereas Stefan blamed Sylvia. Both families had lost their patriarchs, and now the authorities suspected them of money laundering and embezzling funds from a rural Kentucky hospital.

Why do we find it easier to blame each other than work together?

He needed Stefan to ensure his sister's safety. Svie had dissuaded him from coming, but Jules had to understand Baptiste's position before he proceeded.

An uneasy silence made the atmosphere oppressive. Jules pushed aside those emotions and approached Stefan's desk. He settled into an upright leather chair, crossed his legs, and took a deep breath.

"What happened, Stefan?" he asked stoically.

"Sylvia stole from my dad," Stefan replied with a deadpan expression.

This study resembled Herman Baptiste's Kentucky estate. Jules recalled police photos depicting the gory murder scene with their fathers' and brothers' bloody bodies strewn across the room. Jules gripped the chair arms, shifting position in the seat.

"Svie tried to protect our families," he countered. "Why didn't Korlemo and Herman make financial arrangements for the hospital and the ajabu before they left?"

"My father faithfully served the ajabu!" Stefan snapped. "He did not lie."

"But he did!" Jules shouted, jumping from his seat.

Their compatriots sized each other up. Standing behind him, one of Jules' cousins laid a hand on his shoulder.

You can do this. You must.

"I apologize. I'm upset, so are you." Jules gazed at the bookcase. On a shelf above Stefan's left shoulder perched a photo of him, Stefan, and Svie celebrating their college graduations.

Friends forever. Until life intervened.

"So much has happened," he said, distantly.

They all graduated from Ivy League colleges the same year. Abigail followed in their footsteps the next year. Their families had been so proud. In the photo, they hugged each other sporting silly, hopeful grins.

How did it all end?

Jules continued, "Stefan, you received copies of the material Svie discovered at the hospital. Secret accounts Herman maintained for Korlemo. Money hidden from the ajabu for years. The week..." He swallowed.

"Before our families' murders, Herman moved money from an overseas account. Why didn't he mention the transaction at quorum? Why didn't he tell us he planned to relocate Korlemo that evening?"

"I don't know." Stefan lowered his head. "But my father wouldn't do anything to hurt your family—or the ajabu." He rose and glanced at the same photo as Jules. "I can't believe my father would betray our people,"

Stefan said *sotto voce*, "Six months ago, we were best friends—all of us. Now, Abigail and I are the only children left of Herman Baptiste. And you and Sylvia the last survivors of Gerard Senegal." He shook his head. "How did we get here?"

"You believe Korlemo made him do it?" Jules asked.

"Korlemo?" Stefan asked distantly. "Why would he ask my father to deceive the ajabu?"

"Because he's a selfish bastard."

"Listen—"

"Please." Jules raised a hand, motioning Stefan to stop. "Korlemo has always controlled your father's decisions, and you know it. He doesn't care what happens to any of us. Has he contacted you since he fled Kentucky?"

"For security."

"Of course, for that. But for anything else?"

Jules wandered around the room. "Korlemo's greed and hubris initiated this tragedy. He cursed our families instead of admitting defeat at the hands of a woman." He glanced at Stefan. "You know the legend, as do I."

"We are blessed, not cursed." Stefan opened his arms, encircling the room. "Look at us. We surpass bindimèn in strength and wisdom. Both man and animal. Would you rather simply be human?"

"I would rather be me. Determine my own destiny. Not have my life dictated by a pathological sadist."

One of Jules' cousins said, "Gentlemen, this conversation is not productive. What about the present situation?"

"Where's Korlemo?" Jules asked Stefan.

"Safe."

The two men glared at each other.

"Where, Stefan?"

"It doesn't matter."

"Is he going to send for the other families?"

"No, but he has agreed to provide for them." Stefan returned to his desk and fidgeted with a pen, avoiding Jules' questioning stare.

"The ajabu in Kentucky are struggling. Those families need financial assistance immediately," Jules said. "And who'll protect them?"

Stefan glowered under a knitted brow. "I cannot. The FBI surveillance has stretched my resources."

Jules sat in front of Stefan's desk. "Then why protect Korlemo?"

"I'm not."

"But your associates are."

"Our family has protected Ibori for centuries. It's our obligation."

"And look at the result."

A silence fell upon the room as Jules and Stefan glowered at each other. The same cousin broke the silence.

"Guys," he said, "we have to make plans. Forget who's at fault. How do we proceed?"

Everyone turned toward the door as Abigail entered the study. Those seated rose. Jules walked over and took her hands in his.

"Abigail."

He barely spoke before she hugged him deeply, then kissed his cheeks.

"It's been too long."

Only after she sat in a chair before the antique wooden desk did everyone else sit except two guards positioned near the exit. Jules took the chair beside hers.

"I'm sorry about your father."

A single tear tumbled down her face.

"We have all lost significant family members." Abigail squeezed his hand. "Is Sylvia safe?

"For now." He shrugged. "Korlemo contacted her."

"Ah, that leech," she said, throwing up her hands. "He's at the center of all this."

Stefan frowned. "Abigail."

"What?" She leaned across the desk. "Would you have me lie among friends?"

"We discussed this," Stefan said through gritted teeth. "It's best not to—"

"Are you afraid of the millennial vampire too?" She chuckled. "Korlemo's an arrogant fool."

"Not now," Stefan pleaded.

Rolling her eyes, Abigail said, "Fine." She faced Jules. "Besides, we have serious matters to discuss."

"Exactly," said one of Stefan's cousins. "Where are we with preparations for—"

Stefan raised a hand, giving the man a terse glare. "First, we need to know where Jules stands on our project."

A scowl crept along Jules' brow. "I don't understand."

"It's simple." Stefan circled around the desk, hovering over him. "Do you remain dedicated to our goals, or have your allegiances changed?"

Jules rose and squared off with Stefan. "Since when has my commitment to this project ever been in doubt?"

"Since your sister stole from our patron." Stefan sneered.

"Korlemo has never been trustworthy," Abigail interceded, stepping between them. "Sylvia protected the ajabu." Looking at Jules, she asked, "How does she plan to distribute the money to the families?"

"She can't contact ajabu in Ramsey without alerting Korlemo." Swiveling around and glaring into Stefan's face, he said, "Someone gave Korlemo her cellphone number. So, she's definitely not safe."

"Not me," Stefan said, meandering over to a side bookcase. "My father swore me to protect Korlemo, but I wouldn't kill for him."

"And Sylvia is our friend—our sister," Abigail said, eyeing her brother.

"I have no beef with Sylvia," Stefan said, "I simply wish she had warned us."

"She didn't have time," Jules said. "Korlemo gave no warning."

Stefan frowned. "Why was he anxious to leave?"

"That witch," Abigail said. "Dad told me a witch warned Korlemo to leave."

"Well, her prediction came true," said one of Stefan's cousins.

"Humph." Abigail crossed her legs. "How did she know the mwindaji would attack?"

"Are you sure of their involvement?" Jules regained his seat beside her.

She nodded. "We found silver bullets lodged in the walls. Besides, those who survived reported seeing the murderers dressed in black and carrying machetes. Hallmarks of mwindaji."

How did the mwindaji locate Korlemo in Kentucky? There must have been a leak in his or Stefan's office.

"Getting back to present matters." Stefan ambled around the desk, gazing down at Jules. "We need your cooperation to complete the project."

"I need assurances Svie will not be killed."

"We have no dispute with her—or any Senegal." Stefan reclined against the wall positioned between two floor-length windows, slightly disturbing the drapes. "So, are you with us or not."

"Where's Korlemo?" Jules asked, glancing sharply at Stefan.

"Why do you care?"

"Because he's a threat to Svie."

"Tell Sylvia to come here." Stefan grinned. "We'll keep her safe."

No chance.

Jules turned to Abigail. "If Svie sends you the money she took from Korlemo, will you distribute it to the families in Ramsey?"

"Of course." Abigail laid a hand on his forearm. "But we need your help. We're at a crucial point in our arrangements."

"Exactly where are you with the project?" one of Jules' cousins asked, stepping forward. The other cousin stood at his side.

"It's confidential," Stefan said, not bothering to visually acknowledge either man.

"We have a right to know," the same cousin said.

After a deep inhalation, Stefan eyed the man. "Know your place. This operation exceeds your," he enunciated slowly, "limited capabilities."

The man's jaw clenched. "We are lupasteri too."

"But not of sufficient importance to share this information!" Stefan hollered. The draperies shimmied. Then silence.

Jules' cousins retreated to the center of the room.

"Blame the mwindaji," one of Stefan's associates asserted. "They destroyed our lives. We should concentrate on our shared enemy, not squabble with each other."

"William is right," Stefan said, loosening his shirt collar. "The mwindaji have become a serious problem. If we do not unite and defeat them, our families will be extinguished.

"If you want our cooperation," Jules said, looking at Abigail, "we need to be included in the plans."

Exchanging a glance with her brother, she said, "We trust you, Jules. However, there has been a breach in security."

He frowned. "And you suspect us?"

"Last week, someone trailed our associate from the Manhattan office" She scrutinized his face. "They trailed him all the way to Finger Lakes."

Jules's brows rose.

One of his cousins said, "We weren't in—"

"Hush," Jules said, angling his head upward, admonishing his cousin with a glance.

Stefan leaned forward. "We suspect the mwindaji, or—"

"Or?" Jules regarded Stefan.

"Or a rogue compatriot." He crossed his arms. "A competitor."

"I believe you suspect me." Jules sized up Stefan and Abigail in turn.

"We don't," the latter replied, "except your sudden unwillingness to assist—"

"We simply want to be included in the arrangements," Jules' second cousin interjected, speaking up for the first time. "Why won't you and Stefan confide in us?"

"There is no *us*." Stefan sauntered around the room, keeping his gaze on Jules. "You, me, and Svie developed this project in college. Remember?"

Jules nodded. "I do. But I also recall a different purpose—an equalitarian one."

Stefan shrugged. "Plans change."

"Agreed." Jules headed for the door.

The guards surged forward and blocked his egress. Jules' cousins, bristling, strode up beside him.

"What's this?" Jules swiveled around, regarding Stefan.

"We need your cooperation," Stefan said as his temple twitched. "Tell me Korlemo's location."

"Don't worry about the vampire. He won't hurt Sylvia." Stefan rested on the corner of the desk. "I promise you."

"Yet you threaten me and my cousins." Jules considered the guards.

"A minor delay in your departure." Stefan waved dismissively at the guards, who retreated away from Jules and his cousins, though still blocking their egress. "I require information."

"Where's Korlemo?"

Stefan sighed loudly. "You sound like a broken record."

"In Michigan," Abigail said.

"Abigail!" Stefan yelled.

"It doesn't matter," she said, addressing her brother. "Nothing matters but the project." She turned to Jules with a slight grin. "Please. This is important."

For a second, Jules considered.

Did Abigail lie? Even if I find Korlemo, will Svie be safe? What if Stefan warned the vampire to flee?

It didn't matter. He and Svie had discussed the situation and decided not to cooperate. The project had grown out of control, and they wanted no part of—

"Your answer?" Stefan asked, cupping his chin.

Jules shared a glance with each of his cousins. Both men gave a slight inclination of their heads.

"No."

Stefan peeked over Jules' shoulder at the guards. Jules stepped forward a second before the guards seized his cousins.

"Let them go!" he shouted.

His cousins and the guards morphed into werewolves and a struggle ensued. Chairs and furniture were overturned.

"Stop it!" Abigail yelled.

The guards released the men but watched Stefan for directions.

She glanced at Stefan. "Is this necessary?"

"I apologize," Stefan said. He faced the guards. "Step away from them."

Obeying their orders, both guards returned to the doorway and remained in werewolf form.

Stefan removed a gun from the top desk drawer and pointed it at Jules's chest. "Will you reconsider?"

"Put the gun away."

"Yes or no."

"No."

Stefan shot one of Jules' cousins in the forehead. Brain tissue sprayed the left side of Jules's arm. Crumbling onto the floor, the young man regressed to bindimèn form. His body twitched once. Blood pooled around his head.

Jules rushed Stefan. The latter raised the gun and pointed it at him.

"You're insane." Jules's heartbeat pounded.

Walking around to the front of the desk, Stefan said, "I'm committed to a cause. A principle you—and Sylvia—once supported."

Quickly surveying the room, Jules considered how to extricate himself and his remaining cousin from the situation.

"Don't." Stefan motioned with the gun. "There is no escape. You both will remain here until you provide the information we require."

Abigail took a step forward. "Jules, please. No one has to die. Give us the documents."

Glancing at his dead cousin, Jules said, "People have already died."

With a sneer, Stefan said, "And others will, too, if you refuse to cooperate."

"What guarantees—"

Pop.

Jules' remaining cousin's head exploded. He dropped to the floor on Jules's right side.

Gasping, he said, "You're as psychotic as Korlemo."

"He's the past." Stefan chuckled, making a fist. "We are composing a future."

"We need your help," Abigail said. "Join us. Reunite our resources and build the organization we discussed in college."

"You told Korlemo about Svie, didn't you?" he asked.

"I did," Stefan boasted. "Bait to bring you here."

He sat down behind the desk. "Are you sufficiently motivated to assist us, now?"

"Go to hell," Jules said. At least Svie was safe. *I hope.*

"Fine." Stefan motioned to a guard. "Take him."

The lights went out.

Chapter 36

PETER TAPPED NYESHA'S SHOULDER and motioned for her to go left. Using night goggles, he touched a knob and slowly turned. As the door opened, Peter spotted a burly man, arms crossed, stationed immediately inside the door. A woman stood near the desk, three men to his left, and a man behind the desk.

With his fingers, he signaled the number and position of the room's occupants. He rushed inside with his team close behind.

"What happened to the lights?"

"Who's there?" someone asked.

There wasn't time or need to answer. Peter jabbed a syringe into the burly man's neck. A thick claw clapped down on his right shoulder, tearing the sleeve. After a short scuffle, the hand slumped off.

Mwindaji charged inside and scuffled with the occupants. Furniture knocked over. Screams and shrieks rang out. Three men managed to briefly transform into werewolves before they were shot with sedative needles.

"Now," Peter said into a cellphone, quickly removing the night lenses.

The room lit up.

Inside the study, he counted three unconscious men, two by the entrance and one near a bookcase. Behind a wooden desk, another man crouched beside a chair. In front of the desk, an average-sized woman with auburn hair sat in a leather chair. A slim man with jet-black hair smoothed back with gel stood in the center of the room.

"Mwindaji." The man behind the desk sneered and stood erect.

Peter circled around two bodies surrounded by pools of blood. Approaching the desk, he appreciated the wood and admired the craftsmanship.

Not bad, for werewolves.

"What do you scum want?" the man asked, snarling at Peter.

Speaking through a voice adjuster, Peter asked, "Where is Korlemo?"

"Fuck. Not this again."

Peter shared a look with Nyesha. She shrugged, then held a machete under the woman's neck. The latter spat at her. Nyesha struck the woman on the side of the head with the butt of the machete.

The man behind the desk started forward.

"Don't," Peter warned. "No one has to die. We only want information."

"If you changeover," Nyesha said, "I'll slice your neck clean off your shoulders."

Glowering, the woman clenched the chair arms but remained seated.

"Please, I don't know anything," the man with jet-black hair said. "Let me leave."

"Werewolf or vampire?" Peter asked.

Before the man answered, the woman said, "We are lupasteri." Her chin jutted forward, and she glared at Peter.

Exchanging a glance with Brian, Peter slightly shrugged. With a slight nod of his head, Peter signaled Aaron. They immediately began searching the room.

They pulled books off shelves and rummaged among the volumes. Peter strapped the machete to his backpack and shoved the man behind the desk aside to peer through desk drawers.

Instantly, the man morphed into a werewolf and pounced on Peter. He managed to slice Peter's chest before Nyesha shot him in the throat.

"No!" the auburn-haired woman screamed. She rushed from her chair and cradled the fallen man.

Gurgling, the werewolf reverted to human form.

Clutching his chest, Peter retreated from the werewolf and collapsed near a bookcase.

Brian motioned to Aaron. "Help him."

Aaron assisted Peter, who spoke into a cellphone. "I'm down."

"Is it bad?" Makeda said over the phone.

"Bad enough. Anything on your end?"

"Time's up. We need to clear out," Brian said, speaking into Peter's phone.

"On our way up."

Peter hung up.

"What about them?" Nyesha asked, pointing at the woman and man bleeding on the ground.

"Leave them." Peter covered his wounds while blood leaked around his hand.

"Wait." Brian held up a folder. "Look what I found." He handed the papers to Peter, who waved them away.

"Grab everything in the desk. We'll review the papers later."

"Let's go," Brian said.

"Please," the man in front of the desk said, "take me with you."

For a moment, the mwindaji stared at him, then glanced at each other.

Blood soaked Peter's shirt. Clutching his right arm close to his chest, he motioned Brian closer.

He whispered, "Why would a werewolf want to come with us?"

Brian pointed. "Maybe it has something to do with the two dead guys over there."

"Those are—were—my cousins," the man with slicked-back black hair said.

"Apparently, not all werewolves get along with each other." Peter cringed in pain.

"Not our problem," Nyesha said.

Again, the mwindaji started to leave.

"I'll tell you where Korlemo is," the man said, rising and following them to the door.

"No way," Nyesha said.

"He's lying," Aaron said.

"If you leave me here, they'll kill me," the man said.

Chapter 37

Z EKE AND MAKEDA RUSHED into the study.

Makeda noticed Peter bleeding and dashed to his side. She removed gauze and dressings from her backpack and treated his wounds.

"Ready?" Zeke asked, looking at Aaron, who half supported Peter.

"Let's go," Peter said, wincing as Makeda wrapped gauze around his chest.

A slight, tall man with dark hair followed. "I'm telling the truth. You must help me."

"What's going on?" Makeda asked no one in particular.

"Werewolf feud." Nyesha pointed at the dead bodies. "They killed these two before we arrived."

"We're not werewolves," a woman beside the desk said. She cradled a dead man in her lap. "We are lupasteri, and you will pay for this."

Makeda's brow raised.

Nyesha said, "She's a spitter."

"Who cares," Aaron said, "let's go."

Nyesha addressed Makeda, pointing to the man following them. "Apparently, they planned to kill this guy next."

"Give me a minute," Makeda said, handing Aaron the dressings.

Peter regarded her. "What?"

"Trust me."

"Five minutes, then out." Peter exited the study assisted by Aaron.

Nyesha grimaced. "Let him die with his kin." She departed.

Chapter 38

O

NCE THE OTHER MWINDAJI left, Makeda studied the pleading man. He wore an expensive tailor-made suit with a boutique hairstyle. Thin but fit, Makeda concluded he worked in finance or not at all.

"Who are you?" she asked.

"None of your business," the woman said, releasing the now-de-
ceased man from her lap. "You mwindaji will pay for this."

"Tell me your name," Makeda addressed the man.

He hesitated.

Gauging what to reveal.

From his shaking hands, she realized he desperately wanted to
leave.

"Later, I—"

"Name?"

"Don't," the woman said, striding up behind him.

Makeda removed her machete and pointed it at the woman. She
glanced at the man. "Tick tock."

"Jules."

"Surname." She noticed the woman slowly creeping forward.

The man shut his lips.

"Fine. Work it out with her," Makeda said, pointing her chin at the woman.

"Wait, it's Senegal," he said, reaching forward and almost grabbing Makeda's arm. "Now, can we leave?"

"Why were they going to kill you?"

"Don't make a mistake, Jules," the woman said.

He glanced back at her. "Like killing my cousins—or betraying Svie."

"I didn't."

"Stefan called Korlemo with your approval."

A minuscule grin formed along the woman's mouth. "We wouldn't let Korlemo hurt her. We needed you to come here."

"Why Abigail? To kill me, too?"

"Convince you to..." She glanced up at Makeda. "Stay. We can work this out."

The man faced Makeda. "We need to leave. Security will arrive soon."

As Makeda pivoted toward the door, the woman evolved into a werewolf and sliced at the man's head. He managed to duck as Makeda's hands shot forward and slammed Abigail into a wall beside the windows.

Dazed, Abigail looked up at Makeda, speaking groggily, "You're a witch."

"I'm not a witch."

Makeda grasped Jules' arm. "Come on."

Abigail gasped. "Zauber."

"One moment." Jules hurried over to the dead men in the center of the room and removed items from their pockets. "They were family."

While she waited at the door, Makeda's burner phone rang.

"Now," Zeke said.

"On my way," she said, ending the call. "If you want our help, we need to leave ASAP."

Using the wall, Abigail crawled off the floor. "Wait, zauber. We can help each other. I'll pay you—handsomely."

"No thanks."

Abigail chortled, blood dripping from her mouth. "Do your mwindaji friends know you're a zauber? I doubt it. They'd slit your throat like they murdered my brother."

Jules ran up to Makeda. "I'm ready."

"Why are you looking for Korlemo? So, you can help him again? Zaubers created that *mobowou*. Returning to your master?"

Makeda swung around. "No one controls me."

"Zauber are servants. Anyone who pays you—controls you."

"Chekate." Makeda lifted Abigail off the ground and tossed her across the room.

"I make my own decisions."

She grabbed Jules by the arm, and they fled.

As they raced across the cobbled driveway, Jules said, "Thank you. I really appreciate this."

"Don't thank me yet," she said, yanking a black bag over his head. Makeda plunged a syringe into his neck.

Jules tore at the bag, trying to remove it. His hands elongated. Hairy skin bloomed along his arms and his fingers clawed.

A moment later, Makeda slung his limp body over her shoulder and hurried into the idling RV.

They sped down the drive and zipped onto the street. Past the thicket where they had parked earlier, Makeda noticed a car's headlamps flip on.

Chapter 39

THE RV JOSTLED AS they sped away from the Baptiste estate. Makeda braced herself while stitching a laceration across her brother's chest.

"You brought him?" Peter asked, pointing at an unconscious Jules Senegal.

"He has information we need." She tied off a stitch and applied antibiotic ointment to his wounds. "Besides, they would've killed him if we had left him there."

"Good," Carolyn said, handing Makeda a needle and glass vial.

Peter frowned. "What's that?"

"Antibiotics," she said. "Stop moving."

Brian helped her settle Peter on the queen bed in the rear of the RV. He asked, "What do you have in mind?"

"He's also the brother of the hospital administrator," Makeda said.

"You sure?" Peter's eyelids drooped from the sedative she gave him.

Carolyn said, "This could jeopardize the entire team."

"How? He's unconscious and blindfolded."

"I don't care. He's a liability."

The RV entered a park nestled a mile outside the Great Swamp National Wildlife Refuge.

Makeda regarded her brother. "You disagree?"

"What can he tell us?" Peter asked, squirming on the bed.

Makeda adjusted a pillow under his arm.

"He might know the location of the embezzled money."

"Is that why you brought him along?" Peter asked, a slight grin on his face.

She shrugged. Makeda didn't want the mwindaji to kill Jules, and she truly believed he had valuable information.

But will he divulge it?

"You can't bluff to save your life." He winced. "Ouch."

"There's something significant going on here, and I believe he knows what it is."

"I trust you," he said before dozing off to sleep.

In a patch of woods located in the Great Swamp Wildlife Park, mwindaji surrounded Jules. They wore their characteristic black uniforms with face masks.

With the voice adjuster, Zeke asked, "Why did your friends want to kill you?"

Clumsily, Jules rose to his feet and perused the surroundings. He lightly touched his neck.

Zeke motioned to Thomas, who handed Jules a flask of water.

"Thanks." Jules drank hungrily.

"Why—"

"They aren't my friends."

"At one time they were." Zeke sat on a folding chair and invited Jules to do likewise. "What happened?"

Jules guzzled water and handed back the empty flask.

"Have you had time to think up a lie?" Zeke asked.

"This is ridiculous," Nyesha said. "Why don't we simply bury this guy and move on."

"Because that's not who we are," Makeda said.

"No," Jules said. "What about Ramsey?"

"What about it?" Nyesha asked. "How many people did you and your friends murder for food?" She strode up to Zeke. "I'll be in the RV."

He nodded. To Makeda, he said, "This was your idea."

"Jules, you asked for our help," Makeda said. "Keep up your side of the bargain."

Dusting off his slacks, Jules said, "I'll happily pay whatever expenses you—"

"Expenses," Zeke said. "Dude, we saved your life. Or did you want to be plant food like your cousins?"

Jules flinched.

Makeda touched Zeke's shoulder. "I got this." She faced Jules. "What are you hiding from them?"

Jules' gaze widened.

"If they simply hated you, they would've killed you and your cousins simultaneously. But this…" Makeda tried to remember. "Abigail used your cousins to influence you. Therefore, you must have something she wants."

She approached Jules. "What is it?"

Zeke left the circle. Makeda walked over to Brian.

"He's not going to talk," she whispered.

"What do you want to do?"

"Take him for a ride."

After a momentary hesitation, Brian nodded. She gave him instructions about where to find supplies. He departed into the RV.

Hauling Jules by the arm, Makeda escorted him up to an old clunker situated beside a broken road sign and covered with tree branches.

Tying Jules' hands behind his back, Brian slid the man inside the car before taking the wheel.

While Brian situated Jules inside the car, Makeda explained about the car lights.

"Think someone followed us?" Zeke asked.

"Possibly."

"Safety first," Carolyn said.

"Dad and the others already left. We'll head out."

Nyesha pointed at the RV's door. "What about our prisoner?"

"He's not a prisoner," Makeda said. "We saved his life. Now, he needs to keep his promise."

Zeke asked, "And you and Brian will make him talk?"

"We'll call you after we dump him."

"Now you're talking." Nyesha climbed into the passenger's seat.

"If we don't hear from y'all in an hour…" Zeke said.

"Send in the Marines."

Makeda dashed out of the RV and slid into the back seat beside Jules.

With two beeps of the horn, Brian drove away and onto a narrow dirt road. Not until he entered the highway did he flick on the car's headlights.

"Where are you taking me?" Jules asked, his voice muffled by a black hood.

"At the house, you agreed to provide information." Makeda gazed out the rearview window. A lone set of headlights followed.

'Did you see that?'

"Yep. You called it.'

Addressing Jules, Makeda said, "Apparently, I misjudged your veracity." The removed his hood.

"Humph," Jules grunted, leaning his head against the side window. "Mwindaji are not known for keeping their word."

"And werewolves?"

She spied a slight grin on his face.

"Let's simply be you and me for now."

"Oh. You want me to be honest while you're wearing a mask and talking via a voice manipulator."

Makeda removed the voice box.

"But not your face."

She grinned. "We haven't achieved a sufficient level of trust—yet."

With a flick of a knife, she cut the ropes binding his hands.

Messaging his wrists, Jules thanked her and settled back into the seat cushions.

"This has been a long, horrible day," he said.

"I'm sorry about your cousins."

He gazed into her eyes. "I believe you mean that."

"Despite what you think, mwindaji only kill monsters preying on people."

"You consider us monsters?"

"Anything that will eat you qualifies as a monster."

"Bindimèn eat cows, chickens, and fish. Would you consider yourself a monster?"

"To the animals we eat, yes."

He laughed. "Perhaps we all have monsters inside us."

"Let's get back to the sharing part of this relationship," Brian interjected.

Makeda glared at him through the rear mirror, but he avoided her gaze.

"There's something here beyond Korlemo. Why did this Abigail woman want to kill you?"

"She..." Jules's gaze wandered out the window. "We were once close. All of us. We had these ideas."

"College graduates dreaming of saving the world?" She smiled. "That's not unusual."

"We didn't want to save this world as much as our own."

"What do you mean?"

He cut her a side glance.

"I read several papers from the study desk. They mention politicians and other influential people."

Jules remained silent.

"Nothing."

He cleared his throat. "I'm grateful to you and the other mwindaji for saving my life, but—"

"But it means nothing now because you're safe." Her head tilted slightly.

"I grew up with Abigail and Stefan, and they tried to kill me. They killed my cousins." His chin trembled.

Myaisha gave him space, waiting for him to compose himself.

"Believe me, Korlemo is the least of the mwindaji's concerns."

She frowned. "There's a greater conspiracy, isn't there? Does it involve mwindaji or bindimèn?"

Silence.

"Jules, are werewolves plotting against humans?"

"Do you know what lupasteri are?"

"I've heard the name."

"Well, you have a lot to learn then."

Makeda wanted information, but she didn't want to reveal her lack of knowledge. Therefore, she decided upon a different approach.

"Where's your sister?"

Jules' eyes gaped.

"You're Dr. Sylvia Senegal's sister, right?"

"How did—"

"There's a slight resemblance. And the name is not common."

He nodded.

"Is she safe?"

"Enough."

"Why did she take the money? She could've embezzled from the hospital anytime. Why then?"

"Sylvia is not a thief." Jules sat up straight. "She took money for the Ramsey families. Korlemo left them destitute."

"Yes, he has."

The look Jules shot her made Makeda recoil.

"Because of the mwindaji"

"Because werewolves and vampires used the hospital to feed their appetites."

He sighed. "People made mistakes."

"Feeding on people is not a calculation error."

They sped along for miles before Makeda said, "If your sister truly wants to help the families of Ramsey, I know someone she can contact."

Jules eyed her, a curve in his doubtful mouth. "Who would help us?"

"A pathologist. Now the hospital administrator. Dr. Bones has hired many werewolves and vampires as long as they agree not to eat patients," she added.

Jules chuckled. "You surprise me." He leaned toward her. "Do the other mwindaji know you're a zauber?"

Makeda's back stiffened.

"I see," he said. "They don't."

He stroked his chin. "How long do you plan to keep it secret?"

From the highway, Brian merged onto Interstate 95.

"We'll drop you off at the next exit," Makeda said. "I'm sure you can contact your confederates from there."

They completed the rest of the trip in silence. At 2 a.m., Brian pulled into a closed gas station. Makeda handed Jules a bag.

"These belonged to your cousins."

Jules accepted the bag and exited the car. "Why did you help me?"

Brian excused himself and walked over to the side of the building.

Her brow raised.

'Bathroom.'

'Watch your back.'

'Heard.'

Makeda addressed Jules, "Because there's something significant going on here. And while we don't trust each other, I believe we share similar goals."

After checking the items in the bag, Jules said, "Abigail said Korlemo resides in Michigan. She didn't give any specifics."

"Thank you."

"Be careful. The Baptistes have influential connections. They've made a fortune in armaments. If they're protecting Korlemo, you'll face a lot of firepower."

"Understood."

"Oh, there's also a witch involved."

"Who?"

He shrugged. "I don't know anything about her except she's helping Korlemo."

'She's here.'

Suddenly, a car zoomed toward Makeda and Jules. Both jumped aside but in different directions.

The car jolted to a stop, and a werewolf charged Makeda.

Makeda brandished her machete, swiping the air in front of the charging lycan. Assuming a fighting stance, Makeda swished the weapon.

Leering with saliva pouring down its mouth, the werewolf howled and stepped toward her.

Brian raced from the side of the building and lobbed two shots at the lycan's feet.

Jules burst in front of the werewolf, frantically waving his hands. "Don't shoot. Please! It's my sister." He swiveled around. "Svie. Don't. They saved my life."

Regarding him quizzically, the hulking beast leered at Makeda.

"It's true. Stefan is dead. He wanted to kill me."

A cloudiness formed in the werewolf's eyes. Its body shook and morphed into human form.

"Dr. Senegal." Makeda lowered her machete but kept it at her side.

Brian brought up the rear with the Senegal siblings between them.

"You?" Sylvia Senegal wiped her mouth with the back of her shirt sleeve.

Jules rubbed his sister's back. "Stefan killed our cousins at his residence in New Jersey. If the mwindaji hadn't showed up—"

"He'd be dead with your cousins," Brian interjected.

Sylvia collapsed to her knees. "I can't believe it."

While Jules tended to his sister, Brian entered the car.

'We need to meet up with the team.'

'I know, but we need information about this conspiracy. Don't you want to know what—or who—caused those giant bats to chase you?'

'Fine.'

"The conspiracy," Makeda said, getting Jules and Sylvia's attention.

Frowning, Sylvia regarded her brother. "What did you tell them?"

His shoulders slumped. "We want it to end. The mwindaji could help our cause."

"Or use it as an excuse to kill ajabu."

Makeda's hands rested on her hips. "We came to stop you from eating bindimèn."

"Did anyone miss those people? We ate transients and drug addicts."

"And the Hoppers?"

"Don't judge us." Sylvia glowered. "Bindimèn never needed an excuse to murder us."

Jules entwined his arm with his sister's. "She said there's someone in Ramsey helping ajabu."

"Who?" Sylvia asked Makeda.

"Dr. Bones."

Sylvia's brows raised. "Perhaps. He's a fair man."

The three of them stood in a circle sizing up each other.

'If we don't get on the road, the team will come looking for us. And they *will* kill those two.'

'Right.'

"Time to go. You have a ride, so…" She strapped the machete on her backpack and stuck out her hand.

Jules and Sylvia shared a look before they each shook her hand.

She removed her face mask. "Bye." Makeda trotted over to their car.

"Wait." Sylvia hurried to her car and retrieved a legal pad. "Here."

Makeda quickly glanced at the document.

"Numbers to overseas accounts."

"Is there anyone Dr. Bones can share this with to help your…" Makeda searched for the correct word.

"Ajabu is the community of werewolves and vampires," Jules said.

"Any ajabu Dr. Bones can trust?"

Sylvia and Jules gave her a few names.

"Great." Makeda hopped in the passenger seat.

Before they drove off, Jules handed her a ring.

Her raised eyebrows, questioning him.

"A token of friendship. I'll know who I owe a favor to if I see my ring again."

With a nod to Brian, they drove off.

One they entered the interstate, Brian asked, "What next?"

"Pull over at the next rest stop," she said. "First, we change the license plate. Next, we call the team."

A half hour later, she and Brian drove down Interstate 95 South, snacking on items they purchased from rest stop vending machines.

"Did Peter say what they found in the desk drawers?" Brian asked, slurping soda.

Makeda wiped crumbs from her mouth. "They found over a hundred thousand dollars in cash and a ledger."

Brian's brow creased.

"They'll share the ledger with Daniel. Hopefully, chasing the money will lead to Korlemo."

"Hope so."

Another hour passed. Makeda swapped with Brian at their next fuel stop.

As she re-entered the interstate, he asked, "How did he know you're a zauber?"

Makeda explained what happened inside the study.

"You'll have to teach me."

Speaking distantly, she said, "I'm still learning myself."

Brian frowned.

"Sorry. My mind's elsewhere."

"What about this lupasteri conspiracy?"

She shook her head. "Not sure, but I intend to find out."

Who will provide an honest answer? Yewande, no. Eldridge, umm. Samuel.

But would he risk alienating Eldridge from Yewande or incurring either's wrath?

Chapter 40

SEQUESTERED IN HER BEDROOM closet, Zainabu carefully whispered an incantation over her grandmother's book of spells and replaced it inside a trunk. Once she locked the trunk, she reattached the beetle-shaped talisman to her necklace.

"Two locks are better than one."

Knock, knock.

"Who is it?" At a leisurely pace, she finished dressing, wrapping her microbraids into a bun on her head.

Bam, bam, bam.

She dashed from the closet and opened the door. "What?"

With a mocking bow, the security officer asked, "Did I wake you, princess?"

"Rhogan, what do you want?" She exited the bedroom and locked the door.

"Sherman wants to talk with you," he said, walking beside her as they descended an elegant spiral staircase.

"It couldn't wait?"

"Naw," Rhogan said, twirling a toothpick along his bottom lip. "Told me to get you straight away."

Zainabu stormed down a hallway leading past the garage and into a detached in-law suite. "Sherman?"

She searched the living room, which doubled as an office for the head of security. Not finding anyone present, she yelled, "Sherman!"

"I'm coming," a male voice said. Half a minute later, a middle-aged man entered, zipping up his trousers. "Can't a man take a shit?"

Rolling her eyes, Zainabu asked, "What's the emergency?"

Wiping his hands on his trousers, Sherman walked into the kitchen. "Want coffee?"

Her nose wrinkled. "Not if you made it." She hopped on a kitchen stool. "Rhogan said it was important."

Chewing on a donut, Sherman said, "The mwindaji hit Baptiste's place."

Zainabu gaped. "In Ramsey?"

"No, the son's place in New Jersey."

She weighed this information while tapping her middle finger on the countertop. "Do you know how they found Baptiste's house?"

"Nope. Heard it secondhand." Sherman sipped coffee. "During my rounds, I heard two of them wolves talking about it."

She leaned forward. "Go on."

Speaking with a mouth full of donut, Sherman said, "Well, they were whispering, it was time to leave 'cause they needed to take care of their family."

Did this alter her plans? Korlemo would be furious. Or would he?

Zainabu considered the possibilities to capitalize on the opportunity. The vampire seemed less connected to Stefan than to Herman. Zainabu considered the implications when she noticed Sherman studying her.

"If the mwindaji found Stefan Baptiste, they can find Korlemo."

"Makes sense." He sneezed and wiped his nose on his sleeve.

Zainabu winced and tossed a box of tissues at him.

"Did you talk to Stefan, confirm details?"

Sherman shook his head. "No time. I just overheard the conversation. Told Rhogan to get you and came back here before—"

"I remember."

"Breakfast," he said, blowing his nose like a trumpet. "Besides, Stefan's dead. I heard them wolves say that much."

"They ain't wolves. They're werewolves," Rhogan said, entering the kitchen.

"Like I fucking care. Animals are animals."

Rhogan glared. He swiped the box of donuts and sat at a café style table in front of the windows.

"Do you have contacts with the Baptistes?" Zainabu asked Rhogan. Because he didn't answer, she clapped her hands. "Hey. You listening?"

"No," Rhogan grunted while eyeing Sherman.

"Where are the other security guys?" Zainabu asked the latter.

"Right now, five guys patrol the perimeter. I assigned them *werewolves* out back. At least, that's where I saw them before I came in."

Scratching his head, Sherman poured himself coffee. "Who knows. They probably playing tag in the woods with the bunnies." He sneered at Rhogan.

Zainabu sighed and slid off the kitchen stool. "Come on." Zainabu directed Rhogan to follow.

Once they left the in-law suite and returned to the main house, she said, "I need you to contact the Baptistes—or someone associated with them. Find out what happened. What the mwindaji did and what they learned about Korlemo."

"Why you asking me?" Rhogan said. "Sherman's head of security."

"Figure head," she said, leading him into the study. "I hired him for cover, but Stefan recommended you."

They stared at each other for a second before Rhogan asked, "What do you need?"

"Find out if Stefan revealed our location here in Michigan."

"He wouldn't do that," Rhogan asserted, thrusting his chin forward.

"You don't know what someone will do under the right circumstances."

"True." Rhogan shrugged. "Anything else?"

"See if you can convince those werewolves to stay."

"They won't. If their clan was attacked, they'll return home." She frowned. "You can't be sure."

"This time I can." He placed a clean toothpick in his mouth. "Besides loyalty, they hate Korlemo. They stayed because Stefan asked them to as a personal favor."

Zainabu lightly squeezed his arm. "Try. And tell them it would be to their advantage—financially."

"I'm not wasting my time."

She studied his face. "How much?"

He snickered. "To get them to stay or to ask?"

"Don't push too hard, Rhogan. There are limits," she said, gritting her teeth.

"Not when you're protecting a millennial vampire." He grinned, revealing a tiny gap between his front teeth.

Zainabu's foot tapped along the floor. "How much?"

Staff milled around as they discussed arrangements. Zainabu proceeded toward the study. Korlemo needed to be informed.

She wanted to give him the news. Strengthen his opinion of her as a reliable source of information—good and bad. Before she departed, Rhogan pulled her back by the arm. Glowering at him, Zainabu yanked her arm free.

He released her, raising his hands in surrender. "Don't get touchy."

"What?"

"If I can't convince them?"

"No loose ends. Korlemo's location must remain secret."

He saluted with two right fingers. "Yes, boss."

Before Rhogan headed for the backyard, Abioye scurried over to them.

"Can I speak with you?" he asked.

Unsure who he meant, Zainabu asked, "Which one of us?"

Gazing at Rhogan, Abioye said, "Well, either."

Her eyes squinted. "Why? What do you want?" Zainabu didn't feign patience. Living with the Ibori taught her Abioye had little influence over Korlemo and a lowly position in the household. He spent his time simpering over his neurotic wife and dowdy daughters.

Abioye's face relaxed. "My family hasn't... Well, we need blood. No one has provided our allotment for a week."

"I'm sorry," Zainabu said, "but it's not my responsibility. Have you spoken with Korlemo?"

In an apologetic voice, Abioye said, "He told me to speak with you." His eyes appealed to Rhogan.

"Right now, I have to take care of something for the boss lady. Later, I'll see what I can do."

"Oh, thank you. I would greatly appreciate it," Abioye said before scampering off.

Rhogan shook his head. "Hard to believe he's related to Korlemo."

"The brothers differ significantly."

"No joke." He left.

Zainabu headed for the study. Her hand hovered over the door when a thought occurred. *Where's Enu?*

"He bears watching."

She'd eliminated Zorulo. It required great expense. Fortunately, with the generous salary Korlemo provided, she'd been able to acquire the necessary materials.

It would take tremendous guile to remove a vampire of Korlemo's strength. She only needed to send Zorulo back to *duka mali*. Korlemo must be physically killed. A difficult task given his longevity and prowess.

And Dayo. She sighed.

Tread carefully.

Korlemo's affection for his wife surprised Zainabu.

How to kill Korlemo without arousing Dayo's suspicions?

"And Enu's no fool." In fact, he was quite intelligent. But where did his loyalties lie? Though he displayed obeisance, Zainabu doubted his sincerity.

"He doesn't trust me."

Too many enemies in this house.

"First, talk to Korlemo. Next, find out what Enu has been up to."

Chapter 41

T REES SPED AWAY ALONG the narrow country road.

"Drop me at the gate," Makeda said, glancing at Meria.

"Why?"

"Because there's a family meeting, and you're not invited."

Meria executed a sharp turn. then a sudden stop in front of a six-foot wire fence. "That's not fair. All day I've shuttled you around looking for apartments. Now you send me away like a chauffeur."

"We've discussed this before," Makeda said, exiting the sedan.

"We've been best friends since kindergarten," Meria said, addressing her through the open car door. "I know about the mwindaji and your sorcery."

Makeda frowned. "See, that's the problem." She slammed the door shut. "You don't know how to keep quiet."

As the passenger window scrolled down, Meria asked, "Have I ever revealed your secret to anyone?"

Her face softening, Makeda said, "No, you haven't. You're a great friend."

"See. I'm almost family."

"Yes, you are."

"So, how about a favor for a sister?" Meria raised her eyes suggestively.

"I'm not casting a spell on a nurse because you don't like her."

"It's not that. She's incompetent and should be disciplined."

"And you wonder why I won't teach you magic."

"I'd be a good witch."

Chuckling, Makeda said, "You'd cast spells on anyone who caused you the tiniest inconvenience."

"I would not." Meria leaned across the seat. "Is Daniel here or in California?"

"He won't be back until the holiday. He has a company to run."

"Dammit," Meria said, striking the dashboard. "We should plan a girl's trip to San Francisco."

How can I tell Meria that Daniel isn't interested?

"Sure."

"Is he still dating that model?"

Frowning, Makeda asked, "How did you know he had a girl-friend?"

Meria shrugged. "You have your magic, and I have mine."

As her friend drove away, Makeda sauntered up to the house. The idea of her best friend stalking her brother who lived three thousand miles away would take further consideration. Presently, the mwindaji were meeting, and a glance at her watch showed she was late. She ran up to the house.

"Where you been?" Dad asked, giving her a light peck on the cheek.

"Meria and I checked out apartments in Asheville." Makeda removed her shoes, placing them in a closet beside the front door.

He pouted. "You're gonna break your momma's heart. First Peter, now you."

She hugged Dad's arm and escorted him into the living room. "Don't worry. Thomas will never leave home."

He playfully swatted her arm as Makeda greeted her cousins.

People conversed, gathering chairs around a comfy couch decorated with flowery pillows in the center of the room facing a stone fireplace. After grabbing a glass of water, Makeda sat on the ground in front of the fireplace. A Labrador rested on each side of her.

"Everyone, please be seated." Dad rested in a recliner on the other side of the living room. His right foot rested on a settee. "First, I want to thank everyone for coming to Peter's wedding. It meant a lot to him and Brenda—not to mention Judith and I."

"That's what family does," Uncle John said.

"And they had good food," Raymond said from the kitchen where he ate ribs.

Several people laughed.

"Business first." Dad turned to Peter. "What did Daniel find out?"

Because his left arm remained in a sling, Peter asked Zeke to give each person a stapled stack of papers. "I printed enough for everyone. Daniel located several overseas bank accounts. He temporarily moved the money to other accounts under fictitious names until we decide what to do."

Massaging his thin mustache, Aaron said, "What's to think about? Let's split the money."

"It's not that easy," Nyesha said. "You of all people know money can be traced. Besides, do we split the money between families or by person?"

"Daniel moved the funds into new accounts," Aaron said, reviewing the paper. "We can establish their bona fides."

Dad sat up straighter in the recliner. "Is that true?" His wrinkled forehead questioned.

Peter nodded. "But we're talking about a quarter of a million dollars. Someone's going to come looking for that money, and we don't want unwanted attention."

"They'll come looking even if we leave it there," Keenan said, glancing at Aaron, who gave a thumbs-up sign.

"That's why we need a plan," Uncle John said, speaking from the kitchen table where he had joined Raymond.

"Let's leave it for now," Zeke said. "What about the cash?"

"A tad under two hundred thousand in unmarked, non-sequential bills." Peter slid a suitcase across the wooden floors with his foot.

The dogs circled the package and sniffed. They eventually returned to Makeda. She spied a glance at Brian, who smiled.

'Are we going to tell them about the bank accounts from Jules and Sylvia?'

'No, it'll cause new problems, especially since we let them go.'

'Did you contact the doctor in Ramsey yet?'

"I'll call Michael tonight. He and Dr. Bones are friends. Let's leave the mwindaji out of this decision.'

'Your call.'

Brian knitted his fingers together behind his head and reclined against the couch cushions.

"No matter what you say about werewolves, they sure know how to launder money," Aaron snickered.

"James, what do you suggest?" Uncle John asked Dad.

"We split the cash." Dad rose and lifted the suitcase onto the coffee table. He opened the case and began distributing bundles of bills.

"Wait a minute," Zeke interjected.

Joining Dad at the coffee table, he asked, "Are we sharing this equally?"

Dad frowned. "Of course."

"But we don't split the expenses equally." Zeke gazed down upon the bills.

"He's right," Carolyn said. "We pay for Maybelline's gas and maintenance, and Zeke secures silver for our weapons."

Aaron came forward and picked up a bundle of cash. "Y'all never asked for help before."

"Because none was available." Carolyn glared at him.

"Oh, but now," Aaron countered, "we find money, y'all suddenly need it."

The two squared off, when Dad said, "Sit down."

Neither moved.

"I said sit."

Sulkily, Carolyn joined her dad and brother at the kitchen table. Aaron tossed the cash bundle onto the suitcase and retreated behind the couch.

"We didn't take an oath to fight as mwindaji to get rich," Dad said, eyeing each mwindaji in turn.

Mumbling, Keenan said, "We didn't do it to become poorer either."

Dad glowered, and Keenan apologized.

"This..." Dad pondered. "This windfall should be distributed to those with ongoing expenses for our campaigns. Then, we'll distribute the remaining funds equally."

"And the overseas accounts?" Keenan wiped his glasses with his shirttail.

"Aaron and Daniel will work together," Dad said. "The two of them should be able to cleanse it—or hide it or now. As needs demand, we'll use it."

His words hung in the air while each person seemed to weigh their options.

"Time to vote," Dad said. "All in agreement, raise a hand." Because each hand shot up, Dad hobbled back to his recliner. "John, what expenses do you have?"

"Well, Maybelline's around twenty years old. She needs—"

"Uncle John," Aaron said, "how about buying a new RV?"

The look Uncle John shot Aaron made Makeda giggle.

"Just 'cause something's old, doesn't mean it's not useful. Besides, new RVs have traceable technology."

"And," Zeke added, "it's easier to fix the older models and customize them to our particular needs."

"The engineer has spoken." Keenan rose and picked up a bundle of cash. "So, how much Uncle John?"

An hour later, after the cash had been distributed, people wandered around the home engaging in smaller conversations, discussing Peter's wedding, the money, and an assortment of other topics.

In the kitchen, a half dozen crowded around the stove preparing plates of food. Makeda sat at the kitchen island nibbling on a salad. Since the incident with the refrigerator in Ramsey, she acquired a more vegetarian appetite.

"Nyesha, you driving back tonight?" she asked.

"Yeah, girl. I got a date." Nyesha winked. "I'm making a plate to go," she said, covering the plate with cling wrap. "Keenan, you ready?"

From the corner of her eye, Makeda noticed Peter, Thomas, and Carolyn conversing in an isolated far corner of the living room by a window. Curious, she wandered over.

"I'm telling you," Carolyn said, pointing, "she's trouble."

Makeda followed the direction of Carolyn's finger, but with people wandering around she couldn't ascertain who they referred to.

"What do you expect me to do?" Thomas asked. "Talk to Aaron."

"You're closer to Aaron. Y'all are cousins." Turning her back to the rest of the room, Carolyn's voice lowered, "Look, we know your dad's health is precarious. He can't lead this group much longer."

Peter's back straightened, and his face hardened.

Oblivious, Carolyn continued, "She's putting us at risk."

"Who?" Makeda asked, joining their conference.

"Zina," Carolyn said.

As Peter and Carolyn glared at each other, Makeda asked, "What exactly are you worried about?"

Carolyn said, "She's on social media communicating with alleged mwindaji groups."

"She knows about the restrictions," Peter said.

"Apparently not."

"I-I don't want to seem like we're ganging up on her," Thomas said, gazing out the window.

Peter inched closer to Carolyn. "I don't appreciate your comment about Dad."

"Like I care. This concerns the mwindaji, not your feelings."

Stepping between them, Makeda said, "I'll speak with her."

"Good." Carolyn started to leave, then pivoted around. "Because if you don't, she's going to cause serious problems."

"Wait." Makeda waved Carolyn back. "I want to discuss Michael joining the group."

"Why?" Peter asked. "We don't need him."

"Why not?" Carolyn asked, crossing her muscular arms over her chest. "He proved himself in Ramsey."

"He wants to help," Makeda quickly interjected, "and he has connections with law enforcement."

"We're not going back to Ramsey," Peter said. "If they want to live with monsters, let 'em."

"He's not joining to help Ramsey. In fact, he quit his sheriff job. He lives in Atlanta now. But he wants to help, and he understands the gravity of the situation."

"No." Peters' lips shut firmly.

"The sheriff helped us out twice," Carolyn said. "Besides, we need new recruits. Between my dad's bad feet, and your dad's gout, we've essentially lost two members."

"Dad's fine," Peter huffed.

Makeda's left brow arched. He turned aside.

"This isn't about our fathers." As he walked away, Peter said, "It's up to the group."

Within the hour, most of the mwindaji had departed. Makeda helped Dad clean up the kitchen.

"When's Mom coming home?" she asked, rinsing off a dish.

"She's spending the week with your Aunt Mirlande." He handed her a saucepan. "It's nice to have time to myself."

Grinning, Makeda didn't challenge his statement. Surrounded by family and friends at Peter's wedding, Dad had basked in the celebration. The mwindaji left an hour ago, and with Mom gone for another week, the quiet house would leave him feeling abandoned. But an ex-Vietnam vet wouldn't admit to missing his wife.

"Go sit down," she said. "I'll make hot chocolate."

He thanked her and exited the house. From the living room window, she watched him rocking on the front porch.

While pouring boiling milk into a mug, words broadcast in her mind.

'Where have you been?'

Her hand slipped and scalding milk splashed on her hand and shirt. Makeda dropped the saucepan and ran cool water over her hand.

'Don't yell at me.'

'I'm trying to protect you, silly child.'

'I'm not training until you explain why a demon wants to kill me.'

I can't let her know what Samuel revealed.

Makeda wanted to protect him—if possible.

'There's no time.'

'For twenty years, this demon could have killed me. Why now?'

'Because you revealed your location in Kentucky with kasi kasi.'

'That occurred months ago, and yet, I'm here.'

Makeda awaited a reply. When nothing came, she prepared the hot chocolate and joined her dad on the patio.

Remember to call Michael.

She wondered how the mwindaji's decision would affect their relationship. Feelings would have to wait.

Why was a demon trying to kill her great-grandmother? And should she help, or leave Yewande to her own fate?

It hurt to learn Yewande had lied, yet Makeda empathized with her great-grandmother's limited options.

If a demon killed me once, I might become desperate.

Makeda realized Yewande wouldn't be honest unless compelled to do so. She had no leverage though. Or did she?

Chapter 42

I N A MANSION OF vampires and werewolves, the household thrived at night. People entered and exited in search of entertainment or food. Zainabu waited until Sherman and Rhogan departed. She watched Korlemo enter the study with his brother before she slipped upstairs.

Inside her bedroom, Zainabu dashed into the closet, knocking clothes aside. She nestled in a dark corner and dragged a square trunk from behind suitcases. With the beetle-shaped talisman, she unlocked the trunk and removed the book of zaubers.

Once she whispered an incantation and the book opened, Zainabu reviewed the list of ingredients for a binding spell. It wouldn't kill but merely incapacitate Korlemo long enough for her to stab him with the poisoned dagger.

This has to work.

Carefully, she returned the book to the trunk. She looped the beetle talisman onto a gold chain around her neck and exited the closet.

Peeking around the bedroom door, Zainabu hurried into the empty hallway. At the rear door leading to the backyard, she scanned the surroundings. Confident of being alone, Zainabu zipped outside and dashed into the woods.

For probably the millionth time, she wondered why magical spells required herbs to be gathered at night. Busy dealing with the security team, she'd been unable to acquire the other items needed for the binding spell before tonight. Unsure if it would work on Korlemo, Zainabu at least wanted to try.

Who would be a worse taskmaster, Korlemo or Zorulo?

She had dealt swiftly with the demon. He treated her as less than a zauber. *Fool.*

A hundred meters from the mansion, Zainabu slowed to a brisk walk. Bolstered by her success with removing Zorulo, she considered a contingency plan in case Korlemo proved indestructible. Complacency could be a death sentence.

Korlemo's mood vacillated like this Michigan weather.

Presently, the vampire considered her an asset. In fact, he paid her a generous salary to secure his new accommodations and deal with the security detail. Zainabu neglected the former but had hired Rhogan to protect the family. No reason to find Korlemo a new home when she planned to kill him here.

Her chest lightened, and Zainabu practically skipped around the forest searching for herbs and mushrooms. The dense tree canopy prevented little moonlight from reaching the forest floor. With a pocket light, Zainabu navigated between the brush, scanning the base of trees for supplies.

She tucked plantings into a satchel, then noticed a rabbit crouching beside a bush. As the foolish critter nibbled innocently on a leaf, Zainabu deftly knocked it on the head with a stone. After securing the rabbit, she hiked back to the mansion.

Forty meters from the house, Zainabu heard voices. Slowing her gait, she strained to understand the conversation.

"But Father," a male voice said, "you and Mother cannot stay."

A minute elapsed before Zainabu distinguished each voice.

"Take your brothers and sister," Enu said. "Build a life for yourselves. Achieve all you have dreamed of."

"I won't leave you and Mother here," the male voice said. "When Uncle finds out—"

"Do not worry. Your mother and I can care for ourselves. We have for many years even before your uncle condemned us to live as mobowou."

Zainabu inched closer and tripped over a vine.

"Did you hear something?" Enu's eyes scanned the woods.

Seconds passed.

"Come." Enu guided his son toward the house. "We must be careful. Before..."

Afraid of detection, Zainabu did not follow and thus failed to hear the rest of Enu's conversation. But as the pair entered a clearing, she recognized Fatou.

I knew it.

She had suspected Enu of duplicity, but now, she had proof.

Of what though?

Korlemo would demand evidence. Not only was Enu his brother, but Korlemo understood that most of the Ibori household adored Enu. Though they feared the patriarch, they loved the second son.

How can I use this?

On the way back to the mansion, Zainabu considered various scenarios. While she had decided to notify Korlemo of Enu's scheming, a way to capitalize on the information eluded her.

Instead of approaching the house from the side door, Zainabu cut across the backyard, skirting around the pool. The household generally entered from the porch deck, and she wanted to concoct her binding spell before daybreak.

As she passed the pool house, Dayo popped out from behind a tree.

Startled, Zainabu grabbed her chest. "Where did you come from?"

"Look what the night has conjured up. Out cooking up spells? Gathering herbs?" Dayo sneered and pointed at Zainabu's bag. "Planning to poison me again?"

Zainabu maintained one eye on the vamp while advancing toward the door. She didn't want a fight. The binding spell must be completed before dawn.

The fact that I intend to poison Korlemo, not her, wouldn't appease this vicious vamp.

"I didn't poison you. If you'd listened to me, you wouldn't have become ill."

"Lying bitch." The words slithered on Dayo's tongue. "You may have enraptured my husband, but I see the truth."

"You're crazy." Zainabu rushed for the door. "I have to speak with Korlemo. It's urgent."

Snatching her by the arm, Dayo said, "Not a chance. Your influence over my husband ends tonight."

Yanking herself free, Zainabu said, "You stupid cow. I'm not interested in Korlemo. It's my job to protect him."

"He does not need protection from a ghetto witch." Dayo grabbed a handful of Zainabu's braids and tossed her across the grassy yard.

Landing on her hands and knees, Zainabu climbed off the ground. Her chest heaved. "Crazy vampire!" She pushed the air forward with her hands, slamming Dayo against the mansion's stone wall.

Dayo's head smacked the stones. Shrieking, she morphed into a vampire, standing over two meters in height. Elongated, clawed fingers reached forward as Dayo flew at Zainabu.

With a shout, Zainabu recanted a spell submerging the area around them in complete darkness. As Dayo stumbled across the grass, Zainabu crawled along the ground to escape and reach the mansion. Aware of the vampire's acute sense of smell, she released the frightened rabbit from the satchel. As soon as the creature's feet touched the ground, it scampered away.

Dayo chased after it.

During the distraction, Zainabu scrambled up the stone patio. One of Zainabu's shoes crossed the threshold when two clawed hands ripped her off the ground. Like a rag doll, Dayo hurled her across the lawn and into a tree.

After crashing into the tree's trunk, leaves showered Zainabu as she crumbled to the ground. Blood trickled down her arms from scratches caused by the tree trunk. She struggled to rise as the vampire attacked again.

"Enough!" Zainabu cast a series of spells, punching Dayo in quick succession about the face and torso.

Wiping blood from her mouth with the back of her hand, Dayo said, "When I finish with you—fucking witch—you will regret ever meeting Korlemo."

Like lightning, the vampire rushed at the tree, seized Zainabu around the neck, and squeezed.

Chapter 43

ORCHESTRAL MUSIC FILLED THE living room. Korlemo reclined on the couch sipping bourbon.

The pianist finished the composition and performed another. As Richard Wagner's *The Valkyrie* reached a crescendo, Korlemo slammed down his goblet.

"Insufferable." He strode up to the piano. "Give me this." He snatched up the music papers. "I don't want to listen to Wagner."

Trembling, the pianist jumped off the bench. With bowed head, he asked, "What shall I play?"

"Brahms, Rachmaninoff, Chopin."

Trembling, the pianist searched among the sheets of music. "I...I don't see anything by those composers."

"*Are you an imbecile?*" Korlemo shouted, slamming down the piano seat lid. "A musician should be able to play from memory."

"But I'm not a musician," the man said, his voice barely audible.

"Who are you?" Korlemo asked, glaring at the man.

"The gardener."

"What?" Korlemo leered at the man, who retreated and bumped into a wall. "Where's Enu? I need a musician."

As the pianist-gardener fled the living room, Abioye entered.

"Brother, I must speak with you."

"Not now!" Korlemo shouted. "I need a pianist. Where's Enu? It is his responsibility to attend to my needs."

Creeping slowly up to him, Abioye said, "Please, this is important."

"Nothing takes precedence over my peace. How can I relax without music?"

"I will turn on the radio."

"I do not want manufactured noise. A king has musicians to serenade him and calm his nerves."

"Listen." Abioye joined his brother on one of several couches situated around the grand room. "My family is starving."

"What?" Korlemo asked, refilling his goblet with bourbon.

"We have not received our allotment of blood. Nothing for the past week."

Shrugging, Korlemo returned to the couch. "And how does this affect me? Discuss this with Sherman. He manages security."

"I did."

"So, it is handled."

"No, Brother. He referred me to Mr. Rhogan."

Korlemo crossed his legs and removed a piece of lint from his slacks. "I do not see how this concerns me."

"Brother, my wife and daughters starve while you refuse to intervene." Abioye grimaced, his face strained with grief.

"I told you not to marry her."

"Please. Do not insult my wife."

"She is beautiful, but your daughters... They inherited neither their mother's beauty nor the Ibori strength."

"They are lovely like their mother."

"What purpose does beauty serve?" Korlemo regarded his brother. "Outside of securing a good marriage, it matters not."

"My family matters to me," Abioye said, clutching his chest.

"Then you all can sit around and look at each other. Perhaps that will satiate your hunger."

"Why are you being cruel?"

Korlemo chuckled. "Simply toying with you, Brother. What do you require?"

"Food," Abioye said, raising his voice.

"Tell Sherman—"

Gesticulating, Abioye said, "He will not assist me without a direct order from you."

"Hunt on your own," he said, stressing each word.

"My wife and daughters cannot hunt. They are—"

Yawning, Korlemo said, "I know. Delicate and beautiful." He walked over to the piano.

"Why must I beg for simple sustenance?" Abioye asked, following behind him.

"Unfortunately, you married foolishly. Your wife gave you daughters." Korlemo tapped along the piano's ivories. "What can a daughter do for her father other than to marry well and provide a dowry? You should have unloaded them years ago."

Tears pooled in Abioye's eyes. "If I must beg, I will. Please. My family needs—"

"Food! I heard you!" Korlemo shouted.

Sherman ran into the living room. "Yo, boss."

"What did you say?" Korlemo glowered, rising from the piano and baring his canines. "I have explained before not to address me disrespectfully. This is not—"

"Shut up and listen," Sherman said, his eyes gaping. "Your wife is killing the witch."

Chapter 44

Korlemo's nostrils flared. His eye sockets deepened under a growing overhead brow. He glowered at Sherman and began his vampire changeover when Sherman's words penetrated his conscious mind.

Dayo was attacking Zainabu.

He snarled. "Where?"

Vampiric speed carried Korlemo to the backyard before Abioye or Sherman.

"Dayo, no!" He bolted over to his wife, who clutched Zainabu about the throat.

Ineffectively, the latter punched the vampire, but the blows landed like raindrops in the ocean.

"Release her!" Korlemo ordered.

Without looking at him, Dayo said, "No." Her grip strengthened.

Zainabu's eyelids fluttered, and her lips purpled.

At his full vampiric stature, Korlemo easily dwarfed his wife. He snatched Dayo by the wrist strangling Zainabu and bent it backwards.

"Ouch!" Dayo screamed, releasing Zainabu.

Crumbled on the ground, the latter coughed and sputtered.

Sherman rushed to Zainabu and helped her stand. Abioye remained on the porch gawking.

"Let me go." Dayo struggled under his grip.

"When I give an order, I expect it to be obeyed," Korlemo said, glaring at his wife.

"No one gives me orders," Dayo said, wrestling to free herself.

"I do," Korlemo gloated.

Dayo bared her teeth at him. "How dare you take the side of a witch over me."

Throwing back his head, Korlemo howled, gnashing his teeth. "While she serves my will, she lives."

He released Dayo. "Now, please, my precious, this jealousy must end. We can live together peacefully."

Sherman assisted Zainabu to the porch and settled her down in a chair. Korlemo bent down to pick a satchel off the ground.

Instantly, Dayo leaped at Zainabu. An inch before the women connected, Korlemo caught his wife by the arm.

"Let go. I will teach this bitch who's in charge."

As Dayo thrashed around in his arms, she slashed his shoulder.

Korlemo screamed. "No more!" He pitched his wife across the yard and into the swimming pool.

Dayo crashed into the pool like a stone. Splashing, she flailed in the water. From the side of the house, Enu dashed to the pool's edge and lifted her out.

Cursing and vowing vengeance, Dayo allowed Enu to cover her with a towel. Drenched and shuddering, Dayo strode up to Korlemo.

Her dark eyes bore into his. "You broke your honor."

Korlemo regressed to his bindimèn form. "Dearest. This is unnecessary."

She shook off his arm and pointed at Zainabu. "That bitch wants you dead. Ask her what she was doing in the woods."

Rising off the patio chair, Zainabu stuck her chin forward. "Collecting herbs."

Dayo sneered. "To poison me."

"I didn't try to poison you," Zainabu sputtered, her voice grainy.

"Liar."

Before Korlemo intervened, Dayo ripped a gold necklace off Zainabu's neck.

Too late, Zainabu reached forward. "Give it back."

"Try and take it." Dayo's eyes slit with a daring glare.

Coughing and fingering her bruised neck, Zainabu said, "I'm a zauber. We collect herbs."

"A witch collects herbs at night to create binding potions or poisons," Dayo insisted.

"Oh, now who's the witch?" Zainabu said snidely.

Dayo bustled forward, but Enu intervened.

"She is right. This *witch*," Enu emphasized the last word, "wishes you harm. Remove her while you still possess your faculties."

"Zainabu has shown no disloyalty to me or my family," Korlemo said, trying to comfort his wife.

Dayo slapped his hands aside. "Then why did I become ill?"

"From drinking the blood of alcoholics," Zainabu said.

"An alcoholic bindimèn would not make Dayo unconscious or ill to the point where she required medical intervention." Enu handed Dayo a fresh towel. "Please do not insult our intelligence."

Straightening her back, Zainabu said, "Fine. I'll leave."

"Wait." Korlemo followed.

"Let her go," Dayo ordered, dropping the towel to the ground and proceeding after him.

In a flash, Korlemo swung around, leering into his wife's face. "This zauber saved our lives in Ramsey, and she located Sylvia." He did a minor changeover, displaying his incisors. "If she leaves, will you do for me what she does?"

Smirking, Dayo said, "But of course, my husband. I have been stroking your ego for the past thousand years."

Korlemo raised his hand to strike Dayo when Enu grabbed his arm.

"How dare you touch me," Korlemo demanded.

Stoically, Enu said, "I will not allow you to abuse your wife." He scowled at Korlemo before releasing his arm.

"Forgive me." Korlemo took Dayo's hand and kissed it.

Shouldering past him, Dayo entered the mansion, and Enu assisted her upstairs to the master suite.

"I will send Nambi," Enu said and departed.

Water dripped from Dayo's afro. Nambi helped her undress. Korlemo stood at the doorway, observing the two women.

"Can I run you a bath?" Nambi asked, unzipping Dayo's dress.

Shaking her head, Dayo gazed in the mirror, inspecting bruising along her cheeks. "My husband sided with a witch over me. What does life mean to me?"

Korlemo hurried over and kneeled beside her chair. "Untrue." He kissed her knees. "I have loved no woman since the day we wed."

Dayo glanced down at her hand. A gold necklace with a beetle charm dangled between her fingers. She tossed it on the countertop.

"What is that?" Nambi asked.

"Cheap trash. I don't know what your ghetto witch does with her money," she said, looking at him, "but she doesn't spend it on quality jewelry."

"What can I do to show my undying commitment to our love, my sweet?" he asked, palming her hands in his.

"I want her out of this house." Dayo raised her chin.

"Done." Korlemo kissed her lips.

Nambi smiled. "Shall I return the necklace?"

"No," Dayo said, picking it up and studying it. "If she wants it, she can come beg me for it." She cut a glance at him.

Korlemo nodded. "Agreed."

Dayo grinned and squeezed the necklace in her hand.

Chapter 45

Two dark stretch limousines cruised down Sixth Avenue away from Central Park. August in New York City broiled. Buildings trapped hot air inside and blocked any cool breezes. Abigail intended to be in and out of the city expeditiously. She checked her Patek Philippe watch.

"Pull over at the next corner. We can walk from there." Dressed in knee-high boots and an above-knee wrap dress, Abigail exited the car surrounded by four people.

They entered a brick building with a doorman. Inside, a security officer approached, his hand hovering over a weapon. One associate spoke with the officer while Abigail and the others walked over to a hall with two elevators.

An elevator arrived and whisked Abigail and her three associates away. With a small ping, the doors opened and deposited them on the tenth floor. As the doors parted, three werewolves exploded out of the lift and across the hall. They flew into the office before the guard managed to secure the steel-reinforced double doors.

One of the werewolves clutched the man's head in a wrestling hold and snapped his neck. The guard crumbled onto the polished tiled floors as people scattered into the office space. Cries and pleas rippled throughout the floor.

Abigail followed, stepping disinterestedly over discarded bodies. Along the way, she snapped her finger directing her henchmen who to kill.

People were snatched from their desks. A few attempted to flee but Abigail's men systematically corralled and exterminated them.

Strutting behind them, Abigail bellowed commands. With the outer office secured, she stormed through a wooden door at the end of a long hallway decorated with plaques and trophies. Abigail ignored the photos of herself, Stefan, Sylvia, and Jules. Their friendship had ended. Destroyed by...

Abigail immediately realized she had no idea what had changed Sylvia's and Jules' opinions about the project.

Doesn't matter now.

She pointed. One of the werewolves kicked the door aside. It splintered and crashed to the floor.

"Kill him." Abigail pointed at the clerk seated at the reception desk.

The werewolf who broke down the door leaped at the man. The clerk managed to shoot the werewolf in the shoulder.

With a minor grunt, the werewolf chomped into the clerk's throat. The man's head lolled backward. Blood spurted across the desk. The werewolf spit out the trachea and inspected his wounded shoulder.

Abigail's stride didn't waver. Shrieks, screams, and footsteps trailed behind her. She trekked down a shorter hallway and up to a door with a bronze plaque that read *Chief Operating Officer, Jules Senegal.*

Quiet descended around her. With a brief glance down at her hand, Abigail squared her shoulders and turned the knob. Inside, she paused.

Bright sunlight streamed in from a wall of windows. Blinking as her eyes adjusted, Abigail surveyed the executive suite.

"Where is he?"

She stomped over to the desk and rifled through drawers, tossing papers everywhere.

The injured werewolf joined her.

"Check the bookshelves. Look for hidden recesses."

He did as ordered.

Abigail checked her wristwatch. "Damn. We're almost out of time."

She collapsed onto a plush leather chair and viewed papers strewn across the floor. "Where would Jules have hidden—"

Knock, knock.

Someone entered, but Abigail didn't bother turning around.

"Anything?" she asked, gazing out the pristine windows at the Manhattan skyline.

"Nope." A young man with locks, wearing a three-piece tailored suit sat at the desk across from her.

Eventually, Abigail swiveled the leather chair around and faced him. "I hate your hair. It looks like shit."

"I hate your style. It lacks finesse."

"You mean this?" She pointed to the papers lying at her feet.

"And out there. Such a waste—and unnecessary."

She shrugged. "Perhaps."

"Have you ever heard the phrase, 'You catch more flies with honey?'" he asked, extending his legs under the desk.

"And I can kill a ton of mwindaji with a bomb rather than a gun." She rose and paced around the office. "But guns are in greater supply, and I want the people who killed my brother."

"The mwindaji killed Stefan, not these people."

"They helped Jules escape. Kill them, find him."

"Well, he's not here. What next, Cuz?"

She frowned. "Don't call me that."

"Now, you're giving *me* attitude?"

"Knox, we have to find Jules."

"Why can't we proceed without him?"

"Because Jules has the information required for the next phase. And he's the sole person who can contact all the cells. He holds vital information."

Two werewolves entered.

"The place is locked down. Who do you want to question first?"

"Anyone in management."

One of the werewolves shook his head. "No go. Only clerical staff remain. Jules dismissed everyone else a week ago."

Abigail frowned. "Who told you that?"

A burly werewolf entered, dragging a shivering man along the ground. He slung the man along the carpet up to the desk.

"Tell her," the werewolf demanded in a garbled voice.

"Umm." Trembling, the terrified man froze.

Kneeling beside him, Abigail touched his shoulder. "Don't be afraid. I won't let them hurt you."

Gradually, the man's tremulousness decreased. Abigail helped him to a chair and offered him water.

"Now," she said, sitting beside him and crossing her legs, "what can you tell me about Mr. Jules Senegal."

"I-I don't know anything." The man gulped water. "He only hired me last week."

"For what?" she asked. "What's your position here?"

"Answering phones as an office clerk."

While he finished drinking, Abigail nodded. "Do you know any of the long-term employees?"

"Most of the staff are new hires—like me."

"Have you met Mr. Senegal—or his sister?"

The man shook his head rapidly making his eyes jostle. "I didn't know he had a sister."

"I see." Abigail rose and slowly circled the room. "Tell me about the past week. Have there been many phone calls?"

"No, not business calls anyway." He placed the glass on a side table. "A few wrong numbers."

"What have you been doing then?" she asked, spinning around and scrutinizing the man.

"Well, we've been shredding documents, filing, mailing packages."

Abigail's gaze sharpened. "Where have you mailed these packages?"

Slightly cowering, the man said, "To the addresses provided by the supervisor."

She approached the man, holding his gaze. "Where's this supervisor now?"

"I-I don't know."

As the werewolves closed in, he mumbled, "Probably at lunch."

Sitting beside him, Abigail asked, "Do you know how to contact the supervisor?"

Sweating, the clerk said, "No."

"Well, we'll simply have to wait for... Is it a man or woman?"

"Woman."

She grinned. "Then we'll wait for her to return."

With a nod, Abigail directed the werewolves to escort the man out of the private office.

"Wait with him in the back of the limo. When the woman returns..." She clenched her fist.

One of the werewolves nodded and escorted the clerk out. This time, they permitted the clerk to walk on his own two feet.

At the desk, Abigail stared out the window.

"Thoughts?" Knox asked.

"Sylvia disguised as the supervisor?"

"Possible. Highly unlikely." He stretched and strolled around the office. "Jules knows you're desperate to get the information. He wouldn't chance you finding Sylvia."

"True. But Sylvia thinks she's clever. I can imagine her returning to the office, verifying all valuable information has been removed."

Knox shook his head. "No way."

She spun around. "Doesn't matter. We'll stick with the plan." Abigail consulted her watch. "The authorities will be notified soon."

After retrieving her purse, which she had absently tossed on the desk, she headed for the exit.

"I'll leave two guys to help you. Give the supervisor an hour to return. If she does, bring her to the house."

"Otherwise, kill the worker and return to the estate."

She cleaned a drop of blood off her boots. "Correct. Deal with the remaining staff and gather anything possibly related to Jules or Sylvia.

Before Knox replied, she departed.

Chapter 46

I N THE DARK ROOM, light from a television illuminated a tiny area of the floor. Sufficient illumination for Sylvia to navigate around the room.

It looked tolerable in the dark.

Accustomed to well-apportioned accommodations with servants, this roadside motel barely qualified as housing.

No time to grumble. Focus on your enemy and strategize next steps.

Papa would be proud of her. Or would he?

Sylvia's precipitous actions caused the present feud with the Baptistes. The mwindaji served as a mere distraction which allowed her time to flee. Korlemo hadn't forgotten though. The longer it took for him to find her, the greater his rage.

Life doesn't rewind.

She had to move forward. Concentrate on her and Jules.

"What're you watching?" she asked, perching on a corner of the queen-sized bed.

"News," Jules said, increasing the volume.

"Turn on the light."

Jules switched on the bedside lamp.

Sylvia regarded the multi-floral bed comforter. Her expression soured. "This place is a dump."

"It's cheap." Jules leaned forward.

"Anything from the office?" she asked while completing a crossword puzzle.

"Shush. They're talking about the raid."

The television broadcaster announced, "Authorities haven't determined a motive behind the violent attack on employees at Senegal, Mangus, and Courtland. The boutique investment firm handled a limited client base with..."

Sylvia learned nothing beyond what their business partners messaged.

Jules decreased the volume. "The media isn't saying much, but the authorities—"

"Aren't our concern," she said, tossing the crossword puzzle aside. "We need to know what, if anything, Abigail discovered."

"I dismissed any staff aware of key details. They're hiding out."

"Abigail's clever." Sylvia absently stabbed the bed comforter with a pen. "And ruthless."

"Unless someone talks, she'll get nothing. I kept pertinent details hidden. Mom said never trust anyone a hundred percent."

Sylvia's eyes misted. "Except family."

Jules playfully tossed a pillow at her.

"Don't." She sniffed it. "It stinks."

He chuckled, scooted back against the headboard, and perused a takeout menu.

"Hungry?"

She moaned. "Not for that crap."

"Hey." He discarded the menu and moved beside her. "We'll overcome this." He lifted her chin. "We have to."

With a lopsided grin, she said, "Because we're Senegals."

"Exactly." He kissed her forehead. "Look."

Jules retrieved a suitcase from the closet, opened a front compartment, and displayed its contents. "Passports. Burner phones. Cash. Everything we need to start over."

"With the Baptistes on our trail. Oh, and let's not forget Korlemo."

"They know security and weapons, but we understand money and influence." He rubbed her shoulder. "We'll survive."

She gazed into his face. "I wish you'd come with me."

He stood and ambled around the diminutive space. "Can't. This originated with us. It's our responsibility to dismantle the program."

"Why? Without our intel, Abigail can't proceed."

"You weren't there as she stood by while Stefan executed our cousins. She's obsessed."

Sylvia grasped him by the arm. "It's dangerous. A fanatically committed Baptiste with access to weapons *and* Korlemo."

"Obsession limits her outlook." Jules gently removed her hand. "Besides, she hates Korlemo like we do."

Jules absently picked up the menu. "Once I know you're safe, I'll work on destroying the organization."

"How?" she asked, leaning on her hip. "Individuals, institutions. It took time and a lot of negotiating to reach this point. Other people became involved who have serious interests in seeing our program succeed."

"We started this—you, me, and Stefan." Jules tapped the menu. "It would've created a world where lupasteri existed freely, without restrictions or discrimination."

"They bastardized it." Sylvia's jaw clenched. "They twisted it to their personal machinations to destroy bindimèn and control mobowou."

"We made a mistake, but identified the error."

"Did we?"

Jules frowned. "What do you mean?"

"Stefan wanted lupasteri to dominate the United States. He's dead, and we have no idea what he's done. Can it be stopped?"

"If we move quickly. We wanted lupasteri and bindimèn to live symbiotically. Stefan and Abigail perverted our goals to create a superrace. A path toward lupasteri domination."

"I believe they've already converted key personnel toward their inclinations."

Jules sighed. "It originated with us. We must destroy it."

"You don't owe anyone an apology, especially not bindimèn." Sylvia arched her back in a yoga pose. "Did you forget? They butchered our father and brothers."

"Would you expect less given the fact we've been feeding off them for decades? Centuries. Well, practically since forever."

"Survival of the fittest."

"Darwinian?"

She waved dismissively. "You know what I mean."

"Do you regret not helping Stefan and Abigail?"

"No, they're fanatics. But that doesn't mean I sympathize with bindimèn."

Sylvia flopped on the bed and continued the crossword puzzle.

"They saved my life—at least the zauber did." He stretched out on the bed beside her. "She could've left me there."

"They traded your life for Korlemo's location."

"No." He stared at the ceiling. "She understands there's a larger problem."

"Hardly."

"You worked with her at the hospital, right?" His wide gaze observed her face. "Tell me about her."

She chuckled. "A zauber mwindaji. Talk about an oxymoron."

"I believe," Jules rolled over on his stomach, "she's different."

From the corner of her eye, Sylvia scrutinized her brother. "What do you mean?"

"Not sure. But something about her made me hopeful." He shook his head. "She's powerful. Knocked Abigail right on her ass."

Sylvia laughed. "Wish I'd been there."

His smile faded. "Stefan shot our cousins point blank in their foreheads. He would've tortured me. I don't want to imagine what he would've done to you."

She smacked his back. "Forget it. We're here. And I'm fine." She checked her watch. "Or will be in four hours."

Jules sat up. "This place *is* a dump. Why don't we head out to the airport?"

"Okay." Sylvia packed up their few items. "Sure you don't want to come with me?"

"Positive." He slipped on a sports coat and joined her by the door. "Once you're out of here, I can work freely and not worry about my baby sister."

Chuckling, Sylvia switched off the hotel room light. "Don't underestimate me because I'm younger than you. I'm a force on my own."

On the taxi ride to the airport, Sylvia asked, "You're thinking about that zauber, aren't you?"

"I'm reviewing our plans." His earlobe twitched.

"I know when you're lying."

Jules stared out the window.

She laid a hand on his shoulder and lowered her voice. "The enemy of our enemy remains an enemy." Sylvia's gaze bore into his.

Jules gave a slight nod, but she worried.

As he paid the cabbie, Sylvia exited and gathered their luggage. Side by side, they entered the airport terminal.

"Why didn't you continue on to the international terminal?" he asked.

"I want to make sure you catch your flight."

He received his boarding pass and walked over to a snake-like line of people awaiting screening.

"Go on. They won't let you near the gate without a ticket."

Sylvia studied his face. "Stay away from that zauber."

"Why would I bother with her?" Jules said, his eyes widening. "I know what needs to be done." He glanced up at a scrolling screen of departing flights. "Hurry or you'll miss your plane."

But she didn't move. Instead, Sylvia squeezed his arm. "Listen to me."

His face softened. "Didn't I listen when you told me about Korlemo?" Jules patted her arm. "Once I finish dismantling the program, we'll meet up."

"Agreed?" She held out her hand.

"Absolutely."

They exchanged their secret handshake from childhood. Afterwards, Jules pointed to her ring.

"Remember, Dad gave you this because you're stronger than all of us."

Tears welled in her eyes.

"You must survive Svie, for Papa."

"For the Senegals."

Sylvia watched her brother approach the security checkpoint.

He's not done with that damn zauber.

For a moment, she considered possible actions.

Follow Jules. Kill the zauber.

Her glance fell over the three-jeweled ring from Korlemo's grandfather. The voice of her father echoed in her head.

"Screw it."

She exited the terminal. Jules took priority over her safety.

Chapter 47

B EEPING FROM THE ALARM interrupted Makeda's peaceful slumber. She checked the time and reset the alarm. Propped up on smooth, silk pillows, she gazed out the window.

Blue-black sky hid most of the forest, but she viewed sinewy tree limbs snaking up the side of the cabin. She inhaled and relaxed under the blanket. A warm arm pulled her toward the center of the bed.

"When did you wake up?" she asked.

Michael kissed her neck. "A minute ago."

She wrapped an arm tightly around his waist. "We should get up."

He rolled over on his back. "Why? I haven't rested this well in weeks."

"Rest?" She chuckled. "We've been up all night."

"Yeah, but making love doesn't count as work."

"Not if you simply lie there."

"Wait a minute," he said, sitting up. "I did my part."

Laughing, Michael scooped her up in his arms, kissing her lips.

On the other side of the door, Daisy whined.

"She wants to go for a walk," Michael said.

"You've become quite attached for a man who never wanted a dog."

He frowned. "Is she a problem?"

She smiled and ran her fingers along his curly afro. "I grew up around dogs. They're like family to me." Stretching, Makeda swung her legs over the bed. "Well, let's go give Daisy her exercise."

Sweat trickled down Makeda's back as they jogged up the trail.

"This isn't fair," Michael said. "I'm walking Daisy."

"Don't blame her." Makeda whistled, and Daisy ran to her side. "You've become soft working in an Atlanta office. Even hauling a backpack, I'm faster than you."

Panting, Michael said, "True. We don't get time to exercise like before." He scratched Daisy behind the ears.

With Daisy at her side, Makeda sprinted up the trails. At a bend, she admired the view while he caught up. She patted the German shepherd's head.

"Daisy doesn't want to stay in a stuffy apartment all day. You should let me take her home. She'd love to play with other dogs."

Rolling over on her back, Daisy allowed Makeda to rub her belly. "See. She likes me."

Michael reached the crest of the trail. "No way." He bent over, breathing heavily. "You're not taking my dog."

"I thought you weren't a dog person." She grinned.

"Well, now I am." He retrieved Daisy's leash. "She's my dog. Right, girl?"

Woof.

Makeda shrugged. "For now."

They rested together on an enormous boulder, viewing the vista. Trees flowed down the mountainside and into the valley below.

Michael yawned. "I'm hungry and sleepy."

"Did I keep you up too late last night?"

He hugged her lower back. "How about we walk?" Michael said, gently restraining Daisy.

"Sure." Makeda lightly pecked his lips.

As they descended the trail, Makeda's thoughts flowed from Michael, to home, then Yewande. She hadn't told Michael about the mwindajis meeting, nor about her decision to move out on her own.

He'll appreciate the privacy, but he'll worry about my safety.

Makeda hadn't reached a decision on telling him about sorcery. Their fledgling relationship had survived Ramsey's monsters, but her being a zauber?

And what about sorcery?

She hadn't been able to reach Samuel. Either he deliberately ignored her, or Eldridge warned him to avoid her. Despite what they said, Makeda had decided to embrace her heritage as a zauber and continue working with the mwindaji. She simply hadn't figured out how to do both.

I'll be the first mwindaji zauber—but not if I can't find someone to train me.

"What's going on?" Michael drew her close.

Makeda inhaled the piney air to fortify her resolve. "I need to tell you something."

He glanced over at her. "Okay."

Not easy but it should be.

"You see—"

"Stop it!!"

The shout made them pause.

"Let me go!"

A second later, Michael raced between trees toward the cries. Makeda and Daisy trailed him, speeding through the underbrush and woods. The path opened onto a parking lot where several walking trails converged.

Makeda spotted a man and woman tussling beside an SUV. The man held the woman by the wrist. She held a key in her free hand. Inside the SUV, Makeda noticed a couple kids and another woman.

"Quit it," the woman begged, wrestling to remove his grasp.

"You're not leaving," he snarled, wrenching her forearm backward.

"Ouch! You're hurting me."

Michael crossed the clearing and raced up to the fighting couple.

She paused, detecting a familiar scent. A strong, feral odor filled the air. Makeda recognized it didn't come from Daisy. She first smelled a similar but more earthy scent when the mwindaji tracked a group of lycans in North Carolina around Cape Fear.

As they approached the melee, Daisy's coat bristled. The German shepherd emitted a low growl.

"Steady, girl," Makeda said, rubbing Daisy behind the ears.

"Let her go," Michael insisted, rushing up to the man.

The woman used the moment of distraction to peel the man's hand off her shoulder and rush toward the SUV. A second man, dressed in camo and construction boots blocked her from entering the car.

"Harold," she pleaded, "stop. Not in front of the kids."

"You can't take them from me!" Harold shouted, placing his back against the car door.

"Wait," Makeda said as Michael stormed over to the man. But he hadn't heard or chose to ignore her warning.

"Move." Michael bustled between Harold and the woman.

Harold sneered at Michael. "This isn't your business, boy."

The second man stepped up behind Michael. They boxed him in around the car. "Y'all better leave while ya can."

At the edge of the parking lot, Makeda remained close enough to assist Michael, if necessary, but provided distance if the men decided to leave.

Michael glanced in her direction and she slightly nodded.

"I'm making it my business." Michael pivoted toward the woman. "Can I help?"

Trembling, she hesitated. Strain was etched into her downturned mouth and watery eyes.

"Yes," she feebly croaked.

"What do you need?" Michael asked.

Harold placed a hand in a trouser pocket. Makeda inched closer. The second man spotted her and tromped over to her and Daisy.

As Harold's hand slowly came out of the pocket, Makeda yelled, "Watch out!"

Michael spun around and grabbed Harold's hand, wrenching the man's arm up and around his back. A pocketknife dropped from the man's grasp as Michael wrenched his arm backward.

The second man lashed out at Makeda. His fist flew directly at her face.

Makeda dropped Daisy's leash. She squatted, avoiding his lumbering strike, and kicked his legs out from beneath him.

At the SUV, Michael slammed Harold into the side of the car. It rocked and the kids inside cried.

Frozen, the woman gawked.

"Get in," Michael ordered, hauling Harold away from the SUV.

As if a lightbulb went off, the woman jumped in the car and sped away, kicking up rocks and debris.

Makeda watched the children's moon-shaped eyes gawking as the SUV turned left toward the park's exit.

"Let go of me," Harold demanded.

Once the SUV's parking lights vanished, Michael released the tussling Harold and pushed him aside. The second man, who had already slunk away from Makeda, now joined Harold.

"Y'all gonna regret messing with us," Harold said as he rubbed the arm Michael had twisted.

"I doubt it," Michael said. "Nothing good comes from hurting a woman. You're lucky I'm not sheriff here. I'd lock your ass up for assault."

"Law can't touch us." Harold walked over to a Jeep parked on the other side of the parking lot.

"Careful," Michael said, "you might find out differently."

Harold grinned, sporting a front gold tooth. "I was 'bout to tell you the same thing."

Makeda came forward, touching Michael's arm. "We should go."

Lightly shrugging off her hand, Michael said, "I'm not afraid of this scum."

"Humph. Let's see how brave you are, boy." Harold signaled his friend, who strutted toward them.

The odor intensified. Makeda gently pulled Michael's shirt. Daisy growled and barked, baring her teeth.

"You don't understand. These guys are—"

Before she finished, Harold and his friend transformed into grotesquely huge werewolves.

"Ah, hell," Michael mumbled.

"I tried to tell you," she said, retreating toward the trees.

He gazed at her. "How did you know?"

Barking and snarling, Daisy stood protectively in front of Makeda and Michael.

Bulky crooked teeth garbled Harold's speech. "Now, you'll see what happens when you interfere in other people's business."

The second werewolf howled. "Yeah. Teach this boy to mind his business."

Michael bristled and took a fighting stance. "Any ideas?" he asked, glancing at Makeda.

She handed him a lance. "Try this."

His brows rose questioningly.

"Mwindaji are always prepared," she whispered.

Harold dropped onto all fours and charged. Michael extended the lance and fought the werewolf off. Daisy bit Harold's leg, clamping down with a snap.

"Aww!" Harold kicked at the German shepherd, trying to shake her loose. "Let go you, stupid dog!"

The second werewolf surged at Makeda. She sidestepped his assault and ran into the woods. His noisy clambering between the trees prevented her from hearing Michael or Daisy. Her pulse beat in her ears as she raced up the inclined path.

Heavy breathing from the werewolf drummed in her ears. Twice, he had swiped at her. Makeda zigzagged up the mountainside, placing distance between them and Michael.

Before she reached the clearing, the werewolf dropped from a tree branch, blocking her path. Braking suddenly, Makeda grabbed onto a nearby tree to stop herself from pummeling over the side.

Drooling, the werewolf leered at her. "I haven't eaten human in a month." His burly arms clutched at her.

Cautious of her footing, Makeda dodged his reach.

"This is gonna be good." The werewolf's tongue licked the fur around its mouth.

"Not for both of us."

As he bolted toward her, Makeda summoned her maji and pushed forward. Without making physical contact, she propelled him into a sapling. The immature tree broke, and the werewolf tumbled to the ground.

Roaring, it crouched and attacked.

With her fists, Makeda rapidly punched the air, delivering multiple blows to the lycan's torso.

Dazed, the werewolf halted, shaking its body. "You're a witch."

"You are as stupid as you look." Makeda sprinted up the mountainside.

The werewolf gave chase. At the summit, she stood atop an enormous boulder.

Mockingly, Makeda said, "Are you tired? Poor thing." She pulled a dog treat from her backpack. "Perhaps doggy would like a treat."

In a tackling stance, the werewolf rushed forward.

Makeda held her position. Like a hot wind, the lycan's fur brushed her skin as she somersaulted forward over the beast and onto the path.

Propelled by the velocity of his charge, the werewolf flew over the boulder and tumbled down the mountainside. His cries shattered the once peaceful forest.

After a quick glance below, Makeda sped down the trail.

In a wide arc, Michael swiped at the lycan. Makeda noticed a cut on Michael's flank but no active bleeding.

On the opposite spectrum, the werewolf bled liberally from oozing leg and arm lacerations.

"Get off me," the werewolf howled. With a strong kick, it walloped Daisy. The German shepherd whimpered and slogged aside.

Poking at the werewolf, Michael slipped, lost his balance, and fell on his butt. The lance rolled away out of his reach.

Free of the dog, the werewolf seized the opportunity and pounced on Michael. With his arms, Michael covered his face.

"Ubumi!" Makeda yelled, entering the clearing. She lifted the werewolf off Michael and threw him across the lot.

A dust cloud engulfed the lycan as it slammed onto the dusty gravel.

Makeda dashed for Michael. Daisy limped to his side.

Shaking off dirt and rocks, the werewolf staggered to its feet. "Now, you both die." Like a sumo wrestler, it prepared for another charge.

Sunlight glistened off the silver lance. Daisy crouched beside Michael. He began crawling over to the lance lying three yards away.

As the lycan galloped toward Michael and Daisy, Makeda yelled, "Chekate!"

In a snap, the lance rose off the ground. Using Baoumali, she directed the implement forward. As if she had hurled the pole by hand, it pierced the werewolf's chest.

"Ahh!" The werewolf screamed, clawing at the lance.

Michael gawked. "How'd you do that?"

Makeda did reply but watched the lycan.

Incrementally, it managed to remove the lance. Tossing it aside, the werewolf staggered forward.

Raising her machete, Makeda braced for an assault.

Moaning, the werewolf slumped to the ground feet away from Michael.

The lycan rolled around on the gravel, clutching its wound. In time, it reverted to human form.

Meanwhile, Makeda assisted Michael to a tree stump. She removed items from her backpack and treated his flank. Whining, Daisy rested at his side.

"Got any water?"

She handed him the backpack while dressing his cuts.

Michael cupped his hands, forming a well as Daisy drank.

Periodically, Makeda checked on the lycan, making sure he no longer posed a threat.

"Thanks," Michael said, rising and examining his injuries.

They held each other a moment, gazing upon Harold, who slowly bled out.

"This is crazy."

"It was." She checked his wound. "We need to clean your cut. I have antibiotics back in the cabin."

He eyed her. "Mind telling me how you did that?"

"Later. We need to dispose of him before someone enters the parking lot."

"Yeah. It would be hard to explain a silver pole and a hole in the man's chest."

Makeda retrieved the lance, retracting and securing it in her pack. At the same time, Michael unwrapped a tarp. She inspected Daisy's leg before helping Michael.

"You seriously carry this gear everywhere?" he asked, struggling to maneuver Harold onto the tarp.

"An unprepared mwindaji doesn't live long."

They worked in silence.

Not until they headed up the trail, did Michael ask, "How did you know?"

"I tried to warn you."

"Are you going to answer my question?"

"Let's finish this first." She avoided his gaze. This wasn't how she wanted to explain sorcery to Michael.

They reached the boulder as the sun reached its zenith. Makeda rested as Michael rolled the dead man over the cliff.

He rubbed his injured side. "Ready?"

She nodded. "Time to head back."

"I meant are you ready to explain how you guessed they were werewolves."

"Wait until we get to the cabin. This isn't something to discuss in the open."

Michael hobbled into the living room and crashed on the couch. He reclined on pillows and stretched his legs out along the coffee table.

Since she cleaned up first, Makeda had prepared lunch.

Daisy looked up from her bowl for a moment, then returned to eating.

Makeda carried a tray into the living room.

"Mind moving your feet?"

Once Michael took his feet off the table, she set down the tray.

He guzzled the entire glass of water and devoured the sandwich. "Who knew killing monsters created such an appetite."

She picked at her food. Makeda considered how to explain what happened.

Tell him everything or simply enough to satisfy his immediate curiosity?

Makeda cared for Michael and valued their relationship, but she carried a lot of baggage, not to mention a demon may or may not be after her.

No, she believed Samuel. It made sense Yewande needed her to kill the demon. But why would a demon want to kill her great-grandmother? Should she help? Thoughts tumbled across her mind.

Where to begin? I wouldn't be surprised if he walked away.

The sandwich hung limply in her hands. Makeda's appetite evaporated.

Once Michael finished his sandwich, he exhaled and rested on the couch cushions.

"You haven't answered my question."

"They have a specific smell. Earthy. Like a wet dog, but stronger."

He extended his arms along the back of the couch. "And the throwing a spear without touching it thing?"

"Magic."

His brows raised.

"Actually, sorcery."

"I see." Michael rubbed his chin. "You're a witch."

"Sorceress. We're called zaubers in Baoumali." Makeda offered him her sandwich which he accepted.

Between bites, he asked, "When were you going to inform me?"

Not any time soon, if I had a choice.

In the kitchen, Makeda filled Daisy's food and water bowls. After a quick washup, she carried glasses of soda to the living room.

"This isn't easy." She sat beside him. "I grew up mwindaji, but sorcery is new."

"I exercised and ate." He lifted her legs onto his lap. "Perfect time for a story."

"I wanted to tell you. Promise. But I hadn't found the right time."

He chuckled. "There is no right time."

She studied his profile while drinking. After a long swallow, she said, "I don't understand all of it yet."

He frowned. "Explain."

She sipped water. "Zaubers are rare. Our abilities vary."

"Your brothers?"

She shook her head. "Only me."

"No surprise."

Makeda smiled. "My great-grandmother taught me sorcery before she died."

No reason to share Yewande's brutal murder at this time.

"I didn't restart lessons until Ramsey."

"Perfect timing." He chuckled.

"Like I said, I'm learning, more each day. There's much I don't understand."

"Enough to save my ass."

"It's a nice ass."

He laughed and lifted her onto his lap.

Makeda placed her hand on his chest. "Kidding aside. I care for you, Michael. Too much to let you get involved if you aren't prepared."

"I'm prepared," he said, kissing her neck.

You think so.

Makeda realized Michael had no clue about the serious nature of their work.

Why did this have to happen today?

She climbed off his lap. "Let me check your cut." She examined his shoulder.

"The bandage needs to be changed."

Michael grinned mischievously. "Are we gonna play doctor?"

"I'm a nurse." She cleansed his wounds. "If I had medical school debt, I wouldn't be traipsing across the country with the mwindaji."

"Do you regret it?"

"Which?"

He gazed into her eyes. "Either."

Makeda secured his dressing. She started to return supplies to the bedroom when Michael touched her arm.

"Come." He patted the cushion beside him.

You can handle this. She braced herself.

"Tell me."

"The mwindaji had a meeting. I told them you wanted to join."

He leaned forward "And?"

"Are you sure? It's dangerous."

"I worked in law enforcement."

"There's no medical benefits or retirement. If you're hurt on a mission, or die…" Makeda bit her lip, afraid to envision that possibility.

"I understand."

"No, you don't. Your family will not be told what happened to you. The mwindaji will cover up your death to protect the team, the organization."

"They rejected me."

She held his hand. "They accepted you."

"That's good, right?" He scooted closer to her. "You don't want me to join?"

"I don't want you to die." Her lips quivered.

Michael's finger delicately stroked her cheek. "When I left business school, I accepted a six-figure salary at a prestigious advertising firm. After 911, several of my friends, guys I grew up with, enlisted. Most returned home, but they had changed. You understand."

Makeda nodded.

"I joined the police force to protect and serve, not in a foreign land but at home."

His intense dark eyes bore into hers.

Like a gentle squeeze on her heart, Makeda felt the importance of his words.

"Until Kentucky, I never imagined monsters existed. Drunks, abusers, murderers. But inhuman creatures blew my mind."

"Ramsey created an unusual situation even by mwindaji experience."

"If people are being victimized, I want to help."

"Would you want to join if I wasn't an mwindaji?"

Michael looked at her, then gazed distantly.

Makeda held her breath. She needed to know the answer but simultaneously didn't want to know.

"Yes."

She exhaled.

"Listen, because this next part is vital."

He sat up straighter. "Okay."

"Mwindaji kill witches and zaubers."

His gaze widened. "But you—"

"My family doesn't know I'm a zauber."

I'm not going to tell him about Mom or Brian—just in case.

"And if they find out?"

She shrugged. "Not sure, but it wouldn't be good."

"Wow." He scratched his head. "That's messed up."

"Incredibly."

He frowned. "But they wouldn't kill you if they found out."

"My family wouldn't, but others might. If people find out, it will place my family at risk."

"I see."

Makeda's head lowered.

Michael raised her chin. "I can keep a secret." He kissed her lips. "A girlfriend who can slam a werewolf into the pavement. That's hot."

She laughed. "You're weird."

"But you like it freaky, right?"

They laughed. Daisy came over to the couch. Michael shared the rest of the sandwich. The German shepherd carried the treat to the fireplace and ate.

"No bruises on you," Michael said, examining her arms and legs.

"A gifted zauber isn't hurt by a scummy werewolf."

He massaged her legs. "Anything else I should know?"

"Currently, you're up to date."

Part of the truth isn't a lie.

"About you, I mean."

Daisy snored.

"Want to go see a movie?" she asked, reaching for the paper.

"How about we take a nap? Daisy's not the only one who's tired."

"I have pain medication if your shoulder or side hurts."

"How about a shower?" Michael's brows rose suggestively.

Makeda chuckled. "What is it with men and shower sex?"

Rubbing her arm, Michael said, "It's sexy."

"Then you can watch me shower."

"If done together."

"Forget it," she said, walking into the bedroom.

Shutting the door, Michael asked, "Why not? It saves on water."

"Oh, now it's about conservation." She sat on the edge of the bed. "My hair will get drenched, and it'll take me hours to dry and braid it."

"I'll do your hair." He twirled her long curls between his fingers.

"Sure. And I'll end up looking like Buckwheat."

"Seriously, I know how to braid hair," Michael said. "I have four sisters."

"You're going to do my hair."

Michael dramatically removed his shirt before tossing it on the bed. His hands glided up her blouse, tracing the arch in her back before resting at her hips. "Promise."

Her brow arched. "Time for relationship ground rules."

"Well, since I know you can throw me across the room, I better listen." He kissed her lips. "Okay."

"First, no sex in the back seat of a car."

"What about the front seat?" he asked, nibbling on her fingers.

"Second, no sex in the woods."

"Is that a zauber thing?"

"I don't like chiggers up my butt."

"I'd remove them."

"Next."

"What if you get to be on top?"

Makeda tried not to laugh as Michael made silly expressions. "Condoms will be used at all times."

"Always?"

"Yes."

"Even if I get a note from my doctor?"

Laughing, she pushed him aside. "Goofy."

"Admit it, you're turned on."

Though she didn't answer him, she was.

They kissed, expectantly undressing each other.

"So, what about a shower?"

Makeda hugged him around the neck. She spoke directly into his ear. Her voice was soft and alluring. "Ask me in the morning."

"Yes, ma'am."

I'll tell him about the money for the ajabu later.

Michael lifted her by the buttocks and brought her pelvis up against his. Makeda wrapped her legs around his waist and melted into his embrace. At the moment, Michael remained the sole thing on her mind.

Chapter 48

Zainabu stared into the bathroom mirror. Dark circles encircled her puffy eyes. Blue bruises dotted her cheeks and neck along with red pinpoints. She lightly palpated the enormous handprint from where Dayo strangled her neck last night.

"Damn." She splashed water on her face. Once dried, she applied concealer to her face. Zainabu wandered into the bedroom, rubbing lotion along her neck.

"What next?"

She sat on the edge of the bed and considered options. With the money she received from Korlemo, she'd live like a queen in Gao or Ansongo.

In Kondoro, not as lavishly.

Before she accepted Zorulo's offer, Zainabu vowed never to return home. Her ancestors had lived in Gao and Ansongo for centuries. Unfortunately, ancient traditions persisted. Zainabu wanted to live in the present, not hampered by outdated customs.

Given she had stolen her grandmother's book of zauber spells, Zainabu doubted she'd be welcomed. In fact, her aunts would surely punish her for the theft.

She could live anywhere, in Africa, America, or Europe. Zainabu pictured Korlemo's tantrum if she left. With Dayo's threats on her life, he shouldn't be surprised.

"Maybe I should get rid of Dayo. It would be easier than killing Korlemo."

But the vampire's devotion to his wife made Zainabu dismiss the idea. Inside the bedroom closet, she began packing.

Best be prepared for anything.

Bending down to retrieve her shoes, she noticed dirt on one heel. Returning inside the bathroom, she used a towel to clean the shoe. As she wiped away dirt, a smoky figure rose from the soil.

Zainabu gawked at the elongated disfigured face. It resembled Edward Munch's *The Scream.*

"Boo."

She dropped the towel and shoe.

The face swayed as if buoyed by a breeze. "You missed." Instantly, it vanished into the ether.

Racing into the closet, Zainabu dove behind the suitcases for the chest.

Knock, knock.

"Shit. Not now!"

Where's my trunk?

Once she shoved aside the suitcases, Zainabu reached for her talisman. "Oh, no."

The battle last night with Dayo flooded her mind. Suddenly, a memory popped into her head. Dayo had ripped the necklace off during their fight.

The person at the bedroom door pounded and shouted, "Hey!"

"Hell." Zainabu left the closet and whipped open the door. "What?"

With a toothpick dangling from between his lips, Rhogan said, "His majesty wants to speak with you."

"In a minute," she said, starting to close the door.

He inserted a foot between the frame and the door. "You think that's wise? I mean, pissing him off." Rhogan twirled the toothpick along his tongue. "He's the only thing keeping Dayo from sucking you dry."

Grinding her teeth, Zainabu locked the bedroom door. "Where is he?"

"Study."

Shouts reached her as they descended the staircase. Korlemo's voice drowned out all others.

Inside the study, the vampire stood beside the oblong desk arguing with two men flanking the entrance. Zainabu detoured around the men and strode up to Korlemo.

"How can I help?"

"These ungrateful," he spluttered, "children insist upon leaving. They refuse to acknowledge their obligation to serve the Ibori."

The older of the two men hovering near the door said, "Stefan's been murdered. Abigail needs our support."

"She does not require your assistance," Korlemo said, retiring behind the desk. "Others can offer her comfort." As an aside, he addressed Zainabu. "A drink."

Hurrying to the wet bar, she prepared his bourbon.

"The mwindaji murdered Stefan," the same man said. "She needs protection, not sympathy."

"Yes. An unfortunate circumstance." Korlemo consumed the beverage. "Abigail has multiple resources at her disposal. I have only you two."

The same man approached the desk. "We came at Stefan's request. Our obligation has been fulfilled. We owe the Ibori nothing."

The second man said, "We're leaving."

Rising, Korlemo shouted, "I demand you remain and provide security to me and my family."

"We're done," the man closest to the desk said, following his associate out of the room. "Screw this."

They had barely exited when Korlemo whirled around the room, spilling bourbon along the floor.

"Unacceptable insubordination and disrespect." His hands clenched as he ranted. "All because Herman sent us to this desolate hole."

Careful not to cross his path, Zainabu asked, "What do you wish me to do?"

Korlemo's fingers elongated and pointed at the study door. "Punish them."

Zainabu glanced over at Rhogan, who slightly inclined his head.

"Done." She exited the study behind the security guard.

She needed to dispense with the guards and return to her room. If Zorulo remained on tafa buni, she wouldn't live for much longer.

How did I mess up the incantation?

Had she recited the chant incorrectly? Zainabu recalled the soil on her shoe.

"Dammit. I removed part of the magical soil."

Sherman joined them on their way to the garage. "What's wrong, princess?"

"I'm not in the mood, and neither is Korlemo."

"Now what's wrong?"

"Where have you been?"

"My job," he said, scratching his crotch. "You think it's easy guarding this place? I had to find food for Abioye. He's been driving everyone crazy."

"Not my problem," she said, overtaking Rhogan.

"Not mine, either," Sherman said. "I'm a guard, not a goddamn hunter for a bunch of bloodsuckers."

In a line, they entered the garage where the two men who earlier argued with Korlemo stowed gear inside the rear of a Humvee. The older guard glanced up.

"Don't try to persuade us," he said to no one in particular. "My brother and I are outta here. Korlemo's insane."

"Perhaps," Zainabu said. "But in his house, he gives the orders."

"He orders you around," the younger man said, "but we don't answer to a leech like him."

The older man glowered at her. "Back off and no one will get hurt."

Irritated by Korlemo, Zorulo, *and* Dayo, Zainabu wanted to unleash her anger. Two werewolves would do nicely.

"Oh, people will get hurt." She signaled Rhogan, who tapped the button lowering the garage door.

Cracking his knuckles, the older man approached her, jabbing her chest with a thick calloused finger. "I'm warning you. Lift the garage door and walk away."

Glancing at the man's finger, Zainabu said, "I don't like threats."

"And I don't make them lightly," he snarled. "Didn't you get your ass whooped bad enough last night by Dayo?"

The young man snickered. "Scamper away, little witch."

"Fine." Zainabu raised her hand. "Ubumi." The older man rose a foot off the ground before she slammed him into the side of the Humvee.

Scrambling to his feet, the man began a metamorphosis into a werewolf when Rhogan shot him in the head. The shot reverberated around the garage, splattering blood and brain tissue along the side of the Humvee.

Zainabu covered her ears and glared at Rhogan.

The younger man transformed into a werewolf and attacked Rhogan, slashing him across the chest.

"Dammit!" Rhogan grabbed his chest as blood oozed down his shirt.

The young werewolf backslapped Rhogan against a workbench. He then growled at Zainabu and leaped forward.

"Chekate." Zainabu gave a command and tossed him aside.

Bleeding, Rhogan morphed into a werewolf and grabbed the younger werewolf by the feet. He spun him in a circle before flinging him into a cement wall. Tools and chipped cement rained down upon the young werewolf.

"This isn't a game," Zainabu said, "finish him."

At which, Rhogan retrieved his gun and popped the werewolf twice between the eyes. Two large bloody spots imprinted on the wall as the werewolf slumped to the ground.

She glanced at Sherman and before entering the mansion said, "Clean that up."

Gesticulating and shouting, Sherman said, "Like hell. This isn't what I signed up for." He grabbed Zainabu's arm and spun her around. "I want my money. Now. This shit show sucks."

Zainabu's mouth opened to reply when Rhogan pumped three bullets into Sherman's chest.

She glowered at him. "You might have shot me."

Rhogan shrugged. "But I didn't."

Zainabu inspected her blouse, sprinkled with blood and body tissue. "Take chances with your life, not mine."

She entered the mansion, then poked her head back into the garage. "Oh, and—"

"I know. Clean it up."

"Consider the Humvee a gift." Giving him a tight grin, she returned to the study.

Korlemo circled the perimeter of the room, muttering and fuming. "I will not tolerate disobedience." He looked up as Zainabu entered. "Have you contained the problem?"

"Eliminated, as you requested."

He sighed and rested in a cushioned chair behind the desk. "Excellent."

She joined him, standing at his side. "They will no longer disrespect you or your family."

"As usual, I can count on you."

"It's early in the day to be kissing the witch's ass, my husband," Dayo said, storming inside the study. She glared at Zainabu, who retreated behind Korlemo.

Absently, her hand rubbed her throat.

Dayo reclined on the sofa in the center of the room.

Korlemo rose and sat beside Dayo, taking her hand in his. "Listen, my love. This disagreement between you and—"

"Hush," Dayo said, placing a finger to his lips. "The mere mention of her name makes my blood boil."

Zainabu failed to hide her eye roll. Dayo glared at her.

Korlemo kissed Dayo's hand. "Your happiness is paramount. So..." He approached Zainabu.

Her shoulders stiffened.

Will he kill me to please Dayo?

She was no match for both vampires at once. Zainabu searched for an avenue of escape. Daylight streamed through the windows.

Flee out the window and down the front lawn.

Incantations flew around Zainabu's head as she prepared to battle two thousand-year-old vampires.

"I have given this much thought," Korlemo said.

Rhogan entered. "I disposed of Sherman and the other two guys." His gaze bounced from Korlemo to Zainabu.

Korlemo's brows rose.

In answer, Zainabu said, "Sherman had become a problem. We addressed it."

"Ah. Fits nicely with my plans." He returned to Dayo's side. "A wife's home should be a castle. Since you displease my wife," he looked at Zainabu, "you must leave."

Dayo grinned widely.

"However," Korlemo said, raising a finger, "I need her to manage our affairs."

Zainabu smirked at Dayo, who shot back an intense snarl.

"So, for the foreseeable future, Zainabu will be restricted to the in-law living quarters. I will consult you as necessary. From this moment forward, you will be prohibited from the house."

He regarded his wife. "If you discover her on the premises..." Korlemo slightly bowed his head. "Do as you wish."

Purring, Dayo said, "Thank you, my husband."

He gave her a tiny peck on the lips. "Anything for my queen."

Besides wanting to heave, Zainabu had packing to do. "Fine. I'll get my suitcases."

"No," Korlemo said, "Rhogan and the servants will retrieve them." He stood. "I said you must leave immediately."

"But I need—"

"The servants will pack your clothes."

"Wait. I..." She paused, not wanting to mention the book of zauber spells in the trunk.

Korlemo herded her toward the study door. "I depend upon you, but my wife's vengeance must be appeased." He whispered, "Go now. We will discuss the situation later."

Zainabu started to reply, but he held up a finger.

"No, no. Later." He shut the door in her face.

Standing outside the study, Zainabu considered how she could return to the bedroom and retrieve her trunk.

And, oh, let's not forget, figure out why the binding spell didn't work.

Suddenly, the study door opened, and Rhogan exited.

Before he shut the door, Zainabu observed Dayo on the couch. Between her fingers, the vamp dangled the gold necklace with the beetle talisman.

"Bitch," Zainabu said, not in a low voice.

The door closed as Dayo beamed.

Chapter 49

MAKEDA ROLLED DOWN THE window, hoping cool air would keep her awake. She glanced at the speedometer, under eighty, and the gas level hovering above a quarter tank. If she hadn't received that urgent call, she'd be at home curled up in bed. Actually, she needed to find an apartment.

However, Samuel had insisted—no begged her to return to Memphis. She prayed Eldridge was fine. Her first instinct had been to contact Eldridge via kasi kasi. Samuel warned her not to.

Why?

Had the two men quarreled? Had they separated?

Doubtful. They acted committed to each other the last time she had visited. Time had passed though. The situation may have changed. Eldridge may have discovered Samuel had met with Makeda and a rift developed between the couple. Her departure had not been on good terms.

A green highway road sign signaled she had entered Memphis city limits. Samuel told her not to come by the house. Clearly, he didn't want Eldridge to know about their meeting.

This can't be good.

'I'm in town,' she messaged Samuel.

No reply.

Makeda glanced at the directions he provided.

'Samuel, I—'

'Hurry. I'm waiting.'

At the interchange, Makeda switched onto Interstate 240 which led her to Interstate 55 toward Jackson, Mississippi. Around noon, she arrived at a small café not far from the Memphis airport.

She parked. A jumbo jet climbed into the clouds. Between the airplane noise and traffic, Makeda struggled with kasi kasi.

Once inside the restaurant, it took a moment to locate Samuel. He sat at a table off to the side in the rear next to the kitchen. A glance at his face made her rush to his side.

"What's wrong?" she asked, sitting across from him.

"Keep your voice down." He surveyed the room.

Makeda frowned. "Is someone following you?" She slowly eyed the patrons.

Energy buzzed around the café, which had an indoor and outdoor section, both packed due to it being lunchtime. Because they sat near the kitchen, servers walked by frequently.

"Should we go somewhere private?" she asked, leaning across the table.

He shook his head. "I chose this place because it's close to the airport. It will interfere with anyone trying to overhear us—audibly or via kasi kasi.

Because a waitstaff approached, Makeda didn't respond. They ordered tea and sandwiches. Ravenous, Makeda attacked the sandwich in seconds. She noticed Samuel's gaze.

"Sorry." She wiped her mouth. "I just finished a twelve-hour shift before you called."

He laid a hand on hers. "Thank you for coming. I apologize for the urgency."

Regarding his hand, Makeda appreciated a sallowness to his complexion. She studied his eyes, though anicteric, they appeared dull.

"You're ill."

He nodded.

Makeda recalled the tremors in his hands. "Tell me." She scooted the chair closer to his.

Samuel gave a tiny smile. "It doesn't matter, child. I've lived a glorious life."

"Did you consult a specialist? We can find a healing zauber."

"You think I haven't tried?" He sipped tea. "I'm a zauber who can heal."

"But not yourself." Her gaze drifted across the parking lot, recalling the story about her grandmother. "My grandmother died from cancer. She was a healer."

"Apparently, Mawu does not permit zaubers to heal themselves." Samuel glanced upward. "Forgive me."

He sat up straight. "I invited you here to discuss other matters."

Cupping her mug, Makeda braced herself.

"Let's dispense with pleasantries and pointless hopes. I am dying. I'm prepared. Eldridge remains my single concern."

Her face fell. "He's sick, too?"

"No. I want you to take care of him after I die."

Tears welled in her eyes. "Of course."

"How can you promise when you don't understand what will be required?"

Did he want her to move here and care for Eldridge?

As if reading her mind, Samuel chuckled. "I'm not asking you to relocate to Memphis. Eldridge can attend to his daily needs."

Her shoulders relaxed.

"He needs a friend." Samuel squeezed her hands. "A true friend. Someone who will take risks to ensure his safety." His gaze bore into her eyes.

Makeda stiffened. "You're warning me."

Samuel nodded.

"About someone in particular?"

"Yes."

Glancing quickly around the area, Samuel whispered, "There are certain rituals I want you to perform after I die."

Her body slightly withdrew. "I'm going to need details."

He inhaled and squared his shoulder. "It sounds gruesome, but I want you to eviscerate—"

"Eviscerate!"

"Shush." He glared at her.

Makeda bit her lip. "Sorry."

"Have you heard the term zamba dufa?"

"No." She shook her head. "Wait. That's a protection spell."

"Correct. If you bury a piece of yourself, it will keep out unwanted presences."

"Presences?"

"People, werewolves, vampires, zaubers."

"This is about Yewande."

He held her gaze without replying.

"Why would Yewande hurt Eldridge?"

The question remained unanswered while the waitstaff refreshed their tea.

"Well?" she whispered.

"I explained before Eldridge's history with your great-grandmother."

"She saved his life." Makeda's gaze narrowed. "Now, you're suggesting she would hurt him."

"Yewande is not a zauber to cross." Samuel raised and lowered his brows.

"She saved Eldridge's life. Why would she kill him?"

Samuel's chest caved. "Because E has become powerful. The longer a zauber lives, their strength grows. And if Yewande cannot control him, she'll kill him."

"Ooh. Kind of like *Highlander*."

"Excuse me."

"A TV show. If you kill someone, you assume their power or strength."

He grimaced. "No wonder E refuses to have a television in the house."

"Am I right?"

"No one will gain his powers. Yewande simply doesn't appreciate having her authority challenged. It's her side or death."

"Has he ever refused her?"

"Not until you arrived," he said with emphasis.

"And you want me to promise to," she lowered her voice, "cut out your organs and plant them around your house?"

"I do. The procedure must be completed before embalmment or the ceremony will be futile."

"Oh, of course. No problem." Makeda reclined in the chair. "I'll simply walk into the morgue and ask them to step aside while I remove the choice bits."

He scowled. "This is not a joke."

"No, it isn't." She considered her meal but decided against eating. Their conversation had her mind spinning. She didn't want to vomit.

"I haven't heard from you or Eldridge since July. Then you ask me to speed down here. And now…"

Samuel regarded her, tilting his head slightly. "It's hard to ask anyone to perform such an intimate procedure as I have. I weighed my options carefully."

"And decided I was the best choice?"

He swallowed. Makeda noticed his Adam's apple oscillating. "There's no one I trust above you."

"We hardly know each other."

"From the moment you arrived, I sensed a presence about you. A bravery and honesty rare in these times."

Afraid her voice would falter, Makeda stayed silent.

"You are your grandmother's daughter." His eyes shined.

"Yewande is my great-grandmother," she corrected him while blowing her nose.

"I know."

Makeda's eyes widened. "You met my grandmother?"

"Unfortunately, no. But E did. Perhaps if your friendship with him grows, you can ask him about Deborah." Samuel slyly lowered his lids.

"Cunning."

He smiled. "I made an enormous request and have nothing to offer in exchange but gratitude. Eldridge's safety…" His lips pursed. "I'll risk anything to protect him."

Will Michael and I ever love each other so intensely? What would I sacrifice for him?

"Any legal issues? What if I'm caught?"

"Technically, I don't believe it's illegal. Also, you're a mwindaji. You shouldn't get caught."

"Touché. Illness hasn't dulled your wit."

He chuckled. "Mortality makes you appreciate humor."

They drank tea. Samuel nibbled at his food. Makeda reviewed her experiences for anything to help with breaking into a mortuary.

"Believe me," he said, setting down his cup, "I never imagined discussing this with anyone, especially a young lady I hardly know. But during our short acquaintance, I've gained a lot of respect for you—as has Eldridge."

"Does he know?"

"No," Samuel spoke sharply. He wiped his mouth and neatly folded his napkin, setting it next to his plate. "I asked E, but he refused—despite the protection it would provide."

"Is Eldridge scared of Yewande?" Makeda asked.

"Terrified. He knows what she's capable of."

"Where are his friends?" Makeda asked. "From the pictures in the living room, you both have lived in Memphis for decades."

"You're perceptive."

"Nosy."

"A valuable quality in a zauber."

"You consider me a zauber?"

"Child." He took her hand. "It's not what I think, it's what you are."

"I thought you and Eldridge wanted me to make a choice."

"The choice concerns who you will follow—associate with." He pointed to his heart. "In here, you're a zauber. That's how Mawu made you."

She swallowed hard, holding tears at bay.

"Why doesn't Eldridge have close friends in Memphis?"

"Because they're all dead."

Makeda frowned. "How?"

"The reaper meets everyone sooner or later. They were—like I am—more bindimèn than zauber. Remember I explained how za-ubers—"

"Eldridge is a zauber with strong emi DNA. He's outlived his friends and family." She paused before asking, "How long can a zauber like him live?"

"Until their body succumbs to disease or injury."

They both retreated to their private thoughts.

Samuel said, "For a long time, he only had Yewande. Of course, he associated with other zaubers, but no one closely since his last brother died in the early 1900s. Thirty years passed before we meet."

Makeda gaped, then snapped her mouth shut. "I'm beginning to understand."

"Are you willing? I need an assurance you will carry out the ritual."

"I am."

He handed her an envelope sealed with a gold embossed star. "Inside, you'll find directions, including several of Yewande's personal items: clothing, hair, nails."

Her brow arched.

"Necessary for the ceremony."

"Noted." She accepted the manila envelope, immediately securing it in her backpack.

"And." Tears gathered on his eyelashes. "You'll check in on E, make sure he's okay."

"It would be my pleasure."

His chest relaxed, and he settled in the chair. "It's hard for a zauber with prolonged longevity to maintain friends. If you stay in one place too long, people become suspicious. You have to change your name, your identity. Sometimes move."

She placed her hand on his. The frailty in his hand, and slight tremor, led Makeda to suspect he had liver or kidney disease. This kind, gentle man was dying, and he worried about his partner. Such love and devotion. She choked down a sob and drank her tea.

"I met E as a young man," Samuel said, dreamily, gazing beyond her. "We met at a SNCC meeting." He eyed her. "You do know what SNCC means?

"Student Nonviolent Coordinating Committee. I'm young, not dumb."

Samuel sighed. "It's hard to gauge what young people know today. The work we did, fighting and dying. The Civil Rights Movement is defunct."

"No, it's not."

He chuckled. "I believe the Civil Rights martyrs would disagree."

Makeda didn't want to debate history. "Sorry, I interrupted you."

"Yes, well." He sat up straight. "I was born in Mississippi, outside Jackson."

She nodded.

"In 1963, Civil Rights Movement was on fire. We were determined to demand our rights." He grinned. "SNCC held a meeting in a tiny shack on a sharecropper's farm. E walked in with a group of zaubers, of course at the time, I didn't know who they were. To me, they looked simply like SNCC volunteers. But when I saw E..."

He flicked a tear from his cheek.

"We would meet, privately. He explained what I was. Taught me about zaubers and maji."

"Those were dangerous times."

"For zaubers?"

"No, for gay men."

Samuel nodded. "Triple for a gay Black man. Whites didn't need a reason to lynch Black people. In fact, most times, they did it for sport. You heard about the lynching postcards."

Makeda shivered. She had. Americans mailed postcards depicting their tortured innocent victims strung up in trees by their necks.

Delicately, she asked, "When did you two become a couple?"

"SNCC headed up to Winona in..." He rubbed his forehead. "June of 1963. Cops jailed Fannie Lou Hamer and other civil rights workers. They beat them viciously. My momma became hysterical. Family said she threatened to march up there because she thought I left with those other SNCC workers."

"But you hadn't."

"Eldridge and I slipped away for a private moment. We couldn't socialize publicly, so we snatched any moment possible to be alone."

"They found out."

"Nothing's secret in the South. A church member spotted us."

His jaw tensed.

Makeda noticed an increase in his hand tremor.

"Momma was prepared to die for her son, the civil rights worker, but not the homosexual."

Makeda glanced away and let him have a moment.

"I left with E, and we've been together since. After Medgar Evers' murder, we traveled to Alabama and Georgia. In the house, there's a sketch E drew of the Leesburg Stockade Girls."

She wasn't familiar with the story but didn't want to interrupt his reflections.

"My goodness. We traveled all across the South. Because of his background, how Yewande rescued him from the plantation and the Underground Railroad brought him and his family to Canada, E felt compelled to participate in the Civil Rights Movement. And we made a difference."

Mirth shook his frame. "I remember..." He laughed. "I remember this one White bigot who raised his hand to strike one of the SNCC photographers." Tears poured down Samuel's face as he laughed heartily. "We taught him a lesson he wouldn't forget."

Samuel dried his tears with a monogrammed handkerchief. He slammed his hand down on the table. A teacup overturned, spilling liquid across the plates. "I hate to leave him like this—all alone."

A few people glanced their way. Makeda mopped up the tea.

"Forgive me." Gradually, the tremor in his hand slowed.

He gazed fondly at her. "I recognized you were unique, a trustworthy, gifted zauber. He will need a friend unafraid to stand by his side."

This time, she didn't try to stem the flowing tears.

"Now, we can't have that. One blubbering mess is enough." He handed her a fresh handkerchief. "Chin up. We have plans to make."

Suddenly, Samuel jumped up in his seat. "That bird."

Makeda followed his gaze out to the parking lot. "What bird?"

"I've wasted precious time." He removed a box from his sports coat and slid it across the table. "Take this."

She lifted the lid, but Samuel raised his hand.

"Not here." He pointed to the table edge. "I covered the area around the table and café entrance."

Straining, Makeda noticed black smudges around the entrance. She placed the box in her bag.

"It's from a nommo. I burned the flesh and collected the remains. Mixed with herbs and a few incantations, it will keep prying eyes away—particularly *bdomas*."

"Evil spirits?" she asked, gawking at him.

"Time's short." He dropped several bills on the table and led her by the arm toward the parking lot.

"Who do you suspect of following you?"

Samuel stared at her in disbelief. "Yewande."

"What?" she asked, louder than she meant to.

His glare reminded her to lower her voice.

"Why would she?"

"Because of you."

He remained silent until they reached the Cadillac.

Makeda noticed charms around the doors and windows, including a sizable amount of black soot.

"Tell me, please."

Gazing out the windows, Samuel spoke rapidly, "E didn't want to tell you. He feels obligated to Yewande."

"I don't—"

"Be quiet and listen." He strained, peering up into the cloudy sky. "It's already too late. I'm sure she knows."

"How?"

"Because she's been watching our house since you arrived for lessons. That's why I didn't want us to meet there. But I've been gone longer than usual. Yewande is suspicious by nature."

"Apparently."

"I asked E to warn you, but he's frightened." He waved off her approaching question. "Listen. This is urgent."

"How can I protect myself from—"

"Hush," Samuel interrupted. "Don't say its name."

"Is that how they're summoned?" she asked, moving closer to catch each word.

"There's an African proverb about if you speak a person's name you give them life. I'm paraphrasing, but essentially, speaking a dubwana—demon's—name is a step toward an invitation spell."

"But why does Yewande need me to kill this demon?"

"A great question. E and I discussed it."

Biting her lip, Makeda asked, "But you guys don't know?"

Samuel sighed. "I do not. E might."

"But he won't tell me."

He placed a hand on hers. "Please understand. Yewande freed him from a plantation. Gave him and his family freedom in a time and place where it didn't exist for Black people in America."

A weight pressed down on Makeda's chest. Not simply because of what Eldridge must have endured as a slave, but the knowledge Yewande coerced him to train her to battle a demon.

A hawk soared overhead.

Sweat beaded along Samuel's forehead. "I know it's rude to invite you here and request such a great favor."

"You and Eldridge have been kind and patient. He's—You're both my friends." She patted her backpack. "I will keep my promise."

Samuel kissed her cheek. "Be careful." He entered the Cadillac and started the motor.

Makeda noticed his head slump forward. She knocked on the window.

He raised his hand. Wrinkled, jaundiced skin stretched taut over his crooked fingers. Samuel looked at her with jaundiced eyes.

The window scrolled down.

"It takes enormous energy to maintain a façade of health. I didn't mean to startle you."

"Let me drive you home."

"No. It would upset E. Besides…" He glanced again at the sky. "I don't want to draw Yewande's ire, not before you complete the ritual."

She winced. *What have I signed up for?*

"You're ill."

"Give me a moment. It takes a lot of strength to cast an illusion spell. With my failing health, I can barely kasi kasi." It took a few minutes, but gradually, his appearance improved. Jaundice faded, and his skin became supple. In time, he drove off.

Makeda waited until he entered the main road. She exited the lot and trailed two cars behind him all the way to the house. For a moment, she considered renting a hotel room for the night. Sleep tugged hard at her consciousness.

Instead, she completed a three-point turn and headed home. As she merged onto the expressway, a thought arose. Samuel said the nommo powder would keep away bdomas and dubwanas.

Why would it work on her great-grandmother?

She had no problem staying awake on the drive home as questions percolated in her mind.

Chapter 50

F ALL HEIGHTENED ASHEVILLE'S BEAUTY. A stunning array of colors coated the leaves. With the large assortment of trees surrounding their home, it looked like a rainbow of autumn as Makeda exited the house.

Dogs sauntered around the yard. A few followed her in and out of the house as she packed the car. Makeda lugged her last bag down the porch steps and heaved it onto the back seat of her car.

Thomas placed several boxes in the trunk.

"Bye." He opened his arms wide and gave her a bear hug.

"I'm moving to an apartment in Asheville. It's not far."

Moping, he lowered his head. "Don't see why you need to leave."

She kissed his cheek. "Love you."

He mumbled, "Love you, too," before returning inside.

Makeda noticed tears in his eyes. Doubts circled her mind.

Why move out?

She could be a mwindaji and zauber here. Makeda headed for the house when a squirrel darted across the grass. Two of the Labradors chased it up a tree. With a dissecting gaze, Makeda tracked the critter as it scampered between tree limbs.

Could it be Yewande?

She should've asked Samuel how to differentiate a regular animal from one possessed by a zauber. Makeda wavered, suddenly unsure about leaving.

"Ready?" Dad asked.

He and Mom stood beside the car.

"Yeah."

Mom frowned.

"I mean yes."

"Be safe." Dad pulled her to his chest, hugged and kissed her cheeks. "And come home anytime." Tears pooled in his eyes as he darted inside the house.

Mom scrutinized her from head to toe. "Is this about Yewande?"

"No." Makeda sighed. "I... You were right."

Her chin trembling, Mom said, "First, Peter. Now, you."

"Daniel moved out years ago. Us leaving isn't new."

Mom cried. Makeda's attempt at humor had failed.

"I'm not going far," she said, hugging Mom. "And I'll come back often. At least once a week."

Wiping her eyes on her shirt sleeve, Mom asked, "Why do you want to leave? Did I... Have I hurt you?"

"No. Please don't cry," Makeda said, bawling herself. "I just want privacy."

"Because of Michael?"

"To be alone. Figure myself out."

Crying and shaking, Mom nodded.

Makeda rubbed her arm.

"And don't worry. Thomas will always be here."

At this, Mom laughed. They shared another hug and Makeda departed.

She reached the driveway and turned right onto the main road. But within a half mile, she made a U-turn. Before settling into her new apartment, she needed to do something.

Driving down the narrow county roads was like exploring the inside of a multicolored, decorated periscope. Due to prior experience, she had no trouble locating the turnoff leading to Yewande's home. Her car bounced along the rutted drive.

Makeda parked on the right side of the cozy home. Before exiting the car, a heaviness pressed upon her chest. In the clear sky, leaves shimmered on the trees surrounding the home. A premonition she might need a speedy exit made her leave the keys in the ignition.

Once inside the house, she headed straight upstairs to her great-grandmother's bedroom. Makeda searched closets and drawers. A beaded, South Carolina indigo blue charm rested on the floor in the corner of a bedroom closet. The only significant item she had located.

A necklace? Makeda held it up to her neck. *Too small. Possibly an ankle bracelet.*

Hearing movement downstairs, Makeda hurried out of the bedroom. Without thinking, she slipped the anklet into her pants pocket. She scanned the first-floor front room for the source of the noise. Nothing.

Makeda scanned the kitchen before exiting into the backyard. With haste, she picked select herbs and plantings, stashing them inside her backpack.

A sharp, cool breeze made Makeda zip up her jacket. Her spine tingled. The hair on her arms raised.

She unlatched the strap for her machete and surveyed the grounds. Though nothing appeared, the feeling of being watched persisted.

'Yewande. Are you here?'

She wished to find an item belonging to Yewande in case she needed to perform her own ritual to keep her great-grandmother away.

Would it work in an apartment?

She had to ask Samuel. But his health had deteriorated, and his kasi kasi sounded weak.

I'll telephone. Just because I'm a zauber doesn't mean I can't use technology.

'Yewande, if you're here, show yourself.'

Since she received no response and detected no animals nearby, Makeda walked over to the majestic oak tree at the rear of the property. Gold and amber leaves sparkled like jewels. She wrapped her arms around the trunk and inhaled its pine scent. A branch brushed her shoulder as if the tree hugged her in return.

'Where have you been?'

She spun around to find a cat slinking toward her.

'Busy.'

'With the mwindaji?'

'And other things.'

'It's a waste of time chasing after Korlemo. James has been fixated on vampires ever since your momma introduced him to the mwindaji.'

Makeda bristled. 'Dad acts on his beliefs.'

'He's wasted a lot of time—and lives.'

'I'm not here to discuss Dad.'

The cat purred. 'Good. It's time to get to work. Did Eldridge teach you the spell?'

'We didn't get far.'

Meowing, the cat leaped at her. 'What have you been doing? I sent you to Memphis to learn how to destroy demons. Never mind. I'll teach you myself.'

Circling around the yard, the cat eyed her. 'Repeat after me. Zorulo—'

'No.' Makeda proceeded toward the house with the cat at her heels.

'What?'

'I want to know why a demon wants to kill me.'

Makeda didn't want to reveal what Samuel told her about the demon. Yewande would immediately deduce where she obtained the information.

Arching its back, the cat hopped onto the wooden deck. 'We've been over this.'

'Indulge me.'

'Because you're my great-granddaughter.'

'Then why hasn't the demon attacked Mom, Thomas, or Peter? Why me, why now? The demon conveniently waited until I was prepared.'

'Stupid questions.' The cat licked its paw.

'I'm not doing anything until you answer my questions.'

'Ignorance will be your death.'

'A demon cannot enter this dimension without an invitation.'

Dammit.

Slinking up to her, the cat hissed. 'Who told you that?'

'Tell me the truth, Yewande, or I'm leaving.'

They glared at each other. 'Eldridge has been speaking about matters that don't concern him.'

Makeda stood. 'He didn't tell me.'

'Then who?'

'I'm not stupid. Why do you keep trying to get me to say this demon's name?'

The cat turned around swishing its tail. Its eyes narrowed. 'I need you to kill Zorulo so I can be free.'

'You're trapped? Where? How?'

'Zorulo killed me and confined me to another dimension.'

Makeda sat on the deck beside the cat, stroking its head. 'I'm sorry.'

The cat scampered from her reach. 'I don't want sympathy. Unless Zorulo dies, I cannot leave this dimension.'

Makeda scrutinized the cat. The explanation didn't quite jibe with what Samuel told her.

Why would he lie?

He had nothing to gain. In fact, he had requested her help.

'Where, Yewande?'

'My body died, but my spirit lives in a holding cell of sorts. Doomed to be forever suspended, until Zorulo is killed.'

She frowned. New dimensions or planes. Makeda didn't understand them or how they worked.

How do I uncover the truth? Can't google zauber history.

Samuel gave her pieces of the puzzle, but the overarching picture remained vague. He said certain zaubers live for years unless they die from disease or an injury.

Did being killed qualify as an injury?

Samuel hadn't said where zaubers went after their bodies died. Massaging her temples, Makeda lay on the porch deck gazing up into the clouds.

'Damn, this is confusing.'

The cat sat on her feet. 'It doesn't have to be. If Zorulo dies, I live again.'

'The pictures in Eldridge's house came from the 1800s. If you're older than him...'

An idea coalesced, but Makeda's headache prevented clarity.

'Zaubers can live for years.'

'I know, but if you're older than him… There were no pictures of you in his house.'

The cat strutted away.

'Last time, you mentioned possession.'

Eyeing her, the cat licked its fur.

'You said you can possess an animal. Can you possess a person?'

Branches fluttered in the woods to her left, but Makeda focused on Yewande.

'Answer me.'

'What do you want me to say?'

'Have you possessed people before?'

Makeda followed the cat onto the grass. 'Have you?'

The cat flipped around, arching its back. 'Yes!'

She flinched and stepped aside.

'Want the truth? Here it is.'

In a flash, a roaring bear crashed from between the trees. It charged Makeda.

Swishing the machete, she kept the bear away while scanning the area for Yewande. The bear followed her gaze. It barreled toward the cat and battered it with a paw.

The feline flew across the yard and smacked against the house. Its limp body splayed across the deck like a rag.

'Yewande!'

Growling and gnashing its teeth, the bear lunged for Makeda.

She raced toward the oak tree.

Its hot, rancid breath blew on her neck. Makeda ducked as it swiped at her head. At the base of the tree, she vaulted onto the lowest tree branch. A claw slashed her jacket.

Damn, bears can climb.

As if reading her mind, the animal headed up the tree. The bear tore at the tree's bark trying to scale it.

Maji.

Fire would destroy the gigantic oak tree and probably a significant amount of woodland.

Makeda raised her hands and commanded, "Ubumi."

An eerie smile formed along the bear's mouth. It said, "Maji doesn't work on me."

"Oh, hell." Makeda's stomach lurched. *The demon.*

"You don't have to say my name, zauber. I'm already here." It scaled the tree.

Makeda fled higher. Her pulse soared, and her mind raced.

Where can I go?

She searched for an escape. The oak tree's branches fanned out toward the next tree, creating a bridge. Its leaves rustled briskly. She kissed its trunk.

"Thank you."

Without delay, Makeda dashed across the oak's limbs onto the branches of a nearby tree. In fact, the line of trees together assembled a foliage walkway. She realized it led to the front of the house.

A three-foot gap separated the tree she hid in from the next. She jumped from the oak tree to a nearby pine. The trees leaned closer together, allowing her to hop from one to another. However, another fifty yards separated the last tree from her car.

She glanced back and noticed the bear observing her journey between the trees.

I have to hit the ground and sprint.

If demons were immune to maji, she would have to rely on mwindaji training.

See bear run.

Before Makeda jumped down from the last tree, the bear raced across the yard. Eyeing the bear, she hit the ground and bolted toward the car.

The bear had reached the side of the house as she slid across the passenger seat behind the steering wheel.

The carnivore blasted into the rear of the car, propelling Makeda's head forward. Her forehead smacked the steering wheel. She bit the inside of her mouth.

In the rearview mirror, she noticed the bear posture for another attack. She tasted blood as her tongue probed the gash in her cheek. Despite trembling fingers, Makeda managed to shift the car into drive.

A paw shattered the rear passenger window as the car jolted forward and sped down the potholed dirt road.

"Please don't pop a tire."

The bear gave chase but stopped before Makeda erupted onto the county road. She zipped onto the asphalt. The tires burned skid marks into the road. Makeda sped away.

"Damn. I should've brought the nommo ashes Samuel gave me."

She quickly put miles between her and Yewande's house. Not until she reached a main thoroughfare did her speed decrease.

Should I go home?

Makeda did not relish explaining how the car window broke.

"Hi, Mom. Funny story. A demon busted out my window."

A demon.

But Samuel said a demon must be invited.

Had she mistakenly summoned it?

The cat definitely didn't survive that battering. But how did that affect Yewande? Fears, questions. Her mind juggled a multitude of items.

Suddenly, she slammed on the brakes. The driver behind her honked and gave her a middle-finger salute. Makeda pulled over at a gas station.

Samuel told her the nommo ash would keep evil spirits and demons away. Did he imply Yewande was a dubwana or a bdoma?

He might be ill, but I need answers.

She pulled out a burner phone, then realized she didn't have his number.

"Double damn."

Please answer.

'Samuel.'

Nothing. She waited.

'Samuel. a demon attacked me. You said it wasn't possible.'

Like an unsteady, static connection, Makeda detected a reply without understanding.

'What?'

'It isn't.'

'Well, it happened. A maniacal grinning bear chased me up a tree.'

'Did you use what we taught you?'

'It said maji wouldn't hurt it.'

'And you believed a talking bear?'

She took a deep breath. Her jaw clenched. Getting mad at Samuel wouldn't help.

'The demon that killed Yewande attacked me and I didn't summon it.'

More static.

'Hello?'

'Yewande wasn't killed by a demon.'

Makeda's jaw fell.

'Then where the hell did the bear come from?'

I hope you appreciated *Dark Blood Curse*, the second book in my mwindaji paranormal urban fantasy series. Authors survive on reader reviews. Please leave a book review and share your experience with other readers. The first book in the series, *Dark Blood Awakens*, is available at major retailers.

Sign up for and receive a free copy of *Dark Sun Rising*, Korlemo's origin story, information on new releases, and other satisfying reads.

Information about the Write Club Mysteries series and standalone thriller *Hollow Voices* are available on my website. Reader and writer resources are available on the website. Sign up for MrsDoctor Writes free .

www.MichelleCorbier.com

About the author

After over twenty-five years in clinical medicine, Michelle Corbier now works as a medical consultant. As a member of Crime Writers of Color, Sisters in Crime and Capitol Crimes, Science Fiction & Fantasy Writers Association, Authors Guild, and ALLi her writing interests cover many genres—mystery, paranormal, and thrillers. If not writing, you can find her baking, gardening or bicycling